Don't Dance with Death

A Dark Romantic Comedy

Don't Dance with Death

A Dark Romantic Comedy

HAUNTED ROMANCE BOOK THREE

C. Rae D'Arc

Cover design by: Blue Water Books

ISBN: 978-1-961733-02-2 (paperback)

Published by Bursting Box Publishing
www.craedarc.com
www.facebook.com/c.rae.darc
www.instagram.com/craedarc/

To the misunderstood.
To those who made mistakes
And were sorely misjudged by them

Like the horror genre.

Prologue

They were dark and stormy times when twelve young maids were taken by Lord Oswald, the Tyrant, of Margen. Berwyna Acker was the youngest of five to survive.

Six years later, and at eighteen years old, the spell of forgetfulness still held Berwyna's memories about her captivation by Oswald. It was another stormy night as she sat in her father's farmhouse and stabbed some mesh fabric with her needle. Lining the word "Back" with a black thread, she considered the symmetry of her actions with the phrase on the fabric.

"Do to others what you want done to you, because what goes around will come back."

As to her own knowledge, Berwyna only knew what the reports said. Six years ago, the capital city of the "grim" side of Fairy fell under the tyrant's sorcery. Oswald hypnotized and abducted women. He tortured them and eventually dissected them, but only after his mother, the Wicked Duchess, absorbed their beauty. Berwyna had been victim number twelve before he made the mistake of abducting Pansy Finster. She and Marquis Theodor Fromm vanquished the duchess and her twisted son, and saved Berwyna.

She fondly stitched out words from *Oz's Haunting Survival Book*, with notes by Marchioness Pansy Fromm of Margen.

Berwyna considered herself a survivor for escaping Lord Oswald's captivation, especially without becoming shriveled and sunken by Duchess Abadda. She kept her long, dark-blonde hair tied back in a bun while needleworking. She measured which stitch to make with her dark blue eyes and completed the stitches with nimble fingers. On her wall, she displayed cross-stitches of "Horror's Number One Rule: Avoid drugs, sex, and violence," and "Never Split Up." Her most popular quilt had every single quote on its own square.

"What goes around will come back," she mused as she threaded her needle through the mesh back and forth, back and forth, back and forth. Her mind drifted between desires. Did she want to remember what happened during her abduction? No, surely it was horrifying. But she ached to know how she acted on her first Adventure. She hadn't experienced much in the ways of Adventures since then. Sure, joining her father for trades and tricking gnomes out of their garden was fun, but...Berwyna dreamed of traveling the world.

Her thoughts shifted between daydreams with each stitch: saving a friend in Horror, aiding a detective in Mystery, watching a duel in Western, falling in love in Romance...

Thunder shook her back to reality. Oh, the places she would see if she wasn't the daughter of a lowly farming lord in southern Eimad.

She cut her needle free of the black thread and considered which color to use for the flourishes.

A knock on the front door startled her.

Who was there? Her father and brothers were traveling for the trades. It wasn't a night for visitors as the hailstorm flashed with lightning. Perhaps it was her neighbors, the Saubers, checking on her wellbeing and loneliness. She blushed, hoping it was the eldest son, Urien. No, it couldn't be him. He was still on his fishing trip, seeking an Adventure.

The visitor knocked more insistently, and Berwyna secured the chain lock before opening the door.

"Urien?" She blinked with surprise. "You're back from your fishing trip?" He was a handsome young man with light brown hair and the frame of a hard working cattle rancher. He was a dear friend since childhood, though his occasional compliments of her appearance gave her hopes for courtship.

"Berwyna," he gasped with relief and half out of breath. "Wow, you're a sight for sore eyes. I need your help."

"You don't need to butter me up," Berwyna said with reddening cheeks. She would help him over mountains or seas if he asked. She unlocked the chain to open the door wider. "What do you need?"

"Hey, it wasn't a load of lard, that was real butter," he teased. "Anyway, I found something during my fishing trip and it led me to the Thornwood Forest." He leaned in with an excited secret. Berwyna's breath stuttered at his proximity, admiring the rain dripping off the ends of his hair into his long lashes. "Berwyna, I found a hag who needed help! You know how they always turn into beautiful enchantresses who grant wishes, right? But she needs some mending. Will you help us?"

An enchantress? Berwyna's heart clenched, caught between excitement and fear. What would the marchioness do?

Do to others what you want done to you…

"Bring her in," she said.

Urien's heavy boots squished with mud, and the rolled whip on his belt dripped from the rain. To Berwyna's surprise, Urien didn't escort a feeble old woman into her father's house. Instead, he slumped a sack over his shoulder and dragged in a large bag.

Before Berwyna could ask, Urien excused himself. "I didn't know who else to ask. You're the best seamstress in Eimad and the only one I'd trust with what's going on."

"What's going on?" she asked.

"Let me show you." He shuffled the large bag into the middle of the room and sat down to place the small sack on the table. "I found a box during my fishing trip. Inside was…her." He pulled down the sides of the sack to reveal a woman's head.

Berwyna screamed.

"Thisss little maid," the head spoke, "ssshall put me back together?"

Berwyna screamed louder.

The head threw a glare at Urien and commanded, "Sssilence her!"

"Hey, Berwyna, it's alright. I have the rest of her body in here." He gestured to the large bag on the floor.

Berwyna shrieked, "How does that make it alright?"

Urien stood and placed his hands around her shoulders. She stifled her screams at his touch. Never before had he held her this way or stared at her with such earnestness.

"Berwyna, you know the history of The Three Heads in the Well? Princesses and maids combed the heads' hair and received threads of gold, but their wicked sisters who treated the heads wrongly were cursed with ugliness." As Urien spoke, his hand slowly slipped down Berwyna's arm to shyly touch her hand. "I could take her to a healer," he said, "but you were the first person I thought of. I trust you more than anyone, and if I could choose anyone to reap a reward with me, it would be you. I know you've always wanted to go on a great Adventure and see the world. Well, I finally found our chance! If we put this woman's body back together and prove ourselves worthy, she said she'll reward us with riches, power beyond imagination, and a chance to travel across Novel."

Berwyna's mind fogged between his words and the sensation of his touch. Could this be her long awaited Adventure to travel? And she would travel with Urien. Romances often bloomed during Adventures, and how often she wished to explore one with him. All she had to do was stitch this enchantress's head back to her body. She took a deep breath and did her best to clear her head; it was no more than a commissioned piece.

"Alright. I'll do it. May I know your name?" she asked the head.

The head grinned and hissed like a snake. "Only after you prove yoursssself worthy, I shall reveal my true ssself to you and grant your rewardsss."

Usually, the hags who turned into enchantresses in stories were humble and kindly. This woman had a mischievous glint in her eye. A nagging pit weighed in Berwyna's gut. But she couldn't back down now. If she rejected a helpless hag, she could be cursed with ugliness or toads jumping from her throat.

Gritting her teeth, she set the head in her lap as Urien lifted the body to line her neck. She switched out her needle for her smallest size and grabbed some silk thread. Skin was thicker than fabric, but easy enough to pierce. She wondered how this woman was still alive. She didn't seem to bleed. If anything, the woman had to wield very powerful magic. Maybe she was powerful enough to grant her wish to travel the world.

The hag grumbled as the young man and woman rotated her for stitching. Berwyna struggled to focus on her work as Urien watched her with a tender smile. She tied off her thread, then the woman stood.

She was a full head shorter than Berwyna. Her tattered and torn clothes revealed her scarred and weathered body. She groaned as she rolled her neck and stretched her limbs.

"At lassst," she sighed, and smoke streamed from between her teeth. "Bow before me."

Berwyna shivered. Without a doubt, this woman was a high noble. Dipping into a small curtsy, she asked, "Who are you?"

"Ye are in the presssence of royalty. I once had the title of duchesss, but ye will call me Queen Abadda."

Utmost terror struck Berwyna's core. Abadda. The mother of the monster who kidnapped her. The woman who stole magical abilities and schemed to overthrow the Fairy kingdom.

Berwyna's heart screamed as she realized what she and Urien had done. They restored the woman who used her ability of absorption to steal beauty and other abilities. Her wounds reknit from the healing ability of the Phoenix Queen, her speech flickered with the flames of Oswald the Fire Breather, and the storm outside thundered with powers of Greggory the Wind Master.

For the first time in her life, Berwyna thanked the gods that she didn't have an ability. Urien was also safe. His talent with the whip was purely from practice and training.

However, that meant the duchess had no reason to keep them alive.

The duchess's eyes of bottomless pits squinted at Berwyna. "Thou doth ssseem familiar. Tell me, was thou taken in by my gluttonous ssson?"

Berwyna gasped. "Yes."

"Thou hast a sssweet beauty." Her lips curled into a malicious smile. She reached for Berwyna and hissed inward. The woman breathed deeply, flames flickering from her throat. "You will be wissse to assist me. Those who sssought to subdue my powersss will know my rage. It is time to collect my duesss in a place where none can essscape."

Berwyna's limbs became heavy and the hair that dropped in front of her face drained of color. Somewhere in her weakening consciousness, Urien screamed her name. Her vision faded to black between the shrill laughter of Abadda, the Wicked.

Chapter 1

ARE THEY DEAD YET?

Always be sure a Haunting's dead,
but never check up close
Kill them until there's nothing left to kill
Don't celebrate too early
Behead every haunting. Cauterize beheaded hydras
Don't do anything stupid to bring it back

> -   *Oz's Haunting Survival Book,*
> with notes by Pansy Fromm

THEO

Once upon our happily ever after, I sat in a padded throne and longed for Pansy to sit in the marchioness's identical seat beside me. I wondered where she was while I represented my father to the lords' reports and petitions.

After six years, my wife and flower still grew nervous with each meeting in the presence chamber and preferred other duties if possible. At least her influence was seen in the ivy that grew up the stone wall. Pansy suggested it, hoping to "bring some life into the room." She also did a number on the security, regularly reviewing the protocols and functionality of systems within Ruezdad Castle and all of Eimad City. Perhaps she was currently inspecting them, or experimenting with medicines in her drawing room.

I pictured Pansy in my mind with a small smile. Some things did get better with age. After six years of marriage, there were a couple of wrinkles around her brown eyes. She would turn twenty-seven this week, though a few premature greys speckled her black hairline, testifying to the responsibilities of royalty and parenthood. I had some of my own greys above my ears. They grew while I tried to simultaneously learn two fields of study that were usually taught from childhood: how to be marquis and how to be a wizard.

Someone coughed, and I blinked myself back to the matters at hand. A group of children were suspected of stealing items from the giant district. The giants in Eimad were as civil as they came, though I feared the worst if they captured their sneaky little thieves. I could not bear the thought of my own child falling to such a fate.

The lords and I formulated plans to address the issue with the parents, advertise appropriate activities for the kids, and add *The BFG* to the school curriculum. Hopefully it would be enough, though we scheduled a follow-up meeting next week.

The lords left with plans, assignments, and encouragement. Another day, another crisis averted. As long as the people slept peacefully, my family would also.

The last lord held the door wide for a grizzly bear who stood on his hind legs and wore a knight's armor.

"Master Bahr?" I asked.

The massive warrior bowed. "The young prince remained attentive during our self-defense practices, and he would like to share his progress with you."

"Fantastic, send him in," I said, grinning.

He stepped back to make room for the one person he was assigned to guard. A child stepped into the presence chamber.

Aeron Fromm, the Earl of Margen. My son.

A little man of five years, he was truly a beautiful child, and I cherished that he was half mine. He had my blue-green eyes with Pansy's darker skin tones. His blond hair surprised us both, though it slowly darkened each year. We figured he would have my dark brown hair by the time he reached adulthood. He had Pansy's nimbleness and keen awareness with my eagerness to learn. Pansy worried that he asked far too many questions for his own safety.

"Father?"

"Yes, Aeron?" I asked.

"I want to show you something…if I may?" he added as a formal afterthought.

I pinched my lips, a little annoyed at my son's training. As much as I wanted a casual relationship with my son, the formalities would serve him well as Margen's future duke. I smiled and squatted to his eye level. "Of course. What is it?"

"Hold this," he said, handing me an oak board. I took it with one hand by its center. "No, you hold it wrong. Like this, see?"

My son took the board back and held it up by the edges between his palms. "This is how Master Bahr holds it. Now you try."

I suppressed a grin as my child spoke to me the way his personal guard spoke to him. With the wooden board between my palms, I angled it to the side.

He threw his fist into the board and shouted, "Pah!" I winced as the board broke and bits flew towards my face. My son beamed with accomplishment.

"Look! Look! I breaked the—"

"Broke?"

"Oh, I broke the board!"

"Yes, you *broke* the board. Good job!" I grinned and pulled him into a one-armed hug.

"Can that be my title? Can Eimad call me Aeron, the Best Puncher in Novel?"

"Your title?" I leaned back, surprised. "Are you sure? What if you find another skill or talent and want a different name? To receive a title is a great honor given only to royalty and great Heroes." Besides, any title would be considered a nickname until it was made official on his twelfth birthday.

"Then I want to be a Hero," he pouted.

I asked, "Why is that?"

My son fiddled with his leather bracelet. He liked to wear it all day, though its only magical function was to absorb nightmares. Some kids carried blankets for security. Aeron wore his bracelet.

"Cousin Farris say—" I gave him a look "—*says* they will name me after Mom and call me 'The Unsettling,' which means weird."

I frowned. "Your mother's title is 'The Unsettled,' which does not mean weird. It means—" I considered how to simplify her speed ability and paranoia for Hauntings. "It means she moves a lot. Besides, you are not unsettling. Just because Farris says something does not make it true." I still made a mental note to talk to King Aenirin and the attitude of his youngest child.

Aeron shook his head. "He calls me unsettling because I do not have magic *or* a ability."

That phrase rang far too many familiar bells. I, for one, was ten years old before learning that my visions of auras were unique. If only Lord Freund's ability to see others' abilities had not been stolen by my wicked stepmother, Duchess Abadda.

I vaguely remembered her quote of some dark ability born within Pansy's womb. Unfortunately, confirming the prophecy with anyone was impossible since the only other witnesses were dead. Maybe it was better if Aeron's ability was left unknown.

I swallowed and took my son by his shoulders.

"Aeron, you do not need an ability to be a wonderful, unique, and good person. Regardless of your ability or skills, you choose how to use them, and it is your actions that will influence your title."

"I am boring," Aeron pouted. "I cannot do anything special. If I have a ability, it is useless."

Despite my worries and Aeron's frustration, I smiled at the irony.

"No ability is that simple," I said, "even my ability to see auras. I was a grown man before I learned that the darker shades showed me when someone was in danger. Then it was a couple more years before I discovered why some auras are shorter than others'."

"Oh," Aeron said. "So, maybe I can fly, but I do not know how yet. Or-or maybe I can talk to the moon and stars, but they are too far away to hear me."

I chuckled to hide my concern of discovering his prophesied dark ability. "That would be special indeed. Do you want to meet with the Abilities Counselor again?" Though Lord Freund no longer saw others' abilities, he became an illusionist to create situations and help discern abilities.

Aeron paused, then shook his head no. I struggled to hide my relief.

"No?"

Aeron continued to shake his head. "I do not want to see the scary magic man."

I chuckled. "Oh, Aeron, Lord Freund is not scary. Remember, he made that bracelet for you? Then you stopped having nightmares."

Aeron stopped shaking his head only to fiddle with his bracelet again. For a five-year-old, he stood tall and sure of himself. If not for the subtle fidgeting with his bracelet, I might not have noticed his discomfort.

"Does something else trouble you?" I asked.

"Tutor White will not let me pass my language arts lesson."

"Oh? Why do you think that is?"

"I do not know." Aeron frowned and continued to fiddle. "I ask Tutor White to use the lavatory. She says, 'Is it a emergency?'" Aeron mimicked his tutor's voice. "I say, 'Yes, Tutor White. It is a emergency.' Then she says that I say it wrong. Is it because she is a goblin in disguise?"

My smile cracked into laughter. All these years of rearing our child and teaching him to talk with the help of governesses and private tutors, I had not realized that he picked up Pansy's breathy Horror accent with the harder Contemporary "r." It was subtle, as Pansy's accent had lost most of its flavor over the years, though certain words crept up, such as "dark," "survive," and apparently "emergency."

"What is funny?" Aeron asked.

I brushed my hand over his hair. "Oh, you just remind me of your mother."

Chapter 2

HIDING

- *Oz's Haunting Survival Book,*
with notes by Pansy Fromm

PANSY

After my usual check-ins with Ruezdad's guards and security, I went to my drawing room. As a place designated for "withdrawing" and stepping away from duty, it was my favorite room. Gone were Ruezdad's smells of horses, old stone, and smoke. Instead, scents of sterilization chemicals greeted me. Rows of jars spread across the back wall, filled with herbs, fungi, and chemicals. A floor-to-ceiling bookshelf occupied a front corner with my favorite tomes on anatomy and biology. Drawers lined the sides with tools for standard medicine practice and emergency operations. My rolling gurney was currently pushed to the side with my apron on top. Locked in cases on the side walls, I kept my spare daggers, stakes, and crossbows.

A maid finished her cleaning spell and promptly bowed herself out when I entered. I smiled in thanks, but she didn't look. This was normal protocol between servants and ladies, but I didn't feel respected. I felt ignored.

I opened a bottom drawer to reveal a singular object inside: a softly glowing glass ball. A psychic or gypsy's ball is what I would have called it before. For the past six years, it was my virtual assistant.

"Hey, Sunni," I said, lifting it to the counter top.

"Hello, Pansy," the orb hummed back. "Would you like me to contact Princess Brooke Sayer for your weekly call?"

"Yeah."

"Calling Princess Brooke Sayer."

It hummed a soft tune and waved between a bright and soft glow. I stretched and grabbed a sword for my wait.

It was proper for a lady to practice fine arts in her spare time. I dabbled with paints and the violin, but my pieces weren't works to exhibit. I was a miserable poet and poor singer, but I found solace in dance.

Originally, I took ballroom lessons with Theo. When his duties as marquis took over, I switched to ballet and folk dances. My trainer found that I moved more gracefully with a weapon in hand, so my current routine included a rapier.

I practiced the final steps over and over, swinging the thin blade in a wide arc above my head, then twisting it down to hover only an inch above the rug. Keeping it steady, I finished my routine by lowering myself to one knee.

I stood and did it again…and again. The problem with dancing solo was it gave me too much time to think.

My gaze fell to my wooden, silver, and golden stakes. Their dust testified to my pampered life these last several years. Instead of setting traps and safety alarms around a tiny Horror apartment, I updated the security systems of a castle, city, and duchy. Instead of the frantic work of a paramedic for Haunting victims, I leisurely studied similarities between modern medicine and healing magics. Instead of exercising every day at the dojo and the range, I danced.

The ball's glow became still and Brooke's face appeared within the smokey orb. I set aside the sword and sat.

"Hey, Pansy," Brooke's voice echoed from the ball. "Sorry to keep you waiting."

"It's fine." I waved a hand of dismissal. "I know you and Alun are busy with the Sleeping Valley waking up. Well, more than usual."

Brooke laughed. "You don't even know. What are you up to?"

"Same old, same old," I said. "Some kids are tempting death by stealing from giants. I swear, I'll never let Aeron out of Ruezdad unless it's a trip to see family or Heather in Romance."

Brooke smirked from within the ball. "Come on, what's the Adventure in that? He'll either get into trouble outside or inside the castle. Kids are kids, and if there's trouble to be found—"

"They'll find it," I finished for her. "Sure, our local giants are nothing like the mountain giant I fought with Theo and Di, but...whose dumb idea was it to provoke them? I'm just glad Aeron wasn't involved. Every moment I spend with Aeron I'm worried he'll hurt himself. I'm lucky to have a governess and tutors to count on, but I feel like I'm failing my child. How do you do it?"

"Um, one day at a time? Then thank our lucky stars that nobody died."

I buried my head in my hands and moaned. "I know how to turn everyday items into weapons against Hauntings, but everything *is* dangerous in a child's world. Bookshelves, table corners, silverware, and don't even get me started on stairs! I teach Aeron how to survive Hauntings and Adventures, but sometimes they contradict. And how am I supposed to know if he actually understands it? Like yesterday, we visited King

Aenirin's family and I caught Aeron handling the vases. I told him not to touch them so then he handled the flowers! What if they were poisonous?"

"I don't know," Brooke sighed. "Hey, did you get Heather's letter today? How's she doing? She always seems to know the answers about motherhood."

"Yeah, one second, I haven't read it yet."

I grabbed the letter from my pile of mail and slipped it open. I cleared my throat, then read, "'Dearest Marchioness Pansy Fromm...' She's so formal in her letters. Can you imagine her sitting at her desk, straight back and proper like we're supposed to be?" I laughed and slouched farther in my seat.

Brooke laughed too. "She would make the perfect princess. It's really unfair that we got the titles. What does she say?"

"'I only received your letter this morning—'" My eyes glanced at the letter's corner, dated four days ago. I sent my letter three weeks ago. "'—as a terrific thunderstorm detained all travelers for four days. Autumn has fallen upon us. Chastity and Charity have taken ill, but the doctor promises recovery.' Those twins." I smiled at the thought of them. Little saints, they only fought when competing to please their mom.

Brooke grinned. "They share everything—in sickness and in health, apparently."

"'I took Johnnie and Michael on a walk,'" I continued. "'Little Michael wouldn't let me put him down, but Johnnie enjoyed playing in the fallen leaves. We stayed out until Michael took hold of Johnnie's favorite leaf. Johnnie threw a tantrum, so it was necessary to time him out. Tip for the day, dearest Pansy: it is advised to use time-out for children less as a tool for punishment, but more as an opportunity for the child to cool down and wear off his emotions.'"

"Huh," Brooke mused, "I wouldn't have thought of that."

"Where does she learn this stuff?" I asked. "She's like a super-mom with the perfect life."

"Well, I wouldn't say perfect."

"Why not? Her biggest struggle in life is her six-year-old throwing a tantrum? And she even knows the solution?"

"I bet it's more complicated than that. We only see what she chooses to tell us."

"Everything seemed like sunshine and lemonade when we visited last summer," I said. "I don't filter my letters to her. I think that's why she tells us about her kids' tantrums, as if that's her way to relate."

Brooke sighed and paused. "So, what are your ugly details, Pansy?"

I didn't answer right away. I didn't want to. Some thoughts were easier to write about than to speak out loud. "I…I feel like Theo and I have fallen out of love."

"What?" Brooke's surprise was a small relief. I hoped others didn't notice. "Why do you think that?"

I shuffled, unsure how much to say. "We don't seem to spark anymore."

That was like the hand popping out of the ground as the full zombie threatened to emerge. Theo was always too busy or too tired. Kisses became no more than routine. Expressions of love were simply to meet expectations. With Ruezdad over fifty-thousand square feet, I went entire days without seeing Theo. It was a royal luxury for the marquis and marchioness to have their own bedrooms, so who was I to reject it and ask to share a room with my husband?

Knowing the least of my heartache, Brooke suggested, "You could try spicing things up a bit."

As if I hadn't tried. I could stare lovingly at Theo's blue-green eyes even as he ate in a rush between meetings. Why did Theo need to work so hard? I wanted to lose myself in the peace of his strong arms like when we dated. He was the epitome of royalty in appearance and mannerisms. His neatly trimmed facial hair of these past few years only added to the effect. He was succinct and precise with his words, formal yet friendly to everyone. Even with me.

His perfect public image only threw my imperfections into sharper light. As much as I wanted to join Theo in his meetings with the lords, I gained a reputation as The Unsettled Horror who couldn't sit still for one meeting. I was the commoner upstart who didn't know how to curtsy or hold her knife properly. So they said. Knives were made for weapons, not utensils.

My lost thoughts urged Brooke to continue, "Sounds like Theo needs a day off. You probably both do. Aren't you going to relax for your birthday?"

"We're royalty," I grumbled. "You don't take a day off from who you are. We celebrate Aeron's birthdays, but he's young and the future duke. I'm just the married-in marchioness who's turning twenty-seven." Besides, I never liked big social events.

"What are you talking about? Alun and I find any excuse to relax and get away!"

"What about your duties?" I asked. "Don't you have petitions and reports to go over? Events to host and attend, people to talk to, crafts to learn?" My voice dripped into heavy sarcasm by the end.

"They can wait one day. If anything major happens, we know King Aenirin can handle it."

"Knowing my luck," I muttered, "I'm sure some major catastrophe would strike the moment we decided to take a day off."

"You'll be fine. Remember, Theo was away from Fantasy for *months* while at Heartford. It sounds like you two are totally overdue for some 'you' time."

"Alright," I said, considering a possibility. "I'll try it. I'll talk to Theo during breakfast and ask for some time off for my birthday."

A day off from responsibility. It sounded too good to be true. Maybe we'd practice connecting through Sean's bond again. We had a few practice sessions since using the connection to break Oswald's hypnosis spell and create a sword to defeat Abadda. We discovered that it only worked if we were mutually open to each other. It also worked best when we were emotionally charged from tension or meditation. We hadn't connected in over a year.

I finished my call with Brooke and practiced my dance routine again, considering how to approach Theo with his favorite breakfast and the idea to run away for a day. I thought about it through dinner—which Theo took in his drawing room. Aeron stuck out his tongue at the leafy purples and played with his green potatoes. Despite my eating games and encouragement, we left the table forty-five minutes later with Aeron's meal only half eaten.

I joined Aeron and his governess in his drawing room, full of toy dragons and Adventurers that were magically enhanced to light up and reposition their limbs. Around seven-thirty, his governess bowed goodnight, and I tucked Aeron into bed. As routine, I lit his oil lamp and twisted the wick to give him light for the next hour. I read a section from *Oz's Haunting Survival Book* and checked the daggers in his drawer. Master Bahr took his position to guard Aeron's door before I locked it shut. His door was especially made to lock and unlock from both sides, but only with a key kept by Aeron, Master Bahr, his governess, Theo, and me.

Theo spent the rest of the night behind the closed doors of his father's study, so I went to the kitchens to plan my surprise breakfast before heading to my bedroom.

Breakfast was too late.

That night, I jolted awake in my bed.

What was that sound? Why did I feel a terrible dread?

"Helga?" I asked my literal tree-lamp chambermaid. The lanterns on her branches dimmed awake as she yawned with the knot in her trunk. "Did you hear that?"

"Hear what, my lady?" She stretched her branches and wiggled her three base roots. I threw on my night robe and unlocked my bedroom door to peek into the hall. All was dark and still.

I only had to turn down the hall to see something wrong. Aeron's bedroom door was ajar.

Even if Aeron simply left his room for a drink of water, I taught him better than that. I taught him that wide open doors were as dangerous as closed, but at least they were predictable. If wide open, you could catch sounds and conversations from the hallway better. If closed and locked, it served as a barrier between monsters or fires. With doors ajar, the thin crack left too many unknowns. Did someone hide behind it? Did someone peek through?

My instincts—both Horror and motherly—kicked into motion.

"Guards! Master Bahr!" I called, then tapped into my speed ability to run to Aeron's room.

I flung the door wide to reveal the struggle and terrible truth.

Aeron's bed was disheveled. A cold breeze blew at me from the broken window. The oil lamp from his nightstand was broken on the floor. A drawer hung open. One of Aeron's practice throwing daggers stuck haphazardly into his dresser. The other lay discarded on the floor, grazed with blood.

Aeron was missing.

Chapter 3

DOORS

- *Oz's Haunting Survival Book,*
with notes by Pansy Fromm

PANSY

"What happened to Aeron?" I cried. "He's supposed to be safe here! This is his home! If he isn't safe here, he isn't safe anywhere! What more could I have done to protect him? Put bars on his windows? Lock him in a dungeon?"

I sat crumpled on the floor in Aeron's room. My father-in-law, Duke Konrad Fromm, the Horse, click-clopped up and down the hallway while guards ran around Ruezdad.

"Nay," the duke said. "Kings have tried locking away their children before. It does not go well."

Theo stood at Aeron's bed. He gripped the footboard with white knuckles.

"No, Pansy," he said, "there was nothing else we could have done." I waited for him to comfort me in his arms. How badly I wanted to be held. I knew his heartbeat raced with the same distress signal as mine. He likely needed the support as much as I did. But I waited in vain.

As Aeron's personal guard, Master Bahr wouldn't stop apologizing and growling at himself for sleeping through Aeron's disappearance.

"Your son was targeted," he said. "One does not simply sneak into Ruezdad and kidnap the Earl of Margen without premeditation and scheming. I never sleep on a guard shift. Someone laced my midnight drink with a sleeping draught."

"Whoever did this will pay," I said, clenching and un-clenching my fists.

A loud roar of wind gathered and popped in the courtyard below.

"Finally," the duke muttered. He leaned over the railing to neigh to our visitor below, "Mr. John! Up here!"

"I'm *retired*, Duke Fromm!" an old and familiar voice shouted back up. "You know how many times I've woken up in the middle of the night these days?"

"You fool no one, I know you miss it. You are the best investigator I know, now come up here."

A couple minutes later, Mr. Jonathaniel Mystery (also known as Mr. John, Mr. Nathan, Mr. Nate, Mr. Niel, or Mr. E) came down the hallway. The retired detective of Mystery wore his classic trench coat and fedora hat, but underneath was a juxtaposition of cartoon cat pajama bottoms and a t-shirt that advertised a Thriller film. He stood at the doorway, roaming his eyes over the whole room. They seemed to pause and scan every item until they landed on Theo and me.

"What do you know?" he asked.

We each shuffled uneasily, hoping someone else would jump first with more information. We knew so little. But we needed to find Aeron. My head ached and my heart hammered against my chest. I couldn't rest until he was home.

I spoke first. "I found his room like this an hour ago. The servants are scouring the castle, but Theo's searching spell can't find him within sixty kilometers. I kissed Aeron goodnight at eight, like usual, then locked the door behind me."

Master Bahr stepped forward, making the Mystery detective jump and curse, "Shoot! Or, sorry, you're a bear? Uh, how are you involved with the missing child?"

Master Bahr growled. "I am Aeron's personal guard. I stayed with him until my usual late-night honey tea. That drink normally keeps me awake, but I fell asleep on my way back up the stairs."

"As far as we know," Theo said, "that was the last time anyone in Ruezdad saw Aeron."

"Did he seem troubled at all?" Mr. E asked.

I reflected on his playtime with his action figures, innocent and happy. Aeron. My little Aeron. I shook my head. "No. He smiled and said he loved me when I tucked him in."

"Yesterday afternoon," Theo began, "Aeron asked me if he could be a Hero to gain his title. He expressed distress over his unknown ability."

"He did?" I wondered. "Enough distress to make him run away?"

Mr. E shook his head. "Does this look like the room of a runaway? No, he was taken by force."

I couldn't say if his confirmation was more or less upsetting. On one hand, at least Aeron didn't *choose* to leave. On the other, he was held captive by unknown criminals. Either way, my gut ached to think of how scared he likely was.

"He could have staged his departure," Mr. E said, "but as a five-year-old? I'd say his theatrics are phenomenal. Notice the blood in particular? It's just enough to show there was a struggle, but not too much to be obvious. Could I take a sample of it for testing? Maybe it's Aeron's, but if it's the perpetrator's, it may help us find him."

Theo waved a "be my guest" hand while his wide eyes stared sightlessly at Aeron's bed. Whatever it took to find him.

The retired detective walked around the room and analyzed the window. "Any ideas why it's broken *and* unlocked?"

"I don't know," I said. Theo shook his head.

Mr. E theorized aloud, "The unlocked window suggests the kidnappers had help from inside. But then why break through? Maybe they broke in, but needed more space to carry a struggling Aeron out with them? Or there was more than one kidnapper? Maybe the smallest one broke through to open the window for his or her larger partner in crime?"

"If they had help," Master Bahr said, "it wasn't from the inside. The staff is loyal and loves Aeron as their own."

"You think so?" Mr. E asked. "Even if it's true, this wasn't a one-man job."

"What makes you say that?" I asked.

"Did you notice the contradiction between the clumsiness of the kidnapper, yet the thought out process? It seems they were first-time criminals with an experienced instructor."

"First-time criminals?" I repeated, struggling to imagine the scene. "What would drive someone to kidnap a royal child as their first act against the law?"

Mr. E didn't have an answer. He turned to the duke. "I need a list of enemies and possible suspects. Who has your family offended? Meanwhile, can I recruit some hands to investigate your grounds for tracks? Tracking your son is the first priority. Will a ransom note come? That would give us clues to our kidnappers' identities and change our tactics as it changes the criminal's motives."

Mr. E moved to leave the room, but paused as he passed Theo. My husband frowned and rubbed his hands with uncomfortable thoughts. Mr. E raised an eyebrow. "Do you have something to share, Marquis?"

Theo swallowed and clenched his teeth. "My son...has been taken. I just...fear the worst."

Mr. E nodded. "You two sit tight, alright? I'll ask my former team to send alerts for your son. If he leaves the kingdom, we'll know about it."

I stopped a cry as it left my mouth. The thought of Aeron so far from home in hostile hands made me sick with worry. My little Aeron, so far from home? The idea of him outside of Ruezdad alone twisted my gut. Eimad was a relatively safe city for its size, but for a child alone in the dark?

He wasn't alone. He was in hostile hands. Who knew what they wanted with him? Aeron. My little Aeron.

Mr. E continued, "They'll either hide him somewhere in the city, or take him farther away. Will you excuse me to search the castle while the trail's still hot?"

"Please, Mr. E," I said, "what can I do to help? I'll go crazy if I have nothing to do but think."

"How about you work on that list of suspects? Determining who kidnapped him and why will clue us into where they took him."

I turned to Theo. "Who could hate us that much?"

THEO

As Mr. E went about the castle, my father and I gathered every petition and Adventure report from the last month. The culprit had to be someone in there. I hated to think of the alternative...of a bargain coming back to haunt me. Although I feared to cause unnecessary anxiety, I needed confirmation.

I pulled Master Bahr aside. "Recruit a small team to examine the abandoned mines in Thornwood Forest. Search for any holes or signs of interference."

The bear warrior left with a bow, then I joined my wife and father at the table of petitions.

There was maybe one dissatisfied teen who received a lesser reward than desired, though I did not peg him as the kidnapping nor vengeful type. There were the possible enemies of those who had been conquered or subdued by the Heroes who reported to us, except what cause did they have against us directly? Most unnerving were the occasional reports of children-eating witches or ogres. I took a deep breath and reminded myself that those laid in wait for lost children to come to them and never broke into homes to kidnap.

We went farther, searching our records from the whole year. We found a handful more possibilities, though again, kidnapping our son as vengeance was incongruous. Our adrenaline of the night wore off with each page of research.

"What could anyone gain by taking Aeron from us?" I asked.

Father huffed. "He is the Earl of the Margen Duchy."

"Earl, not marquis," I argued. "I am next in line, not he. Why not take me instead?"

"You are a fully grown man with an ability *and* magic. You can fight back. Children are gullible, curious, and easy to ensnare, which is why we have so many problems with their Adventures. Also, as Marquis of Margen, you have a lot of influence. Someone who has your child has influence over you."

My stomach twisted. I expected a ransom note to ask for money, not a demand. Would they threaten Aeron's life to make me do something? Was there anything I would refuse to do in exchange for Aeron's safety?

"There is no ransom note as of yet," I said with little reassurance. "We can just guess what they want."

Pansy sat at a side table with her glow ball, contacting family and friends. She asked about Aeron's whereabouts, just in case he was with one of them. No one knew, but all offered condolences.

"We shall keep your family in our prayers," my sister said. "By the heavens, I cannot imagine if it was one of my own. What heartless monster could take a precious child? Oh, Pansy, you and Theo do not deserve this. Verily, I would not wish the experience on even an enemy. My husband and I will alert the people of Sword and Sorcery. If you think of anything else we can do to help, do not hesitate to ask."

"Yeah," Pansy said from her collapsed position on the table. Her voice was still hoarse from crying. "Will do."

"Give my love to Father and Theo," my sister said in closing.

The ball glow softened and my wife sighed heavily. "Should I call Heather and Jake just to let them know? I feel like we can use all the prayers we could get."

I shrugged, too drained from research, anxiety, and sleep deprivation.

Mr. E stopped by to report trampled landscaping beneath Aeron's window. Unfortunately, it was too trampled to provide a footprint. He was perplexed that he found just that one section of footprints and no more.

"Perhaps they have flight magic," the duke said.

"Fantastics," Mr. E muttered. "Why do you always have to complicate things with magic? You realize that makes it nearly impossible to track them? No ransom note has shown up either, so who's to know their motives?"

He left without another word, and we returned to our hopeless research. We searched report after petition after claim, *looking* for the times we failed to satisfy our people. While it was good to think of the many we helped, it drained my hopes to focus on those we failed. If we were honest with ourselves, anyone could have been dissatisfied in one way or another. We were imperfect, and sometimes our best was insufficient. The hardest part about ruling was the inability to please everyone.

At least it was something to do. Pansy paced across the room, probably wanting to speed time instead of herself with her ability. Minutes stretched into hours as we waited for Mr. E to return with any news at all. The servants and maids bustled about, helping the search by scouring every nook and cranny in Ruezdad. I knew Aeron was nowhere within sixty kilometers of Ruezdad from my Locate spell, though they begged to help. The door was open to the hall and we overheard their shouts to each other.

"Did you search the food storage?"

"Yes, ma'am. I pulled out the boxes to look behind as well. I take it he wasn't in the entertainment room?"

"No. I'll look in the green room next. Take Wilbur with you to search the cellar."

Somehow, it still seemed quiet. Where was Aeron's laughter? Where was Tutor White's scolding? Where were Aeron's imaginative stories or little whines when he struggled to understand the rules? Where was he? In the hands of someone who hated us enough to hurt an innocent child? I could only think of one person, though I prayed to the gods that it wasn't her.

I stared at the same report for almost a half hour before Master Bahr returned. I stood, ready for some relief.

"Lords and Lady Fromm." Aeron's guard bowed. "Knights Adler and Feld joined me to the Thornwood mines. We found them recently excavated."

Pansy frowned. "The Thornwood mines? Isn't that where we buried the wicked duchess's body? Theo? Are you okay?"

No. I was not okay. I doubled over and struggled to breathe. Everything inside of me tightened. My strength to stand wilted.

"This is all my fault," I said. Abadda was supposed to be gone. We should have been safe. I allowed myself to forget.

Pansy came to my side and rested a hand on my back. "Theo? What are you talking about?"

Curses, how would I tell Pansy? I had avoided this moment—prayed that it would never come—from the second that I accepted the bargain. At first, there was never a good time to tell her. Was there an easy way to say, "By the way, I knew you were pregnant with our son because Duchess Abadda repeated a prophecy about him having some dark ability that she wanted. Oh, and she wanted him badly enough to bargain for him."

I studied Pansy's aura. It was short. Would it spike when I revealed the truth? Swallowing back bile, I forced myself to speak.

"I made a bargain. Duchess Abadda required our first born son before she saved you with the queen's phoenix tears. Then, we beheaded and buried her. I thought she was gone. I did not think she could take her claim on him."

"Claim—you—" Pansy blinked, then exploded. "*What?*"

Her aura grew two centimeters. Curses, she wanted to hurt me.

"It was either him or you!" I said. "Abadda wanted Aeron. She wanted him for some prophecy of sorts. Regardless, he was my only bargaining chip. She cared little for my ability or magic. She wanted Aeron, and she alone had the power to save you!"

"You traded my life for Aeron's?" Pansy shouted.

"Yes!" I cried. "I gave up our unborn son for the opportunity to *have* a son!"

Her fury ebbed into despair. "Why didn't you tell me?"

"To make you *more* paranoid?"

She winced, and I regretted my words.

"Please, forgive me," I pleaded. "No one else knew except Oswald. I made the bargain hoping to destroy Abadda before Aeron was born. I thought she was…I thought…"

Of course, she was never truly defeated. She was immortal. A prophecy once stated that "only the royal bridge between life and death can destroy the root of Ruezdad's evil." We thought it identified Queen Alóvera, the Phoenix, who had powers of restoration and health. After her ability was stolen and she was killed, I hoped that it referred to the Supernatural bond that Pansy and I shared.

Pansy stepped away and sniffed back her emotions. "You thought wrong. Duchess Abadda is a condemned immortal, and now she has Aeron."

I collapsed back into my chair and sobbed. Pansy's cries in the corner only worsened my anguish. First, we lost Aeron. Then, I lost Pansy. I wept until no tears remained. Sorrow overwhelmed me as I sought the oblivion of sleep.

The next thing I knew, something wet rolled over my ear and hair. I lifted my head with an imprint of my sleeve on my face.

Duke Konrad, the Horse, licked me again.

"Ugh!" I sat up and rubbed my face dry. "Father, that is disgusting." He huffed with a horse version of a satisfied smirk and gestured to Mr. E. I blinked at the high window. The sun shined brightly through. "What is it? What time is it?"

"About one in the afternoon," Pansy said from the window, her voice ragged. She refused to meet my eyes. "Roughly ten hours since Aeron went missing."

"Theodor," Father said, "Mr. John has news."

The retired Mystery detective nodded grimly then lifted something for us to see. It was a black and white photo taken from a wide angle. The tile flooring looked like the inside of a public Contemporary building. A mall, perhaps, with the crowds. A young man and two women walked with a child between them.

Aeron!

My gut twisted as I also recognized the taller woman in a long black dress. Duchess Abadda, The Wicked.

Did they go all the way to Urban, Fantasy? What about that sign with a question mark?

Mr. E asked, "Do you recognize this man or woman?"

I leaned in and analyzed the harsh angle and blurry faces of the other two people in the photograph. I wanted to recognize them. I should have recognized them, right? Why would strangers kidnap our son? What was Abadda doing with them?

I shook my head and Pansy said, "No. But that looks like Aeron between them."

"This shot," Mr. E said, "was taken from a security camera in Noir, Mystery, International Airport at 6:43. The rest of the footage shows them boarding a plane. Lord Fromm, Lady Fromm…they took your child to Horror."

Chapter 4

EMERGENCY PACK ESSENTIALS

Even a fully charged phone and finely tuned car can
be unreliable during Hauntings
Always carry a fully charged flashlight with extra
batteries (and/or phone)

> -   *Oz's Haunting Survival Book,*
> with notes by Pansy Fromm

PANSY

My breath caught in my throat. Did I tap into my speed? No. Theo reached for me at a normal speed. Time simply seemed frozen.

Aeron. In Horror.

A flood of memories washed over me: my childhood, my youth, my adolescence. The deaths of my parents, the cruelty of orphanages, the monsters and demons… My only happy memories were with Oz and Sean, but they were both dead. I hadn't realized what a nightmare Horror was until I left it.

My little boy was in Horror with an immortal who killed her own son for more power.

My knees buckled and I sank to the ground. Theo knelt beside me and shook my arm.

"Pansy?" he shouted like it wasn't the first time he tried to get my attention.

"Huh?" was all I could say.

"Are you alright?"

My brain fuzzed around a hundred thoughts; all of them ridiculous and desperate. "Aeron."

"I know." Theo grimaced at the ground. "We will bring him back. Right, Mr. E?"

The Mystery cleared his throat. "Do you recall that Horror isn't under Mystery's jurisdiction? Who knows the risks we'd take on our nations' neutrality to send a covert team to Inferno, not to mention the risks on the team? Do you want me to risk my former investigation team against a full-scale version of what we faced in Heartford?"

Theo stood to stare down on Mr. E. "You will abandon the search because you fear Horror?"

The investigator put up his hands in defense. "What gave you the impression that I have the authority to make such an international decision? Even if I did, who would jump at the opportunity to take a Case in Horror? However, what if our friends in higher places got together? What if they arranged a special undercover elite force to extract your child? Isn't he the eventual heir to the duchy?"

Theo pondered, "How long would that take?"

"Too long," I said. My body worked on its own as I stood and walked to the door. "Time is of the essence and we've already wasted enough."

"Where are you going?" Mr. E asked.

"To pack," I said. "The next plane ticket to Inferno, Horror, has my name on it."

Mr. E sighed. "It's a good thing I'm retired, because the department would fire me for suggesting this. Who else but you two with your experiences would be the best extraction team? What if I accidentally leave my notepad in your bathroom and plead ignorance when my former boss tells me that you've taken the Case into your own hands?"

Theo paused then shook the investigator's hand. "Thank you, Mr. E."

"Good luck," he replied. "Now, where's your bathroom?"

THEO

Pansy looked up as I entered her bedchamber. She noticed the notebook in my hands and returned to stuffing her traveling pack. Her coldness towards me pierced my heart. What a mess I created. Aeron was in danger, and Pansy had every right to blame me. I had to correct my wrongs. The least I could do was accompany her search for Aeron, even if it meant going to Horror. Of all places.

"I figured," I said, "that we should pack and plan together."

She nodded with agreement, then again at the notebook. "Anything useful in there?"

"Not much. Every page is filled with sketch drawings. Most are from former Cases that are quite graphic. Regarding ours, he drew a picture of Aeron's room, and the mess of footprints below his window."

"You're serious?" Pansy scoffed. "He was drawing pictures while he interrogated me at Heartford? Does it date back to our first Haunting? It's likely labeled as the Sean Chase Case."

"No. The earliest is dated a month before his retirement."

"Too bad," she muttered, then scoffed again. "Drawings."

I managed a wan smile. "What he depicts here theorizes that a group of two or more people took our son about three hours after midnight. Judging by how quickly they were spotted in Mystery, he suspects they flew."

"Of course, Abadda has Greggory's wind ability. Then there were the two other people in the picture."

"With the Wind Master's ability, they could fly in other lands, though perhaps they were discovered by Mystery's anti-aircraft weapons. That would explain why they stopped in Mystery to board an airplane."

"If only we still had that sword that beheaded Abadda," Pansy grumbled. "You had to lose the one weapon strong enough to cut an immortal?"

"I did not lose Videliz," I groaned. "We know exactly where it is."

"But we can't get it."

"The wizard said he would preserve it for future generations! How was I to know he would stab it into an anvil, never to be removed?"

Pansy sighed as if every old argument we ever had now compounded onto her frustration for my secrets. How could I mend her broken trust in me when she seemed determined to break it over and over again?

"Come now," I urged, "tell me about Inferno. You lived in a town nearby, did you not? Is it just as Dante described in his original explorations?"

"When I think about how much I've changed these last several years," Pansy said, "I can't say if Horror is exactly how I remember it. Inferno is about fifty miles from Brimstone. Do you think they'd take Aeron to my last home? If so, why? I have no connections there anymore."

"I know not," I said. "We will follow them to Inferno first. Do you want the footmen to help us pack?"

"I'd rather keep our departure secret. We can turn our affairs over to the duke while we're gone, and maybe he'll cover for us."

As if abandoning our duties was that easy. Father and the people depended on us. I needed them to depend on us because a useless royal was a dethroned royal. Hopefully, our absence would be short.

I nodded to Pansy. "Yes, alerting the people of Abadda's return would cause unnecessary alarm when she has already fled to Horror. Also, if Abadda is unaware of our chase, then we have the element of surprise."

Pansy set aside her pack. "Okay, I have our hygiene needs. We'll need to buy new Contemporary clothes. I doubt my clothes from university days would fit me anymore anyway. We'll need jackets. It's colder up north, especially during the fall. Horror's probably all decorated for Halloween right now. Prepare for pumpkins."

Halloween sounded like a dangerous time to be in Horror as Hauntings roamed freely in the streets. If Pansy's birthday was tomorrow, then Halloween was just the day after. I hoped to have Aeron home before then and to celebrate over a small dinner as Pansy preferred.

I opened the door between our chambers and rummaged through my drawers. I was certain I had a set of Contemporary clothes somewhere as I sifted through tunics and lace-up shirts. Likewise, I was sure that I outgrew them. While my arms were more muscular from wand forms and training, my gut was larger from sitting and...not training. Pansy kept her strength with speed sprints and dances, though motherhood emphasized some flattering curves around her bodice and hips.

My fingers reached the bottom of my drawer and slid across the back until they found a small latch. I pushed on it to unlock my hidden compartment on the side of my dresser. I pulled out my mythril arm brace for the Wand of Gandiduz. Even if my magic worked differently in Horror, I wanted every advantage available.

"We may take a transporting spell to Mystery," I said, "then buy any Contemporary supplies there."

Pansy mumbled over her emergency pack and weapons. "My magical crossbow probably won't work outside of Fantasy, but will my revolver work after all this time? How many of which bullets should I take?"

"Take them all," I said, giving little thought to the items I stashed into my luggage. "Who knows what spell, trick, or tool will save Aeron from Abadda?"

Twenty minutes later, we had two small suitcases for Pansy's necessities and anything that I thought we could ever need in Horror.

Pansy and I snuck down the stairs to the stables of Ruezdad only to be caught by an unexpected visitor. My younger brother leaned against the doorframe.

Of my living siblings, I saw Dunstan, the Night Shade *Priest*, the least, though that was expected when competing against Di. Even as my sister lived in the center of Sword and Sorcery, Di and Pansy exchanged letters every week. My only living brother, however, lived in the abbey skirting Eimad, and I could count on one hand how many times I saw him. Dunstan fled after our duel for the duchy's right. It took a couple weeks to find and invite him to return to Eimad as a priest. My first time seeing him in the abbey for Aeron's infancy cleansing was similar to our meeting now.

With all the reverence of a humble priest, Dunstan bowed before us. His light aura was just a few centimeters long. He had many of our mother's features, including her bubble nose, thin eyebrows, and emerald green eyes. His shaved head reflected the afternoon light and his simple cloak draped loosely with just a rope around his waist. Most of the priests of Eimad wore grey or brown cloaks. Dunstan's was all black.

Despite his short aura, I eyed my brother warily and kept my wand ready for anything. Six years ago, I was his age at twenty-four, graduated with my Masters in Political Science, marrying the woman of my dreams, and rescuing the Margen Duchy from tyranny. Meanwhile, Dunstan established himself as a villain through all of Fantasy and morphed his ability to absorb light to also convert the light into heat for fiery punches. As a dangerous attack, it was equally dangerous for him to wield it. Rumor said that our duel was the last time he used it.

I rubbed at my chest where he had burned me. If I turned too quickly, the area still tightened and refused to stretch.

These last six years, my brother reportedly stayed out of trouble as well as a reformed terrorist could. He changed his name to Douglas, The Priest, and denied his relationship to the royal family. He had been disinherited after all. Old enemies crept up now and again, though the abbey's leaders said that he worked hard to learn the path of a priest. The magic came with difficulty because of his ability, still only halfway through the apprenticeship after all these years.

Dunstan straightened from his bow and went straight to the point. "I heard Aeron was taken to Horror by our wicked stepmother."

Both of my eyebrows arched high. Pansy frowned.

"How did you hear that?" she asked.

He scoffed. "Please. One of the maids keeps me informed. Maybe she has a thing for me? Anyway, I know my nephew's missing and your favorite detective left you disappointed. Naturally, you made the irrational decision to take the matter into your own hands. Even if it means going after the woman who plotted to overthrow our entire family and kingdom by tricking us individually, stealing abilities, and becoming a bullbegging immortal. Admit it, neither of you are thinking straight. I care about Aeron, but I'm less emotionally distressed than you two. Let me be your voice of reason."

"You?" I guffawed. "The voice of *reason?*"

His downward smirk said, "Of course, you dolt." Dunstan the Night Shade was hardly my first choice for an ally. Six years ago, he tried to kill me to "save" me from Oswald's wrath. Surely, he had an angle.

"You want to go to Horror with us?" Pansy asked, dubious.

My younger brother folded his arms. "I want a lot of things. I want my only living brother to trust me. I want to go on an Adventure and leave the confines of Eimad Abbey. I want to help you take revenge on the wicked witch who tricked me into becoming a terrorist. I want to woo a couple more women before I lose all my hair—oh wait, too late for that. I shave it."

While his light joke released a laughing grunt from Pansy, I frowned.

"Do you know anything about Horror?" I asked.

He gestured to my wife. "Sure, I read that book of yours. I found it fascinating!"

Pansy rocked back, surprised. "You read *Oz's Haunting Survival Book*?"

While his words impressed Pansy, I narrowed my eyes. "Fascinating" was not the word most Fantastics used to describe the book written by Pansy's brother. "Unsettling" was more common, which Pansy still took as a compliment since her title was the Unsettled.

He gave me a cheeky grin. "Come on, you need me. You're trying to be discreet, but have either of you ever gone undercover or done a covert Adventure? I have. Multiple times. Also, it's in my best interest to keep you both alive. If you die, guess who will be stuck running the duchy? Really, tell me because I don't know which would make Father cringe more, demoting Di from an S&S princess or promoting me to marquis. Sounds like a no-win situation if you ask me."

"Nobody asked you," I said.

"Exactly!" He grinned. "Which means I'm here out of the pure goodness of my heart."

Doubtful. My frown deepened. His attitude was the same as ever, though his interests had apparently shifted these past few years. I had to admit that his experiences with travel and gathering information would be helpful to find Aeron.

Pansy pulled me aside to whisper, "What's his aura like? Can we trust him?"

I glanced back to confirm, then sighed. "It is short. I do not fully trust him, however, he seems earnest. Also, he makes a good point. We need as much help as possible, and who else would join us?"

Pansy chewed on her lip and counted aloud on her fingers. "Among those we trust? Master Bahr would become a mute outside Fantasy, and Lieutenant Greenblade can't leave fairy lands. Brooke and Alun are busy with the Sleeping Valley. Di wouldn't want to risk her pregnancy. Heather and Jake are too far and would likely look for any excuse not to go to Horror. Mr. E made his position clear…but is Dunstan really our best option?"

I made another quick analysis of his short aura. He said he wanted me to trust him. Yes, Dunstan was our best option. I gave Pansy a nod before turning back to my brother.

"Just to clarify," I said, "you understand the risks of joining us? I mean more than the dangers of Horror. As a priest, your magic is bound by your oath to serve only the gods of Adventures. If you become involved in a Haunting, then you will break your oath and lose your magic."

Dunstan waved his hand without consequence. "Yeah, yeah, the bishops give us the talk every blue moon. Don't get cozy with the priestesses, or you'll start a Romance and lose your magic. They go on and on. Not like I have a lot to lose anyway."

"Will our magic work in Horror?" I asked.

Pansy bit her lip. "Horror has magic, but it's mostly used by Hauntings. We'll need to be careful when we use our abilities and magics."

"Along those lines," Dunstan said, "your first tip about going incognito: don't let anyone see you perform any special skills that will reveal your identity. I will refrain from using my awesome ability unless necessary, and the same goes for Pansy's ability. Theo, your ability could be hallucinations for all we know, so you're probably fine." He finished with a cheeky grin at me.

"More importantly," Pansy said, "if anyone sees something supernatural, they'll think we're Hauntings to be distrusted and killed. If we use magic at all, it should be in secret or our last act to escape Horror so nothing can follow us. Isn't there a spell to transport people back to a certain location? We should have our escape plan ready before we leave."

Dunstan nodded. "Teleportation. There's a priest at the abbey who's especially good at crafting the spell."

"Fantastic," I said with little enthusiasm. "We may have one written for each of us to come directly back to Fantasy. That way, we can use them as soon as we have Aeron in hand."

Dunstan took us to the specific priest who penned our tickets home—four teleportation spell pages. The directions to use them were fairly simple. When we found Aeron, we would burn all four spell pages to transport back to the place where they were created, Eimad Abbey. We purchased three more spells that were created on the northern border of Middle Novel to save us time from traveling across Fantasy. I took a couple seconds to calm my nerves as the three pages slowly burned.

We were headed for Aeron. We were headed for Horror. We were headed for Duchess Abadda, my wicked immortal stepmother who wielded multiple abilities and put Margen through chaos with her schemes to take over the world.

The last of the spell pages became black from the fire and we found ourselves at the exit of a mountain tunnel, a couple steps away from Mystery.

As soon as we passed the border into the magicless Mystery, my wand weighed heavier in my arm brace. I tried a quick spell to create a small wind burst. Nothing happened. Dunstan, likewise, complained about a headache.

From the border, we called a taxi to Mystery's international airport. We had to wander the airport's misguided signs with question marks and clues until we found a shop to buy new outfits: Overt Clothes.

"Second tip for going unnoticed," Dunstan said, browsing the t-shirts with pop culture logos. "Blend in with the right apparel."

"This feels like a waste of time," I grumbled. "Who cares what we wear as we fight Abadda and rescue our son?"

My wife cleared her throat. "I'm actually going to side with Dunstan on this one. Our Fantasy clothes are too baggy for snagging and use laces that take too long to remove if caught in snares. We'll stand out wearing these clothes, and anyone who stands out in Horror is singled out by Hauntings. The last thing we want is to be caught in a Haunting that distracts us from finding Aeron."

Chapter 5

APPAREL

Never wear something that could be used as a
choking device against you
Beware of anyone who wears or uses a lot of dead
stuff: bones/teeth, fur, leather...

- *Oz's Haunting Survival Book,*
with notes by Pansy Fromm

THEO

Pansy tried to buy some running shoes for me until I convinced her that I could run just as well in my boots. I had never worn ankle shoes and saw no need to start now. We changed in the bathrooms, and Pansy insisted that Dunstan and I shared a stall for safety reasons. I shuffled uneasily out of my clothes.

"Looks like you've settled into your place as the marquis." Dunstan smirked.

I scowled back. "Is that a comment on the weight or the scars that I gained?"

Dunstan's eyes narrowed on the large burn scar on my chest—the one that he gave me during our duel for the duchy.

He pinched his lips into a line, and his eyes mellowed before they moved to my wand bracer. "What's that?"

"None of your business," I said, stepping into my new pair of black dress slacks. The only people who knew about the true source of my magic were those I trusted and Duchess Abadda. I could trust Dunstan to go on an insanely dangerous Adventure to help me rescue my son, though trusting him with my secrets was a different bridge he would need to build.

"Alright." Dunstan shrugged as he shuffled into a pair of dark jeans. "Then what about that welt?" He pointed at my left arm.

"Oh, this?" I flexed my bicep to show off a red scar the size of a coin. "That is from the time Pansy shot me."

"Pansy shot you?"

"Twice. I have another welt on my leg."

Dunstan gaped. "Have I ever mentioned what a weird couple you are?"

I smirked back and buttoned up my new long-sleeve collared shirt. "She was hypnotized by Oswald and apologized over a hundred times for each."

"Still," Dunstan chuckled, slipping on a black t-shirt with some rock band logo. "I never imagined you with a girl like her. For myself, however..."

My smirk fell to a growl. "Dunstan, if you even think—"

"Down, boy," my brother laughed. "I said 'like' her. Besides, I prefer women younger than me. And just because I'm forbidden from Romances during my apprenticeship doesn't mean I can't appreciate some of the gods' finest creations."

I replied with only a scoff as I finished my ensemble.

Either the styles had changed these last few years or I forgot how simple Contemporary clothes were. My new dress slacks covered my boot's knee-high laces so that they appeared Contemporary enough. I wore my button-up shirt sans the necktie because Pansy said those were just choking hazards in Horror.

I finished my outfit with a black suit coat while Dunstan wore a rain jacket over his jeans and t-shirt.

Although Dunstan and I spent time in different Contemporary lands, Pansy seemed the most comfortable in her change of clothes.

She exited the women's bathroom looking just as she had when I first met her: faded jeans that were neither too loose nor too tight, a black tank top, an easy to remove green zip-up jacket, and, of course, running shoes.

She was as beautiful as ever. She nodded with approval over our new outfits. "We'll need alibis and new personas to blend in."

"I'll work on that," Dunstan said. "You can probably pass as a local," he said to Pansy, then gestured to me. "You'll fit in as a traveling businessman."

"Are you sure—"

"Yes, Theo," my brother cut me off. "This is why you brought me along, isn't it?"

"You basically begged us to take you," Pansy muttered.

Dunstan continued, "I spent a fair amount of time hiding and pretending to be a stranger in various towns. I lived in Frog's Mouth for eight months before someone unveiled my identity. Unfortunately, then, the town needed a blackout for my escape."

I narrowed my eyes at my brother's casual shrug, as if the three years he spent as a vagabond were just a mistake of the past.

"My point is," he said, "I'm the experienced one on the topic of sneaking around."

I frowned. He seemed proud of that.

"Whatever, let's go," Pansy said. I expected her to go to the help desk, or to stop one of the many officers and ask for directions to their security room. Instead, she beelined for our gate terminal.

"Should we not go to the authorities for their security footage?" I asked.

"No," she said. "We can't attract attention or we'll let the kidnappers know we're onto them."

"The officers could help us," I said. "We are visiting dignitaries. Will they not want to help?"

"No, remember how Mr. E reacted? He said he'd be fired for suggesting we take the Case into our own hands. Also, Horror's very independent. Strangers—especially foreigners—are treated with suspicion, and you—" she pointed at me "—look royal even dressed as a businessman. Crap, the locals won't trust you for a second."

"They won't trust the Trusted?" Dunstan teased. "Theo, you're a politician. Doesn't that make you a professional liar?"

I scowled. "No. I may omit truths beyond their understanding or tell them just the truths they need to hear, though I do not lie to our people."

"Omit truths," Pansy scoffed, "like your bargain with Abadda?"

I shrank from her bite. Dunstan missed her accusation and nudged me in the ribs. "The best way to not be caught in a lie is to tell as many truths as possible. Believe me, I know."

Pansy bit her lip. "It's not like we're here to make friends. We only need to blend in enough to not raise suspicion as we ask people about Aeron."

Dunstan stepped between us to wrap his arms around our shoulders. "You have enough to worry about just finding your son. If anyone asks why we're here, let me take care of it."

As badly as I wanted to explain our situation to the police in Mystery, it would have caused a stir to ask for their camera footage. I figured the footage at the Horror airport would be more informative anyway. Rookie mistake.

"Why is security so sparse here?" I asked as we walked through the single Horror exit terminal. The turbulent ride on our small propeller plane left me nauseated as we exited to the taxiway. I had little experience with airports, though compared to Mystery's international airport, Horror's runway was cracked, the service reluctant, and the security lacking. Weeds poked through the pavement and stretched with greedy vines. The two people manning the concessions lounged across their counter, watching the TV that buzzed with static and reported severe dust storms in the Valley of Death. Where Mystery had an officer at every intersection and cameras every five meters, the airport of Inferno had no security manning the exit terminals and cameras that hung from their wires as if some earthquake shook them down.

Pansy spread her arms to slow Dunstan and me. "Slow down, guys. In Horror, there are only two speeds: bored like there's nothing happening, and run for your life. The only reason someone walks quickly with purpose is when they're trying to avoid being noticed. Obviously, it doesn't work, so slow down and saunter."

Dunstan took to the new pace with an easy stride. I struggled to relax. Everything about my natural bearing—from my diction to my gait—was meant to show the people of Margen that I was capable of important duties. Not to mention, this place put me on edge, and I wanted to search quickly for Aeron.

We walked through the terminal without anyone asking for our passports. How were we supposed to find Aeron in this place with so little security?

I muttered to my wife, "I truly find it difficult to believe that you grew up around systems as broken as these. Is there no international check-in?"

Pansy shrugged. "They're more concerned about Hauntings leaving Horror and causing international incidents. If anything dangerous enters Horror, either the Supernaturals take it out or it joins the throngs of Hauntings to be eventually taken out by the locals. But Duchess Abadda's already proved herself to be a Mass Haunting. If we don't rescue Aeron and take her down, hundreds will die before the locals can rise against her. Also, the lack of cameras is normal for Horror. They're more often broken or glitching than not."

"Do they forget to pay the electric bill?" Dunstan asked.

"No, cameras are simply faulty technology to easily black-out, flicker, or trick the eyes."

"And I thought Mystery was weird," Dunstan murmured.

"On the other hand, there are always eyewitnesses." Pansy trailed off as she approached a wandering security guard and held up our most recent picture of Aeron. "Excuse me, sir? Do you recognize this child?"

I laughed to myself. The change was so subtle that her slip into the Horror accent was probably subconscious. She spoke as if every topic was as secretive as a crime and as exciting as taxes.

Hoping to jog the guard's memory, I added, "He would have come through just this morning with a couple others."

The guard narrowed his eyes at my accent. Keeping me in his peripheral, he squinted at the picture and leaned in close. "Yeah, I think I remember him. There were two young folks and a creepy woman with him. Walked way too fast and held the boy between them. Had a dark presence about them. Was glad to see them leave without a fuss."

"Did you see where they were headed?" I asked.

The guard looked up. "You have an odd accent and your questions are Mysterious. Official Case workers don't belong here."

"Huh?" Dunstan stepped up with feigned confusion. "Oh! No, they're just friends of ours. We're trying to meet up, but we lost contact."

"Oh." The guard didn't seem to believe his story, but caved. "I remember they took a cab. That's all I saw."

"Thanks." Pansy nodded with a flicker of a smile.

We picked up our luggage and followed the signs for the taxis. As we stepped outside, I blinked to adjust my eyes.

"What time is it?" I asked. "I thought we landed at four-thirty. How is it already sunset?"

"Oh, crap," Pansy said. "I forgot, we get fewer daylight hours in the north. The deeper you go into the city, the fewer daylight hours you get."

"I think I'm going to like it here." Dunstan smiled.

Pansy wrung her hands with nerves, eyes darting between taxis. "I hoped to do some searching before night fell, but we need to get inside as soon as possible."

Before I could ask what she meant, she dashed to a cabby who stood beside his taxi. He looked bored, but lifted a casual smile as we neared. He helped us pack our luggage in the trunk while Pansy scoped out the back seats.

"It's clear," she whispered to me.

Of what? I set aside my questions and opened the door for her.

"Where can I take you?" the cabby asked.

"What's the least haunted hotel in the city?" Pansy asked, fully immersed in her Horror accent.

"That'd be the Pinnacle Hotel in the eighth circle."

"Perfect," Pansy said. "Take us there, please."

"Sure thing," he said, pulling onto the highway. "What brings you guys to Inferno?"

We shared a suspicious glance between ourselves before Dunstan piped out, "Family reunion."

"Ah, that's nice," the driver said. "Where you from?"

Again, we didn't answer right away and Dunstan took over. "Guess."

The cabby hummed and searched us with his eyes. I would have preferred that he kept his eyes to the road.

He pointed at Pansy. "You're a Horror local, but I can't tell if from nearby. I'm gonna guess nearby. And you—" he pointed at Dunstan, "—are either a Thriller or Regency, Romantic. You…" He pointed at me and paused. "I can't tell. You look like you're from anywhere but here, so I'm gonna guess Mystery or Childrens."

I raised an eyebrow.

Dunstan, however, smiled broadly. "Whoa, you're good," he said, with a look to me that said "play along." My eyebrow went higher, especially when my brother added darkly, "Except I am not a Romantic."

Pansy laughed and nudged him in the side. "Yeah, I said that too, more than once."

"Well," I leaned over to whisper, "he is a priest. Romances are forbidden."

As we left the airport behind, I stared out the window. Soon, we entered a highway that circled the great city of Inferno. We drove as if on the cusp of a funnel, the whole city contained within a giant valley that gently sloped downward to the center. Heavy rain clouds blocked our view of the far end, though the view from the top was quite the spectacle. Yellow city lights lined the streets, reflecting the sharp layers of soil as the city deepened. Our cabby took us under an arch that Pansy called Hell's Gate, then over the River of Woe. Lovely.

We passed well-established neighborhoods and small businesses. I imagined Pansy running through the streets, growing up in a place such as this. With the sun dipping into the horizon, the yellow and flickering street lights offered little to see. The houses we passed were adorned with jack-o-lanterns, orange lights, and decorations of skeletons, ghouls, and witches in yards. At least, they looked like decorations.

It was early for dinner, though there was little activity in the streets. The night life remained limited even when we entered the city.

I remembered the Romantic city of Heartford. The similarities to Inferno were few. Inferno's buildings did not scrape the skies or gleam with bright lights. They were simple buildings, blocky and repetitive. A couple tall buildings cluttered the center of the pit/city, though no light shined from them. If anything, one building appeared iced over and absorbed the light as a black hole.

"That's the Twilight Tower," Pansy said, noticing my gaze. "Inside the innermost circle, it's one of the most haunted buildings in Inferno. It's built over the original location of the Bate's Motel, has a broken elevator that goes straight to the underworld, and has the infamous room 1408."

"What about our hotel?" I asked the cabby.

"The Pinnacle?" he confirmed. "It has five star ratings and hasn't had a Haunting since it was built a few years ago. Located in the eighth circle, it was built to be the safest hotel in the city as it only has ten floors, no balconies, and on-site mechanics and plumbers. Its security is supposed to be top notch too, with a police and fire department across the street."

"Sounds good," Pansy said, nodding with approval.

I leaned over to whisper, "Why are we checking into a hotel? We should be on the trail for Aeron."

Pansy grimaced. "I know, but we need to get inside before night falls."

Descending into the valley, we drove over a wide and dark river which Pansy labeled as "Phlegethon." The land itself seemed to burn, then boil. The cab exited the highway as the ground changed to the blackness of a pit. Strange birds picked at the trees' dead branches. Pansy called the birds Harpies, then pointed out another river in the distance as the River of Blood. How could she say those labels so matter-of-factly?

The last of the sun's rays ducked beneath the sloped horizon as we slowed to a stop at a well-lit building. It looked almost as fancy as a Romantic hotel with all the Contemporary luxuries. A young man in a fancy suit escorted a woman into the hotel. I narrowed my eyes at the mock brand of his suit and the fake jewels on the woman as she slipped her hand into his pocket. They disappeared through the doors before I could call out their dishonesty. Disgruntled, I paid our driver, and we gathered our luggage.

Pansy spoke in a whisper though no one else was around to hear. "Stick to the story from the cab. We're here for a family reunion—which is true in its own way. I'm from Eastern Horror, you're from Mystery, and Dunstan's from Thriller or Regency, Romance."

Dunstan, oddly, winced when Pansy said his name.

"All the Priests of Eimad call me Douglas," he muttered. "Those who know me as Dunstan know me as the Night Terror. Also, I'll take the Thriller story over the Romantic."

"Right, sorry," Pansy apologized, then gave him a pointed look. "But not all Romantics are brainless flirts. You go ahead and pretend you're a Thriller, but as soon as you talk, they'll peg you as a Regency-someplace. You might use contractions and slang, but your posture and accent are too refined to be otherwise."

She did not wait for his response as she took her bag and walked past the electric doors of the Pinnacle Hotel. The lobby was nicely furnished with a modern style. Dunstan's eyes practically drooled over the plush couches and gas fireplace.

"It's been a long time since I've lived with luxuries," Dunstan said.

"Is the abbey so deprived?" I asked.

"No, though sometimes I miss the comforts of Urban."

Pansy walked right up to the check-in desk like she owned the place. The receptionist looked no older than fifteen. Black and blue bruises blotched her face and arms, despite her obvious attempts to cover them with makeup. As if all was well with the world, she smiled and welcomed us.

"Hi," Pansy said. "Do you have any double queens open?"

"Yes," the receptionist said. "I can check you in tonight. I just need your IDs and a deposit."

Pansy turned back to me. She made a show of asking for our cards and whispered under her breath, "Can you secretly enchant them to fit our stories?"

"Can I?" I whispered. "You want me to use magic?"

"It's a quick test to see if it works," she said. "We should keep our identities secret so Abadda won't know we're here."

"Alright," I said. "How do you say 'change' in Latin?"

"*Mutatio*," Pansy whispered before she turned around to hand the receptionist our IDs.

I disguised my wand arm movements by scratching Pansy's back. I translated the Latin word into the language of magic, then concentrated. "*Mudadio*. Pansy Finster, a local Horror. *Mudadio*. Theodor Finster, her husband from Mystery, and—*Mudadio*—Douglas Finster, his brother from Thriller."

An unexpected emotion of mischief rose within me as I concentrated on the illusion. The lie thrilled inside of me, urging me to use my powers for my own benefit. I snuffed out the disturbing thoughts and focused my magic.

"Thank you, Mrs. Finster," the receptionist said, handing back our cards. Apparently, my magic worked in Horror. Though, I wondered about that unexpected emotion.

I pushed the thought aside as Pansy raised an eyebrow at me for labeling all of us under her maiden name. She hid her surprise well as the receptionist handed her a disclosure agreement.

"What's this?"

"Because you're a local," the receptionist said, "we need to confirm your last Haunting was within the last six months. It should only take a minute or two to fill out. We have a reputation to hold as the least Haunted hotel in Inferno. We haven't hosted a Haunting since we opened five years ago."

"That's why we came here," Pansy said.

The clerk shrugged. "Yep. The money we save on cleaning goes into ensuring the safety of our guests."

"How do you confirm a person's last Haunting?" I asked.

Since Pansy was preoccupied with her Haunting History form, the receptionist handed me the clipboard to finish our check-in. She explained, "We send the report to the Hauntings Investigations Unit to confirm. The form alone scares away most liars, which is good, because HIU's busy this time of year."

Pansy raised her head from the form to flash a quick smile. "Sure."

I tried to hide my smirk. The receptionist was a talkative security flaw. Regardless, we expected to be in and out of this town before they even noticed us. I admired Pansy's struggle to lie as she filled out the disclosure about our Haunting in Romance, pretending the incident with her fiancé's poltergeist happened eight weeks ago instead of eight years ago. The receptionist handed over our keycards and a flyer about the hotel. "Room number 229. Information about the pool and breakfast times are in the flyer. Enjoy your stay."

We gathered our luggage and I had to search a bit to find Dunstan. He had wandered to the stand of flyers that advertised places to shop, events to see, and haunted tours. Seeing our readiness, Dunstan picked up a single map and followed us up the stairs to the second floor. He opened it for reading as we walked down the hall to our room. The hotel deserved its five star rating—clean, contemporary upgrades, thick walls, and advanced door locks.

We passed by a young man wearing all black, sunglasses, a thick silver chain necklace, and his hood over his head. I kept my wand ready and watched our auras until he sauntered by.

Pansy nudged me. "Theo, calm down. It's only a punk in a hoodie."

"Forgive me," I said, forcing out a deep breath. "I stereotyped him as someone who might try to mug us."

To my surprise, Pansy laughed. "I'd love to be attacked by someone wearing a hoodie. They're so easy to choke out. Crap, I could really use a good sparring match right now."

She shook her arms and stretched her fingers. Yes, I likewise wanted to work out my tension.

"Huh," Dunstan said with his nose in the map. "Your city's backwards. All other cities that I've visited consider their inner circle as zone or area *one*. Here, it's labeled as the ninth circle and the numbers lower as they go out."

Pansy slid her key into our door lock and it beeped green. "If we run into Dante's ghost, we'll tell him he discovered our city zones in the wrong order. For now, welcome to the eighth circle of Inferno—home of frauds, barrators, thieves, and the demons who torture them."

Chapter 6

DEFINITIONS

Supernaturals are God's helpers.
Hauntings are the monsters that serve the Devil.
Hauntings can also refer to the experiences of
interacting with the monsters.

- *Oz's Haunting Survival Book,*
with notes by Pansy Fromm

PANSY

We dropped off our luggage to our little two-queen-bed hotel room. The mattress boards lay flat on the floor so no one could hide underneath, and there was no door for the linens closet to hide behind. There were no doors over the bathroom cupboards, and the mirror was only large enough to reflect a single face. Flipping the light switches off did little to diminish the light. A large emergency light shined above the doorway.

Dunstan scoffed. "I'm going to absorb that while we sleep. I need complete darkness."

As much as I appreciated the Pinnacle's efforts to keep a Haunt-free zone, I agreed. That light was too bright for sleeping. I glanced through our second-story barred window with no balcony. Our view revealed an overcast sky above and dim lights below. I tugged the curtains shut.

"Theo, can you cast Search?"

Theo sat on the floor and rested his wand hand to his side. He closed his eyes and took deep breaths.

The searching spell had its drawbacks. It searched a kilometer per second, but only revealed distance, not direction. It also had a time limitation. If cast again within twelve hours, the accuracy became unreliable. Theo joked that the spell was made that way to prevent stalkers and hide-and-go-seek cheating.

"So," Dunstan mused, "what's the deal with magic in Horror?"

"I'm actually a little surprised it works here," I said. "Horrors are extreme realists. Anything unnatural is received with skepticism and attributed to the Supernaturals or Hauntings."

"So if someone saw that—" He pointed at Theo, who glowed a soft yellow "—they'd think he was a god?"

"A Haunting is more likely. But possibly a Supernatural."

Theo's eyes snapped open. "Aeron is here."

I dropped beside him. "Where? How close?"

"I counted four seconds before I sensed him, which means he is between four and five kilometers away."

"That's not too far," I said. For the first time since Aeron was taken from us, I felt hope. Aeron was nearby. We crossed half of Novel and ended up in one of the most dangerous cities, but we were hot on the trail. "Let's check the map."

Theo used a compass to draw two perfect circles on our map of Inferno, one at four kilometers from our location and the other at five kilometers. Aeron was somewhere between the two circles.

I laughed a little. "I was surprised when you packed that kind of a compass. Adventurers pack like mothers with a diaper bag."

"What?" Dunstan chuckled. "You don't appreciate the Adventurer rule to always be prepared?"

"I do," I said. "It aligns with my brother's rules to survive Horror, but Hauntings are much more predictable. I generally only need what's in my emergency pack. You guys brought everything but the kitchen sink."

"I packed a portable cauldron," Theo said.

"Never mind." I palmed my forehead. "You remember the formula to find the circumference?"

"Something about pie?" Theo offered.

Dunstan laughed and did some calculations on a notepad with the hotel logo. "I finally found a use for those lessons from the abbey. If your radius is five kilometers, minus the area of four kilometers… Your son is somewhere within this twenty-eight-ish kilometer area."

"Twenty-eight kilometers?" My heart dropped.

How could we be so close, yet so far away from finding our son? My husband looked at me with an encouraging smile.

"We will find him."

"We'd better," I said. There was no other option. "Where do you think we should start?"

"Is this a park?" Theo pointed to a green spot within the search area and sixth circle of Inferno. "We could quickly search the large open area, then try some of the buildings nearby."

"Next tip for covert missions," Dunstan said, "familiarize yourself with the lay of the land."

"We can't go outside," I said.

"Why not?" Theo asked.

"Horror isn't safe after nightfall."

"Night fell before five o'clock."

"Fantasy isn't safe either at night." Dunstan shrugged. "Never stopped me from going out."

"No," I said, "Horror after dark is worse than Fantasy at *midnight*."

That made the brothers pause. All Fantastics knew that midnight was a special time for breaking or solidifying spells, curses, and enchantments. People shifted, potions changed, and promises became fulfilled. Nothing was predictable. The safest place to spend the hour was tucked in bed behind the threshold of a loved home.

Only, in Horror, those spells, curses, and enchantments wanted to kill anything they touched.

Theo shuffled. "What is the likelihood that they will move Aeron before the morning?"

"Slim," I said, "unless they're desperate to brave the Hauntings of the night because they know we're on their trail. That's why we need to avoid attention."

Dunstan grumbled, "And here I was so excited to finally get out of the abbey. If Theo casts his searching spell again, that could narrow our search to specific areas where the circles cross."

Theo nodded, rummaging through his pack. "I cannot cast Search again for another twelve hours. However, I know Locate and could try scrying on Aeron to see his surroundings."

"Don't you need to be within so many feet to use Locate?" I asked. "And when did you learn to scry?"

"Three hundred meters." He shrugged. "And I am still learning Scry."

"Okay," I said. "We can Scry from the privacy of our hotel room tonight. Then tomorrow morning, we'll check out the park. Supposing there's a place private enough to perform magic, we can try a second Search. If Aeron's close enough, we'll use Locate. This is all assuming that Aeron isn't moved. They can just keep moving him and they'll forever be one step ahead of us."

Dunstan put a thoughtful hand under his chin. "Looks like it's time that I act as the party's voice of reason. Pansy, when was the last time you ate? Or slept?"

I frowned back. As if those things mattered when our son was missing.

Dunstan clapped his hands together. "I thought so. You say there's nothing we can do until sunrise? Fine. Then use this time to prepare. Eat, sleep, take a bubble bath—whatever. I think Scry requires a calm and focused mind, so get in the right mood."

Theo and I grumbled from irritation and frustration, but complaining about the situation didn't change it. There was little we could do until sunrise. I couldn't stop worrying about Aeron, but the last twelve hours of high anxiety and no sleep or food really exhausted my body. Some Rest & Relaxation sounded nice.

I unpacked my hygiene bag and went to the bathroom. If we started a Haunting, all hygiene went out the window, but for now, I appreciated the luxury.

After my nightly preparations and checking the faucets for leaks, I stepped out. "Bathroom's open—where's Dunstan?"

"He went out to buy food," Theo said. Based on his position on the floor, closed eyes, and deep breaths, I assumed he was meditating. Too bad his words escalated my nerves.

"You let him go alone?" I shouted.

Theo's eyes blinked open. "Yes? We skipped breakfast and lunch. Dunstan volunteered to fetch dinner."

"Alone?" I repeated.

"Either he went alone or we left you here alone," Theo said. "Of the three of us, Dunstan is the only one who has mingled with villains. We reckoned with his experiences, he can hold his own, and he is our best scout for rumors. Also, he is the least recognizable. Aeron's kidnappers will be on alert for his parents, not his uncle who has stayed in an abbey for the past several years."

"But—"

"He already left. Do you want me to call him back with a messenger spell?"

I grumbled. Using magic openly would only make things worse. "You better pray he doesn't get distracted by some old sage selling adorable little monsters or a lady with pretty jewelry that's likely cursed."

Theo grunted. "Knowing Dunstan, those are real possibilities. Speaking of prayers—" he rummaged through his suitcase "—will you join me for the scrying spell?"

I took a few calming breaths and drank some water before sitting beside my husband. He created a triangle with Aeron's throwing dagger, most recent picture, and a vial of his hair collected from his hairbrush. Theo filled his mini cauldron with water, then placed it in the middle of the objects.

"I've never seen you scry before," I said. "It's kind of, um, occult."

"Magic and wizardry is part of the definition of 'occult,' so your assessment is correct," Theo said, offering me a half smile. "Since my magic is entirely dependent on my wand and this is a newer spell for me, please keep your expectations low."

I lifted my knees to my chest as he began the spell. Frustrated as I was with Theo for his bargain and secrets, I recognized his expression of focused determination. All the efforts he normally put into being marquis were centered on finding Aeron. I enjoyed watching him work—the little line that formed in his forehead when he concentrated, his lips moving carefully as he spoke words of magic, and the tension in his muscles as he slowly gestured with his wand arm.

The cauldron water rippled. I leaned forward, hoping to catch a glimpse of Aeron and his whereabouts. Theo's wand movements stuttered and sweat beaded around his neck. I watched the water. Between the ripples, a blurry scene faded into view, lit with weak fluorescent bulbs, no windows, and dark walls. A dark form with blond hair crouched in the corner.

Before I could confirm the form as Aeron, the vision disappeared. The water became clear and still. Theo gasped for air.

"I think we saw him. Are you okay?" I asked. He nodded and measured his breathing. "Is there any way I can help?"

Theo drew in a couple deep breaths before speaking, "No. Besides, I dare not burden you for help since you are not the imbecile who bargained away our only child."

"You're not an imbecile," I said with a tired sigh.

He grunted in a way that said, "Agree to disagree."

I frowned. Sure, I was still upset, but he was taking the guilt too far.

"You did it to save me," I said. "You wouldn't have needed to give up Aeron if I hadn't been dying. If I hadn't been so stupid to grab that poisonous firethorn root—"

"No, Pansy, it was not your fault. I made the bargain. It was my choice. I…I could not lose you."

Chapter 7

WHEN TO BREAK THESE RULES*

To gain more information, such as the past or
weaknesses of the Haunting
To rescue a best friend
To lure the Haunting to your trap
*Only if you're desperate

- *Oz's Haunting Survival Book,*
with notes by Pansy Fromm

DUNSTAN

I almost skipped from the hotel room. This was my chance to finally prove myself worthy of Theo's trust. I knew that Father would never be proud of me—that ship sailed the moment Mother died from my birth. It was my desperation to please the duke that made me listen to Oswald and Abadda's lies, that made me attack that village of supposed rebels, and that made me a "terror" for the next three years.

However, I hoped to gain favor in my older brother's eyes. He was Father's heir after all.

Theo already showed me kindness by welcoming me back to Margen—to Eimad, no less—as a priest. Of all the crazy things to do, he encouraged me to gain more power...just with a virtuous focus. I wanted to prove to him that I was the man he thought I could be.

Unfortunately, rescuing his son in Horror brought up a secondary goal of mine and left Theo preoccupied. I could just imagine what my brother and sister-in-law were feeling. Their anxiety for their son was thick enough to cut with a knife. They were both wrung like a coil, ready to spring on anything that moved.

Pansy said there was nothing we could do until sunrise. Might as well use the time to refresh with some good comfort foods and good comfortable sleep. Maybe Theo and I could share a philosophical debate like the old days, after I returned. I missed those hypothetical discussions with my brother and hoped to impress him with my new knowledge from the abbey.

Until then, the best ways I could help my brother and sister-in-law included two conflicting jobs: one that would build Theo's trust, and one that would unfortunately threaten it.

Back in the downstairs lobby, I searched for the pamphlet that advertised my second desire: "Custom Weapons. Handcrafted from Horror's best metal workers. Made with licensed silver and gold, and minotaur hide." Perfect.

Ever since my duel with Theo, I realized my need for a specialized weapon. Except, I'd been confined to Margen in all that time, and no one in Margen would make a weapon for The Night Terror.

Horror, however, was a place I'd never visited before. It was a shot in the dark, though I was used to working in the dark.

I called for a cab from the lobby, then waited on the plush cushions for it to arrive. I didn't mind the wait. When leaving the life of lords and obligations, I gained a life of "I'll get there when I get there, and bullbeggar to anyone who tries to hurry me."

My ride arrived with an annoyed honk. The desk clerk and a couple of lobby stragglers watched as I walked to the exit and stepped into the night. Their unblinking eyes and confused whispers followed me as if I marched to my death.

Alright, that was a little unnerving.

My muscles tensed, preparing to use my ability and to fight as I walked to my cab. I recalled my combat training and Pansy's book about Hauntings. Nothing seemed out of the ordinary (at least for Horror), but I remained ready to absorb light and use my burning—

No. I was a Priest of the God of Fire now. Fire was meant to cleanse, light, and warm. Not hurt.

The common misunderstanding of the God of Fire's alignment was actually what led me to follow his line of teachings. I empathized with the misunderstood. I made one gigantic mistake by trusting the words of Abadda and Oswald. I destroyed a town that I thought was full of revolutionists, then was mislabeled as a terrorist until Theo offered me a second chance. I wanted to prove to him that his trust was well placed…though needed a backup plan if I failed.

I hopped into the taxi and showed the pamphlet to the driver. "Can you take me here?"

The cabby gave me a slight double take before he drove away from the curb.

Probably because of my accent. Bullbeggar, I hoped that wouldn't cause problems. If Pansy's accent wasn't so peculiar, I'd try to imitate it.

I had a decent collection of accents up my sleeve, including the slang of Urban, the airy tones of Faenor, the rough mercenary speech of Sword and Sorcery, the twang of Western, and even the questionable inflections of Mystery on a good day. I recaptured my natural accent of a Margen royal while living in the Eimad Abbey for the last six years, but apparently commoners mistook it for the polite crispness of Regency, Romance.

At least I didn't look like a Regency local, dressed in my preferred fashion of Contemporary blacks.

The cabby drove me down dark streets that seemed to only grow darker, with fewer Halloween decorations and orange lights.

Was I supposed to be concerned for my safety? Funny, I didn't have it in me to care. I welcomed the darkness. Here, I wasn't the hated Night Terror who was sought for imprisonment and questioning in a windowless dungeon. I was simply a man exploring the city nightlife and food options for his brother and sister-in-law. Oh, and finding the perfect weapon.

I spotted a banner ahead that matched the advertisements on the pamphlet, but the cabby pulled into an empty parking garage two blocks early. Weeds poked through the many cracks in the cement, and if the lights weren't broken, they flickered weakly.

"Why did you turn early?" I asked, and pointed back. "I saw the shop down that way."

The cab driver turned around and grinned with a malicious glint in his eyes. "Oh, we're in the right place. You're taking a permanent detour."

I sighed with disappointment and *pulled* inward with my ability. The whole garage went as dark as a black hole.

"What the horror?" the cab driver swore and slammed on the brakes.

The power of light coursed through my veins. Three main categories determined how much concentration and energy I needed to darken an area: brightness, size, and distance from me. The first floor of the parking garage was dimmer than my usual areas of absorption, though it was also larger. Then there was the addendum to my ability: the more difficult the absorption, the more hazardous it was to my body to expend as heat. The absorbed light of the parking garage was the right amount to convert into heat and burn this man who tried to dupe me.

No. Never again.

I swallowed the urge, then flung my door open and jumped out. I ran for the exit, lit by the overcast night just beyond my absorbed area. These new clothes and shoes weren't as quiet as my usual bare feet and cloak, though the cab driver seemed too confused and scared for his own safety to chase me.

I stopped at the sharp edge of my blackout, then released the light with just enough time to stick out my tongue at the cab driver before ducking around the exit. He threatened me, so I didn't feel bad about running off without paying the doubled nighttime charge. I continued down the streets with a light jog until I stepped into the weapons shop.

The shop welcomed me with seven red sniper dots centering on my vitals, a glowing pentagram on the floor, and a distant hiss of something big about to boom.

"Er," I slurred and raised my hands in surrender. "Your door wasn't locked. Did I come at a bad time, or are you still open for business?"

A husky female voice called from a dark doorway on the other side of the shop, "Who are you?"

"Douglas, the Priest," I said automatically. It was the name I used for the past six years. Hearing Theo and Pansy use my birth-given name (the one usually tied to the Night Terror) grated on my ego.

"A priest?" the woman asked, stepping into the light with a rifle's muzzle still trained on me. She was a short and weathered woman. Her black and grey hair cropped at her jaw and was combed away from her face with a headband. "What does a priest need for a weapon?"

"I'm not a priest of Horror," I said.

"Obviously. Where are you from and what's your business in Inferno?"

"If I choose not to say, will you shoot me?"

"Maybe." The woman smirked. "Depends on your reason for silence."

My mind scrambled for the right answer. What would Theo say? The truth. Except the truth that I was a Fantastic who served the God of Fire probably wouldn't help me here. Most people didn't know the God of Fire as a benevolent spirit. Again, misunderstandings.

What would Pansy say? I didn't know her well enough to predict her words. All I knew was what others said; she lived her life by her brother's rules.

Then, what would her brother, Oz, say? He was probably the best Horror to emulate, and I read his book.

"I'm trying to hide," I said in partial honesty. "I need a specialized weapon to fight back."

The woman lowered her rifle and clicked a button to stop the countdown hiss, pentagram glow, and sniper sights. My tension eased, happy to pass the test. "Is that how you greet all of your customers?"

"Only strangers who come in after sunset," the woman said, setting her rifle down only when she reached her glass case of throwing knives. "What kind of weapon do you need?"

"A copper shortsword," I said.

The craftswoman tilted her head. "Copper? Not silver, gold, or iron?"

"There's some silver too. And diamonds. And soapstone. I have schematics if you'll let me reach into my pocket." I pointed and waited until she gave a nod. I pulled out the piece of parchment with all my notes, then stepped out of the pentagram to meet her at the counter.

The craftswoman took a good minute to look over the notes. She frowned, grunted, then nodded as her eyes reached the bottom and she looked back up. "You've done your research. What exactly do you need it for?"

"I need a weapon that conducts and stores heat. Can you make it?"

"I can make it." She nodded thoughtfully. "It'll take at least a week."

"I don't have a week." I hoped to help Theo and Pansy to find Aeron before next nightfall. The sooner we found Aeron, the happier everyone would be. However, finding Aeron probably meant confronting Abadda, and I needed this weapon before I could do that.

I leaned over the counter to emphasize my sincerity to the craftswoman. "I can pay for a rush job as long as it's not rushed quality. Your pamphlet lists your network with other crafts-people, such as tanners, jewelers, and stonemasons. I know you won't be working alone on this, and I know from personal experience how professionals such as yourselves can create quality work in a single day. So, how long will it take?"

She swallowed and blinked, possibly wondering if she should set up her security features again. "Two days."

"I guess that will have to do." I leaned back. I could use that time to gain Theo's trust before revealing this secret. "I'll leave that copy of my notes. Hopefully this front half of a deposit is enough to motivate quality work." I dropped a small pouch of gold dust on her counter. Sure, it was unmolded, though pure gold held its value across all of Novel. Except Sci-Fi.

"Yessir," she said, immediately testing the legitimacy of the gold.

I stepped back into the night. The cabby was no longer around to return me to the hotel. Not that I'd hire him again anyway.

Also, I needed to accomplish the task that Theo and Pansy expected. I began to wander, analyzing the city while looking for a restaurant or grocery store. I could walk. I was a wanderer, after all, and it was a nice night. A bit chilly, which was perfect with my jacket. The surround sound of screams in the area were a bit eerie, though I could almost pass them off as music. Analyzing the city map, the black pavement and the long ditch beside the road meant that I was in Inferno's eighth circle, several blocks away from our hotel and close to Aeron's search area.

I picked up my pace and a tune to whistle while walking down the black streets. I gave the ditch a wide berth when little horned demons peered at me from within. Down another block of abandoned quick loan businesses, broken banks, and vandalized accessory shops, I spotted a person in the ditch as one source of the screams. The plump man in a tacky suit ran back and forth in the ditch with the little demons hanging on his sides.

"Hey," I called to the man. "Do you need help?"

The man ignored me and continued his mad pacing and screaming. I considered interfering except that I sensed the man…enjoyed the pain. Besides, I needed to prove myself to Theo. To do that, I needed to scout the area for information and buy delicious food to calm their stress.

Bright lights shone from a convenience store up ahead. My stomach gurgled with anticipation.

I jogged the rest of the block, happy to hear the simple two-tone electric bell greet me as I stepped inside. Unlike the weapons shop, the little grocery stop was equipped only with security cameras and a clear shield in front of the cash register. Maybe there was a rifle back there as the cashier kept his hand below the counter while slowly picking through a pop culture magazine. The glass doors closed behind me and offered a small muffle to the outside screams.

The shop had all the basic necessities, though in limited quantity and quality. Half of the floor space catered to food while the other half divided into hygiene care, medicines and first aid supplies, home cleaning/improvement products, minimal electronic accessories, and a couple racks for basic t-shirts and jeans.

My stomach grumbled, so I grabbed a quick cookie from the attached coffee stand. Either the stand was only known for its coffee, or the cookies in Horror didn't taste as wonderful as I remembered of Contemporary food.

I grabbed a basket and made my way back towards the grocery section, passing by six men who lounged in the eating area. They wore biker jackets with metal spikes and dark expressions with mischievous intent. I knew their type all too well from pretending to be one of them for three years. I never truly belonged with their crowd.

Distracted by my memories, I turned a corner and ran right into a young woman.

She yelped as her basket of fruit and packaged meals spilled across the floor.

"Bull," I cursed. "I'm sorry, let me help with that."

I crouched to retrieve the rolling fruit. I walked it back to the basket and…the most beautiful woman I'd ever met. Her hair was platinum white, eyes the palest blue, and skin as pale as a ghost. She stared at me with those forget-me-not eyes, flashes of fear, confusion, then curiosity crossing her face.

"Sorry," I apologized again, handing over the collected fruit. "I know angels are called Supernaturals in Horror, but I didn't know they were tangible."

She said nothing as she continued to stare at me. I knew she'd heard me though, as her white cheeks shaded pink.

I smirked. "Looks like they can blush too. Doesn't that require blood?"

She cleared her throat with a little cough, then spoke with a hushed and plotting Horror accent. "I'm no angel or Supernatural. And you're no Horror. A Regency?"

"Eim-er-Romance," I slurred, and winced. Bullbeggar, I almost said Eimad and blew my cover. Instead, my words sounded like "I'm a Romance." What was worse?

The angelic woman didn't seem to notice my slip as she stared down the aisle at the group of men with spikes.

"Friends of yours?" I asked.

Her eyes went wide, as if terrified by my question.

Bullbeggar, did I insult her?

"No," she whispered, "they're not my friends."

The wariness in her voice spoke volumes. I glared at the other men as if to warn them that if they wanted to harass this angelic woman, they'd need to go through me first.

"Can I join your shopping?" she asked.

My eyebrows raised a little, surprised and a little apprehensive about taking in a lost pup. That wasn't on my agenda. At least she was a beautiful lost pup. I nodded. If I gained her trust, maybe she could tell me the local news of Inferno. Somewhere in the rumors had to be a hint of Aeron's whereabouts.

She didn't seem to urge me in any direction, so I escorted her through the aisles to the cold meals section.

Picking up a cold cut sandwich under the brand name Last Meal, I asked, "Are these any good?"

"I haven't tried them," she said, "but the fruit isn't all bad. Just watch for worms."

I put the sliced sandwiches into my basket anyway. "I've had enough fruit to last me a lifetime. If these are anything like the packaged sandwiches of Thriller, I'm more than ready to sink my teeth into them."

"You travel a lot then?"

I shrugged. "I used to."

"I used to dream of traveling the world," she said softly, eyes turned to the floor as we walked to the grains aisle. She added to her basket a box of Reverend Brown's cereal with marshmallows shaped as crosses and other holy symbols.

I nodded, sympathizing with the beautiful woman, and grabbed a box of Mad Dash protein bars. "I've heard it's difficult to leave Horror."

Her shoulders deflated a little. "Yeah, I fear I'll never leave Inferno. You're lucky to have traveled so far."

I smirked at the irony. Lucky? For running off as a renegade, for banishment from my homeland, for being chased from town to town? Sure, that was one way to look at it.

I led our walk to the refrigerated section. She selected a carton of eggs (Don't Worry, They're Chicken!), and I grabbed a pint of whole milk (Certified: Safe from Mad Cow). We debated briefly about skim milk vs. whole milk, and I asked if she noticed whether any eggs were broken.

Why was it so easy to picture this same situation as an old couple? Never before had I imagined myself growing old with a woman, though I'd never met a woman who intrigued me so.

Moving on to the freezer doors, she pondered over ice cream flavors and asked, "What brought you to Horror?"

"Er, family reunion." Curses, I used to be better at lying. Still, the conversation seemed friendly enough to steer towards asking for information. "We're not exactly sure where to gather yet. Do you know of any places we should particularly avoid?"

"Um, anywhere in Horror?" She laughed. "You probably should have read *Oz's Haunting Survival Book* before visiting. It says not to attend any large gatherings."

"I have read it. Never you fret, we're following the rules. Our reunion is small, no more than ten people."

She bounced her head back and forth in thought. "I suppose that's safe. You have family here then?"

"In-laws," I said, then flustered. "I mean, through my brother's marriage. I'm not married, or courting anyone, and I should stop talking now."

"I can see why you're single," she teased.

"Oh!" I raised a hand to my heart, wounded. "That hurt," I laughed. "I'll have you know that I was once highly favored among the fairer sex. Before I shaved my head, I wooed heiresses and commoners alike."

"Heartbreaker," she accused.

"Perhaps." I frowned with regret. How many lies did I tell to hide my true identity? How many people did I leave behind when my past caught me? I found myself annoyed at the lies I already told this woman. "Another time, another life. I've obviously lost my touch, scrambling over words and rambling about women of my past. Forgive me."

With a pint of strawberry-blood ice cream in my basket and dark-and-stormy-chocolate-night in hers, I realized our time together was closing. Despite the thawing ice cream in our baskets, I slowed our pace while walking to the registers. "What about you?" I asked. "Have you lived in Inferno all your life?"

She hesitated, shuffling a little uncomfortably as she unloaded her basket for check out. "No. I'm here for a Haunting."

"Oh," I said, understanding her discomfort. "I'm sorry. From what I know of Hauntings, they can be, er, horrifying."

"Yeah, I'd rather not talk about it."

I warred with myself while unloading my own goods. I wanted to keep our conversation flowing—to learn more about the not-angel woman—but my mind kept returning to the Haunting she didn't want to discuss. I hurried to complete my purchase, afraid she'd walk away without saying goodbye. To my pleasant surprise, she loitered halfway to the exit.

74

"Hey, sugar baby," a voice called. One of the leather men waited for his order at the coffee stand and winked at the woman. Her pale cheeks reddened. I hurried to her side. Before I knew what was happening, she grabbed me by my jacket collar to pull my mouth down to hers.

As if this woman's beauty wasn't enough to tickle my fancy, her forcefulness awakened a forbidden desire in me. I never liked whining or pining women. I preferred strong women who acted on their own and were ambitious enough to see plans through.

The kiss lingered, but she released my jacket to let me pull back if I wanted. I didn't. Instead, I shifted my lips around hers, and a wave of something pleasant surged through me. Something similar must have coursed through the woman as she shivered and stepped back.

The group of men cheered us with thumbs up and catcalls. I hardly noticed as the woman took my hand and pulled me outside.

"Whoa," I said as soon as the doors closed behind us. "I *like* Horror."

Her next action almost surprised me as much as the kiss. She laughed. Not in a dainty "oh, you're silly," kind of way, but a snorting, bending over, belly-hugging laugh that lasted a full minute.

"Er, are you alright?" I asked. "I didn't think it was that funny."

She used the outside wall to support herself as she straightened and massaged her cheeks.

"Oh, it wasn't," she said with another snort. "The last few days have been pure insanity, and the idea of a foreigner liking Horror is just a cherry on top."

"Cherries make good pies," I said, then flustered. Bullbeggar, how did she turn me into a bumbler? "Sorry, that was random. I mean, I hope your life isn't so insane that, er…I'd like to see you again."

"Why would you want to do that?"

"Same reason any man would want to see a beautiful face." Confidence: reclaimed.

Her laugh caught in her throat and released a second later as a simple "heh."

"May I escort you home then?" I asked. "These Horror streets are dark and…screaming."

I prayed for every second she considered my offer. I prayed for the extended time with her, and hoped for a local's tour of the city. Information gathering, right? *Right. Stay on track.*

She shook her head.

"No, thanks," she said with a disappointing little sigh. "But perhaps tomorrow afternoon I might need to shop for more supplies."

I grinned. A victory however small was a victory all the same. When I thought about how to find her again, I realized, "Although formal introductions seem a bit belated now, my name is Douglas. Yours?"

"Berwyna."

Chapter 8

WARNING SIGNS

Hauntings who loudly announce their arrival and the
chase are just as dangerous as the sneakers
They're just more cocky about killing you
Stay away from animals (especially if they act weird)

> \-   *Oz's Haunting Survival Book,*
> with notes by Pansy Fromm

BERWYNA

Curses of Great Merlin!

Despite my calm and collected goodbye with Douglas, I
internally freaked out as I walked away from the convenience
store.

What just happened? What did I just do?

Given perspective, kissing a complete stranger wasn't any
more insane than my other actions of the past couple days. No
matter how many times I reviewed the events, I hardly believed
them.

After mending Duchess Abadda, the Wicked, and my loss
of consciousness, Urien had bowed to the witch, promising to
serve her as long as she kept us alive. When I woke up, Urien
was there with a potion and a mirror. All pigment from my
eyes, hair, and skin was lost from Abadda's attempt to steal my

beauty. I also had a new cough, fever, and fatigue that burdened me until drinking Abadda's potion with one of her healing phoenix tears.

So, we lived…at a price.

Abadda's first commandment was to kidnap the Earl of Margen. Of all the insane things in Novel. She wanted me to steal the only child of the man and woman who saved me from Oswald. The marquis was rumored to have an ability *and* magic, and the marchioness was a survivor from Horror, publisher of the book I quoted for my cross-stitching.

When I argued against Abadda's plan, she slammed me to the ground with her stolen wind ability, then burned my hands with her stolen fire breath. Urien shouted to make her stop, but she pushed him away with a mere gust of air. After an hour of pain, she prepared a healing drink from her stolen potion-making ability.

"I can burn thee," she hissed, "over and over, as many timesss as I desssire. Or, if thou will obey me, thou may become strong."

I didn't provoke her for a second demonstration. I drank the healing potion and condemned my soul to her power. As much as I adored and respected the marquis and marchioness, the duchess terrified me.

Abadda planned everything. We waited for Aeron's guard to leave the room, then Abadda laced his drink with a sleeping tonic. Using the Wind Master's ability, Abadda flew me up to Prince Aeron's window, which I broke to grab for the lock. The half-Horror child woke with clumsy movements as he grabbed two throwing daggers from a drawer.

Standing precariously on his widow ledge, seeing his weapons, and considering the ridiculousness of my situation, I pleaded to the child. "Help me. A witch wants me to take you away, but maybe we can hide together."

It was a foolish hope.

The naïve child opened his window to let me in. Before I could climb in and hope to escape from Abadda, she flew into the room in the form of a phoenix with Urien in tow.

"Excccellent," she hissed, transforming back into a woman. She swirled the air in the room to fling away the prince's weapons, twisting his hands and cutting his arm. Blood dripped, but Abadda's wind carried his screams out the window. Urien hesitated and cringed before knocking the child out with a blow from his lamp. Wrapped in Urien's whip, we flew the boy back out the window, the horrible deed accomplished in less than a minute.

"Thou did well," Abadda later said to me. That didn't stop my tears as we flew across the city, mountains, plains, and eventually to the Mysterious Mountains. Abadda threatened Aeron into silence as soon as he woke up. Anytime he talked, she used her stolen wind ability to create a tight column of air around his mouth, sucking away his voice and breath so that no one could hear him scream.

As soon as we crossed the border to Mystery—to a land where magic had no hold—I remembered my abduction by Oswald. I remembered the hypnosis and the frustrating lack of control over my own body, being locked in a room with five other girls, and Abadda's anger when Oswald brought home a girl so young and lowly in station.

He argued that my status didn't matter as long as I was beautiful and...tasted good. I shivered from the memories, then again at my current dilemma.

In secret, Urien theorized that Abadda lost her birth-given ability of absorption from her beheading. Urien told me how she had shrieked in pain while attempting to steal my beauty. She stole my colors, but that was all.

I blushed to recall how my childhood crush said that my new albino state was beautiful in its own way, then how Douglas had called me an angel.

My happy thoughts dimmed as I entered the abandoned office building that served as our hideout. I used every excuse to leave it, to run away from the questionable acts accomplished inside. Abadda was currently out to recruit monsters or something like that. The less I knew about her plans, the less guilty I felt for helping her.

I pushed open the unlocked door. Since our whole purpose for being in Horror was to invite Hauntings to join Abadda's horde of followers, I doubted that a simple deadbolt could keep the monsters outside. The whole building smelled rotten with mold. Discarded furniture and papers stacked against the walls from Abadda blowing clear the centers of the rooms. I purposefully ignored a room to the left, where a group of reanimated liches discussed the sorcerers they served and eventually betrayed. I went straight up the stairs to the room of security monitors. In the joining room, a child sobbed.

I hated myself. The kidnapped had become the kidnapper. My only justification was that we treated Aeron better than Oswald had treated me. Oswald had physically, mentally, and emotionally tortured his women before chopping them up like livestock. Abadda, however, commanded me and Urien to offer the prince anything he could ever want, and gave us the funds to do so. Anything to make him calm. I didn't understand the duchess's demands, but I was happy to take the duty of comforting the prince while Urien worked on Abadda's creepier demands to summon demons.

I spoiled Aeron with candies and sweets from the local grocery store. As much as I stuck out with my albino appearance, I'd quickly picked up the hushed Horror accent between the secrets I kept and dangers that surrounded me. I ventured as far as the fourth circle of Inferno to buy expensive Contemporary toys and the annoying batteries that weren't included. I let the prince watch whatever he wanted on the fascinating little television that was more static than picture.

Except he only wanted to go home and be with his family. It was the one thing I couldn't give him.

I empathized with him. I wanted to go home, but I feared angering Abadda and needed her morning potions to heal my new sickness. In exchange, Abadda promised us rewards and power for helping her. Urien was convinced this path was only the beginning of an Adventure and a quest towards glory. I worried about him and what kind of "glory" could come from such evils.

I hoped to wake up and realize it was all a nightmare. Instead, the nightmare grew worse as night settled in Inferno, Horror. Whether the sun was broken or the heavy clouds simply never moved, the sky was in permanent midnight lighting over our office hideout. An eerie pitch of screams echoed in the distance. The inky roads and walkways were slick as ice. In the limited lighting, every eye was suspicious, every mouth a frown.

Except Douglas's.

I smiled to think of the stranger's handsome face, emerald green eyes, and genuine manners. His crisp and clear accent reminded me to mask my own. His face was familiar, but I'd seen several people in Horror who looked eerily similar to people I knew from Fantasy.

Then, of all the desperate things to do, I'd kissed him. I couldn't say why exactly. Maybe it was my overreacting mind wanting to over-act. Maybe it was my frustration with Urien always hinting at possibilities, but never moving forward. Maybe my villainous acts of late fed into a rebellion to break every standard I'd ever set for myself. Maybe it was a deep, dark, secret desire to control something when everything else in my life spiraled into madness.

Whatever the reason, I didn't regret it. I'd expected the stranger to shove me back with disgust. Instead, he'd responded in earnest.

I replayed the moment over and over in my head, unable to contain my smile.

Urien's footsteps creaked up the stairs. The moment he spotted me, he sighed with relief and I mentally cursed. I was cursed after all. The timing couldn't be worse for a Romance. I was already on a horrific Adventure with Urien.

What would Urien say if I told him what happened? Would he be jealous? Maybe then Urien would finally take a real interest in me. Thinking back on the handsome man with the striking green eyes, I thought, *Urien* should *be jealous*.

AERON

I huddled in the dark of my toy-filled dungeon and silently wept. I missed Mom. I missed Father and Grandfather. I even missed Master Bahr and Tutor White. I missed the comfort of my bed and the warmth of the fireplace. I missed Chef Steve's cooking, even if I complained about anything green he served. The satyr liked weird foods, but I promised never to complain about a prepared meal again.

My bowl of sugary mush sat half eaten next to me. The first bite was tasty, but it became soggy when I paused to play.

The back of my head hurt too. There was a big lump where something hit my head during my capture. I think. It hurt to touch like the scratch on my left arm.

I learned the hard way to cry silently. My kidnappers did not like it when I made noise. Abadda even suffocated me when we were around others. My mister captor ignored me a lot, but my missus captor sometimes treated me like my governesses did. I missed my governesses.

I whispered a prayer to the God of Protection.

"Please, do not let me die here. Please, send someone to save me."

I hated that I was the victim. I wished to be the Hero for my first Adventure, not some dumbo in distress. Instead, I huddled in a dungeon, crying to a fantasy god, so far from home.

The front door screeched open from below, then the stairs groaned from footsteps. I tried to be quiet and hear them from my locked room as my mister captor spoke.

"Just finished the incantation and recruited a skeleton."

"Am I supposed to congratulate you?" my missus captor asked. "Why are you helping Duchess Abadda?"

"You know why," he said. "We need her phoenix tears. Besides, I know it's not conventional, but I feel stronger after the rituals."

Missus muttered, "I preferred learning about Horror from a distance. There's constant screaming outside, and a few men leered at me. I almost accepted one man's offer to escort me back here."

"I'm sorry," Mister said. He did not sound sorry. "It's good you didn't take the escort. It would have revealed our hideout. What did you buy?…Where's the rest? Is this it?"

"I figured I'd get more tomorrow."

"You complain about going out there, then you volunteer to do it again tomorrow?"

Missus' voice raised. "I'd rather be shopping out there than in here with these monsters."

Mister's voice grew louder too. "The point of sending you out to stockpile was to hibernate from society, not integrate with it."

"I…saw something that interested me. But would it kill you to escort me?"

"I can't just drop a summoning after starting. Besides, someone needs to watch the kid."

"The earl?" she corrected, then continued, "What's he going to do? *Cry* his way out of here? That's all he does between eating and whimpering. The door's locked, the wicked duchess is never far—"

"Don't call her that!" Mister's voice lowered and I had to press my ear to my locked door to hear. "Like you said, she's never far. Who knows what she'd do to us if we disrespected her? We should consider ourselves lucky to have come this far."

"This far," Missus muttered. "To Horror? How wonderful! To living off overpriced convenience store products?"

"If you want this to go faster, you could always do some recruiting yourself! I might eat a lot, but I'm the only one hefting any weight in this Adventure!"

"I can't recruit monsters for a cause I don't believe in! What kind of Adventure involves kidnapping a princeling and performing blood rituals in an abandoned building in Horror? We're minions to an overlord and helping her to build an army of the undead!"

"Look, it's not what I imagined either, but the queen promises great rewards."

"The queen promises," Missus mocked.

When their pause stretched into silence, I backed away from the door. As I did, a soft glow broke through the cracks. I scrambled up, fearing my kidnappers' approach. But the light was too white and grew brighter. It seeped *through* the door.

"Gagh!" I scurried to the far end of the room, keeping my eyes on the little ball of light. It was the size of a candle flame, but floated in the air. Its light shone on the muggy mess of my little dungeon.

"Shh-shh!" the light spoke. The light...spoke? "Don't worry, I'm not here to hurt you. I like your reaction though. Some people are far too curious when we appear. It doesn't help that kids sense us more."

I stared at the light and wondered what type of magic it was. "A-are you a messenger?" I asked.

The light wobbled back and forth. "It's one name for us."

The light grew and molded until it became the head of a see-through man with short spiky hair and a skinny face.

"But you," the glowing head said, and smiled, "can call me Uncle Oz."

"Oz?" I repeated. "You are not the Oz who pretends to be a wizard and grants wishes with silly gifts, right?"

Uncle Oz tilted its floating head. "That sounds like a dumb way to make people angry at you. No, I'm your mom's brother. Wow, it's weird to think little Pansy's married with a *kid* now. And look at you! You're like a little man!"

"Oh! *Uncle* Oz! Mom tells me about you. She reads your book to me every night, but I do not want to kill crupted loved ones."

The glowing head tilted again. "You mean 'corrupted?'" Then it beamed brighter. "Good to know she's raising you right. Remember those rules when dealing with these weirdos. I'm gonna help you get outta here."

It felt like forever since I last felt hope. My uncle was here! Someone friendly I could talk to! Someone who could help me get back to Mom and Father!

Uncle Oz flickered. "Actually, do you remember the rule to know your enemies so you can fight them better? See, I have some Fantasy informants who keep me updated on your mom's life, but they failed to mention a good chunk of everything else. Ask me if I'm mad—I'm not mad—maybe a little frustrated and irked and upset—sorry, the point is your kidnappers are strangers to Horror and the Supernaturals. What can you tell us about them?"

I fiddled with my bracelet as I worked through his ramblings to his final question. "Um, I do not know Mister and Missus," I said, "but I know Abadda, the Wicked, died before I was born."

"Apparently not," Uncle Oz muttered. "But she's from Fantasy? For certain?"

I nodded.

"Interesting," my uncle said. "As a revitalized Haunting, she has more devilish powers in Horror. I think that's why they came here. I'm working with some friends to determine why they brought you though. Your kidnapping doesn't make sense. All it did was create enemies of your parents and alert them of their plots."

"Wicked Buttchess Abadda was a bad person," I said. "She stole abilities and hurt people."

Uncle Oz snorted. "Did you call her 'buttchess?' That's hilarious, I'll have to tell the guys."

"She was beat by my parents. My parents are Heroes! Oh! Could you tell my mom and father where I am?"

"Ah," Uncle Oz's laughter faded. "Your mom and dad are kind of hard to contact right now. See, people either need to be especially in tune to the spirits or in the right mood for us to contact them, and, uh, your parents aren't in the right mood. They're worried about you, and they're doing everything they can to come get you. I'll let them know as soon as I can."

"Oh," I said, a little confused, but happy that my parents were on their way.

"That buttchess is coming," Uncle Oz whispered. "I'll disappear so no one can see me, but don't worry, I won't leave you."

Uncle Oz's light disappeared and the air chilled. I wrapped my arms around myself and put my back to the wall for the limited warmth it offered. A whisper in the air teased my ears. I looked around, but could not tell where or what it was.

Then, I heard the hissing voice of the Wicked. "Hasss the boy been calmed?"

My captors didn't answer right away. Someone shuffled, then Missus said, "He's been quiet the last few minutes."

The duchess hissed, "Mussst I do everything? Make him drink this sssleeping drought."

My door unlocked and opened. My missus captor walked in with a paper cup. She looked like a ghost, but the wicked buttchess looked scarier. Abadda floated behind her, twirling her feet to control the air beneath her. I crab-crawled to the farthest wall and struggled to hold back my cries. I did not want Abadda to take away my air again.

"Hey, Aeron," Missus said, as if she was one of my governesses. "It's been a long day, hasn't it? Flying all the way here, playing with new toys, trying new sweets. Are you feeling tired?"

I shook my head. "I am not sleepy."

"You didn't eat your dinner," she said, taking the bowl of mush from my nightstand. She replaced it with the cup that steamed and smelled of flowers. "Will you drink this? It will help you sleep."

I shook my head again, but my stomach gurgled before she left. When was the last time I ate? I was hungry and the drink smelled really good. I drank three big gulps. It tasted as good as it smelled. I was only halfway done before my eyelids became heavy.

Somewhere on the edge of sleep, Abadda's voice whispered over me.

"I sssee your ability to be among the dead. Horror is filled with them. Ssspeak to them. Bring them to me. Dream."

No. I could not do that. I could not dream. I did not want to dream. That was why I had my bracelet. I slumped to the floor and cried as my body shut off for the night.

Chapter 9

GOSSIP AND RUMORS

Never discard ominous warnings
from locals or old people.
Never discount a story, because
Hauntings attack doubters.

- *Oz's Haunting Survival Book,*
with notes by Pansy Fromm

PANSY

I barely ate after Dunstan returned that night with packaged sandwiches, milk, and energy bars. He raised an eyebrow at my alive-and-human test.

"Again?"

"What do you mean?" I asked, brandishing my golden stake.

"On my way back," he said, "I ran into a group of people patrolling the city. Apparently, Inferno has a designated mob called the Virgils to help contain the Hauntings. They looked ready to attack me and wouldn't believe that I was innocently lost until they saw me bleed."

"They hurt you?" Theo asked.

Dunstan snorted and showed off a fresh cut on his shoulder. "Just a flesh wound—agh!"

I poked the gash hard enough to make it bleed again. "Alive and human," I confirmed.

He shielded his arm from me and shouted, "What is wrong with you?"

"That's what you get for splitting up," I said. "Hauntings don't bleed like humans do. It's the surest way to confirm that you weren't taken, possessed, or switched by a Haunting. Did you learn anything while you were out there risking your life and our mission?"

Dunstan grumbled, then shared some details about the city, confirming the presence of small horned demons that tortured anyone who wandered into the canal sewage system. I shuddered, remembering my own escape from a Fantasy goblin in a labyrinth dungeon.

Sleep was my only release from my anxious thoughts about Aeron, but I rolled back and forth through the night, waking every couple hours between nightmares of Aeron dying from starvation, from torture, or from falling into darkness, reaching for me, but sinking farther away. What did Abadda want with Aeron anyway?

Dunstan was awake and showered before Theo even got out of bed.

"Alright! Let's go!" My brother-in-law clapped his hands eagerly at seven in the morning. "We can't waste the limited daylight hours!"

Theo scowled at his brother. "What daylight? Sunrise is still in a couple hours, and I thought you hated daylight hours?"

"I do." He grinned. "However, I ate Contemporary delights last night and slept on a warm mattress. It's a new day! We're in Horror looking for your son with a starting place in mind. Anything can happen!"

"Apparently," Theo muttered. "Dunstan is *happy* in the morning. Next thing we know, Aeron will be waiting for us outside."

We dressed, then went downstairs to the main dining hall for our complimentary breakfast. It was simple and hot, but I didn't eat much. Every bite reminded me of meals with Aeron, sitting at the table with Aeron, touring the kitchens with Aeron…

Dunstan ate enough to fill my portion, smacking his lips and moaning with pleasure with each swallow of Contemporary flavors. He easily ignored my husband's glares with closed, dreamy eyes.

I caught Theo's glance and we shared a mutual irritation; how could he be so happy at a time and place like this?

Having the same complaint felt like reading each other's minds, and I let out a soft smirk. Misery loved company, but it didn't feel quite as miserable when someone empathized.

When was the last time Theo and I shared mutual feelings? Or the last time we felt each other through Sean's connection? We'd never replicated the bond we shared while beheading Abadda. There were times, brief flickers of thought, where maybe I connected with Theo's emotions. Or were they only my own thoughts and emotions?

As soon as Dunstan finished his meal and the sun peeped over the horizon, we grabbed some tools and a cab to the designated park. We reached a large grassy area between houses that sported a small jungle gym with a slide, a basketball half court, and a dozen dead trees that lined a paved walkway along the perimeter.

Theo's eyes shifted over the scene. "This park seems… normal."

"Most of Horror is like this," I said. "At least during the day. It's not as terrible as the stories make it seem. Hauntings strike about once a year and can last a week, but during the other fifty-one weeks, Horror's a decent place to live. As long as you follow the rules."

"Such as staying inside after nightfall or keeping away from certain areas?" Theo asked.

"Exactly."

We stepped from the cab and stuck out like a bunch of disjointed thumbs. The park was large enough for the visitors to spread out, but small enough that we could see all the visitors at once. They were all moms with their kids.

"We didn't plan this well," I said.

"Funny enough," Dunstan said, "we would blend in if we had Aeron with us."

"Thanks," Theo grumbled, "as if we needed the reminder."

My eyes scanned the park for a hidden position. I didn't find one. "There's nowhere concealed enough for Theo to do a searching spell."

"What if you two act like a couple on a stroll?" Dunstan offered. "Then you can scout for a better position for the spell."

We needed to "act" like a couple? I knew Dunstan didn't mean the phrase to be jarring, but a stroll should have been natural after six years of marriage.

"What about you?" Theo asked his brother.

"I don't know, I'll try some pick up lines on the widows and see if they've noticed anything odd in the area."

Theo gave him a downward stare. "As a priest?"

"Hey, don't hate my baldness because you're jealous."

"That was not what I...meant." Theo's comment faded as Dunstan turned off toward the nearest woman of age. Theo sighed and I offered my hand.

"Want to stroll?"

We held hands and began a walk along the perimeter pathway. A few joggers with partners passed us, wearing decent clothes and headbands. They followed my brother's rules to "Never be alone," "Dress for comfort and function, not fashion," and "Keep hair short (and use headbands). Long hair and ponytails are easy for Hauntings to grab." Maybe they read his book. Maybe publishing it had saved lives. I hoped so.

The breeze curled around me as we walked. Was there a tune in the air? The wind song carried memories with it. Memories of Oz and a couple choice friends hanging out with a birthday cake at the dojo or at home. Most people only sang the last verse of the birthday song, but Oz always sang the full version.

> Fine, I guess we'll celebrate
> Even though it's getting late
> And parties after dark lead to disaster.
>
> Everybody grab some cake
> Before Hauntings come to break
> And we find out which of us is faster.
>
> Double check the party list
> Careful when you open gifts
> And maybe we'll avoid another death day
>
> Happy Birthday, you're the best!
> Make a wish and take a rest.
> Keep your candle burni—ing till next birthday!

There was a silly superstition that the first and last people to finish "burning" would be the next people to die. Superstition or not, Oz conducted all singers to end together and avoid the curse.

The breeze drifted by, taking the memories and returning me to the dreadful present where my son was missing. Worst birthday ever.

Across the park, Dunstan approached a young woman walking a dog. Despite his obvious attempts to start a conversation, she sped up and let her dog bark after him.

I smirked. "Looks like his priest magic is safe from Romantic corruption."

Theo chuckled with me, but concern touched his eyes. "I worry that his magic may be corrupted for another reason."

"What do you mean?"

"Abilities can transfer between kingdoms and countries," he explained. "That is one reason they are so resourceful. Magics and technologies, however, do not always transfer well outside of their realms."

"I know that," I said. "But you've used magic in Horror."

"Because Horror has its own spell casters, correct?"

"Most of them are dangerous Hauntings or swindling show people, but yeah, Horror has magicians and witchcraft."

My husband exhaled as if working on a problem with an interchangeable solution. "Every time I perform magic in Horror, it feels…strained. As if it wants to serve a different, darker purpose. When I cast the spell to conceal our identification cards, I felt an inner thrill about the lie. With my searching and scrying spell, there is a dissatisfaction to just find our son. As if the magic here has a tainted soul of its own, it feeds a dark desire to search for enemies and prey. It—" He shivered. "It frightens me."

Interesting. I knew magic was corrupted in Horror, but I hadn't known how. "Just another reason we should be careful to use magic here."

Theo directed me to a bench by the side of the walkway. It was a bit further from the playground and in the shade of a massive tree. "If it helps us to find Aeron, I will push past the strain on my magic. Perhaps I can try the searching spell here."

I looked around, then nodded. I didn't like Theo punishing himself for our situation, but his magic was awfully convenient to search for Aeron.

Theo and I sat. He casually put his arm around me, but didn't hold me close like he used to. Instead, he drooped his head and pretended to sleep as he closed his eyes and palmed the bench, pointing his wand arm to the ground. I counted each second as he cast his spell and glowed a soft yellow. Each second was another kilometer between Aeron and us. Each second was a knife in my heart to think we weren't any closer than before.

A kid with a basketball looked our way and pointed at Theo. Time was up.

Theo's eyes snapped open not a moment too soon. The basketball kid's friends turned to look at us as Theo's yellow glow disappeared.

"Eight to nine," he said.

"Did you bring the map?"

"Dunstan has it."

I nodded and stood. For one frantic moment, I couldn't find my brother-in-law. Then I heard a sharp slap across the park. Dunstan held a hand to his face while a woman stormed away.

"I almost feel sorry for him," I said, biting back a laugh.

Theo smirked and waved him over. "That makes one of us."

Dunstan started across the park, and I felt a tap on my shoulder. I jumped around to find a man standing behind me, wearing a strange set of blinders beside his eyes. They were made of mirrors.

"You have a spirit following you."

Chills crawled up my spine. "Who are you?" I demanded.

The man didn't look at me, but kept glancing back and forth at the mirrors beside his face. He tapped at them, saying,

"They help me see the spirits about me. The one around you seems like a good one, even though he has a stern look to him."

"Him? Who?"

"That one, however…" The crazy man pointed across the park at the ice cream truck. Then he wandered off, leaving us boggled as Dunstan reached us.

Theo spoke first. "What in Merlin's beard was that about?"

"Lunatic?" Dunstan suggested. "Every city has a few. Or is that dude normal in Horror?"

"No," I said. "That was new. I get his logic—mirrors help reveal Hauntings and Supernaturals not seen by the average eye. But to wear them like blinders? That's weird."

"That child's aura is unnaturally dark."

Theo pointed at a little girl reaching for a cone from the ice cream truck. The driver smiled kindly. Until the girl took a step closer and I recognized a murderous glint in his eyes.

"It went darker!"

At Theo's exclamation of her dark aura, I tapped into my speed and ran to the little girl. I couldn't help imagining she was our little Aeron. I grabbed the girl and pulled her away from the truck.

Where were her parents or guardians?

Two trees away, a mom fussed over a baby in a stroller with her wallet out. It was probably out from handing the little girl money for ice cream. I took the girl there and untapped my speed.

"Is this your daughter?"

The mom looked up, not even slightly surprised that someone snuck up on her.

"Maria!" she said to the little girl. "Didn't you want an ice cream?"

The little girl blinked, probably wondering how she moved to her mom so quickly. Without her ice cream. She started to wail.

Mom and daughter reached for each other, and I started back to Theo and Dunstan.

"Um, thanks," the mom said to me, a hint of a question in her voice.

"No problem," I said. "You should probably read the history of *Mr. Mercedes* before sending your child to the ice cream truck again." I didn't wait for her response before returning to Theo and Dunstan. The brothers struggled to stifle laughter.

"Look." Dunstan nudged me and pointed at the ice cream truck. The driver still held the ice cream cone in one hand while his other scratched his head.

Dunstan snickered. "You should have seen his face when the girl suddenly disappeared."

"Oh, crap," I cursed. "He probably thinks the little girl was a ghost now."

"A ghost?" Dunstan scoffed. "That would be his first assumption?"

"It's the easiest Haunting explanation," I said.

Dunstan scoffed. "Serves him right for preying on kids."

"I wonder," Theo said, "if he is a villain targeting children, might he be in league with the young man and woman who took Aeron?"

"Not likely," I said. "They're from Fantasy, and Hauntings never intermingle or share secrets with outsiders. Also, Aeron's nowhere near here. Dunstan, the map?"

He unfolded the map, and we sat on the grass beside the pavement to use the sidewalk as a hard surface.

"I left my compass at the hotel so the circle is imperfect," Theo said. "Still, I counted eight to nine kilometers."

"That overlaps a lot with our first circle," Dunstan said. "If he hasn't moved since last night that would put him somewhere along this crescent."

He pointed to a long area on the other side of the circle from our location.

I groaned. "He's either in the eighth or ninth circle." Was he with falsifiers and frauds or the most traitorous Hauntings imaginable?

"Or they moved him," Theo offered, "and he is somewhere along this new circumference."

Dunstan's bald head wrinkled as he did the math on the other side of the map. "With an area radius of eight and nine, that puts our new search at…fifty-three point four square kilometers."

"I don't know which is worse," I moaned.

Theo put a reassuring hand on my shoulder. "We know he is somewhere along this new circle. Shall we start where the circles intercept?"

"I don't know," I said. "That puts us in the ninth circle. The Frozen Lake of Lamentation is the darkest and most haunted area in Inferno. Dante described it as the bottom of the universe."

"It didn't seem all that bad," Dunstan said. I gaped at him and he shrugged. "The convenience store I went to last night was on the border."

"Good thing you bought enough to last us a few days," I said. "You really shouldn't have gone alone."

Oddly, the man hunched his shoulders, like he was disappointed.

"Then let us try this location first," Theo pointed to the edge of the ninth circle, where both circles overlaid. "Do you think a cab can take us in?"

"You mean to leave right now?" I shrieked. "We're not prepared!"

"How could we possibly prepare ourselves more?" Dunstan asked.

"We need to—" My brain grappled for impossible solutions and various excuses. We couldn't prepare for a place like the ninth circle, where the Frozen Lake of Lamentation seemed as smooth as glass, but cracked like skulls under your feet, where cannibals slowly starved then devoured their neighbors, and where a mysterious munching sound echoed forever just around the corner.

No preparations would be enough, no matter how much training and equipment we took. Preparations would only waste time.

I bit my lip and forced myself to face the facts. "You're right. We have everything we need except personal experience. The best way to gain that is to check it out. Let's go."

Chapter 10

PLACES TO AVOID

-   *Oz's Haunting Survival Book,*
    with notes by Pansy Fromm

PANSY

We went back to the street and hailed a cab. When we told the driver our destination, she jerked with surprise.

"You're not from here, are you?" she asked with a careful look at each of us. "You won't find a cabby in town who'll drive you there. I can take you to the border of the eighth circle, but that's as far as I go in. Sorry."

"That'll be far enough," I said.

She gave me another sideways glance between her focus on the roads. "You have the Horror accent down, but you sure don't act like a local. You should read this book called *Oz's Haunting Survival Book,* by Pansy Fromm. She's one of the few to survive and leave Horror. You should look it up. Might save your life. Sure saved mine last summer."

I pressed my lips tight to hide my smile.

Dunstan chuckled. "It sounds like an intriguing read."

Our cabby glanced back at my brother-in-law through her rearview mirror. "I'll say. You're definitely not from here. Well, this is as far as I go. Careful out there."

"Thanks," I said as Theo paid, and we exited the cab.

Buildings as tall as mountain giants loomed over us, swaying drunkenly. A constant overcast kept the city in shadows, though the clouds hung lower in the center. The threat of a storm loomed. The pavement, sidewalks, and buildings were all black in circles eight and nine. Our cabby dropped us off a block away from the line where pitch black met icy black. The darkness pressed heavily in my chest, depressing my thoughts. Even from a block away, I could smell the rancid scent of rot and decay.

As much as I wanted to be close enough to find Aeron, I prayed to the Supernaturals that he wasn't held hostage in the ninth circle.

The cabby drove off and we took our first steps toward that impending doom. I could run out in the blink of an eye, but that would leave Theo, Dunstan, and possibly Aeron alone to fend off the evils that lurked inside.

"Watch our auras carefully, Theo. Dunstan, I don't know all that you can do, but be ready for anything."

Dunstan sighed. "Are you ever going to call me Douglas?"

"Nope," Theo answered for me.

Rain fell in intermittent droplets and I immediately pulled my hood up. Theo and Dunstan followed suit when it became a steady downpour.

Theo studied the thick gobs of rain on his arm. "This is not rain."

"It's sewage."

"What?" Theo paused with a wet finger almost to his tongue.

"Sewage rain," I said. "It's specific to Horror."

"How revolting!"

Dunstan laughed though his expression agreed with his brother.

A shiver rolled up my spine the moment we stepped into the icy black area. Somewhere nearby (or was it in the distance?) something crunched like a giant beast stepping through a slimy forest. It was the sound that inspired Dante to describe the devil munching on three of the world's greatest sinners. No one really knew what it was or where it came from. I never expected to hear it firsthand. The faint but steady crunching pricked my nerves. I prayed to the Supernaturals that Aeron was somewhere else.

"Theo," I asked, "how are our auras? Can you do your Locate spell and say if we need to be here?"

"I can," he said with a shiver. "Although our auras appear safe, I agree. We should leave as quickly as possible. This place creeps like a stalking wolf."

"It's not so bad." Dunstan shrugged. "I expected worse from the ninth circle of Inferno."

I raised an incredulous eyebrow at my brother-in-law as I stood guard beside my husband. Theo removed a hound's paw from his pocket and began to whisper words from the language of magic.

Dunstan gave his own incredulous stare. "Wizards keep the weirdest things in their pockets. Wait, is that a dog's foot? Theo! How could you?"

I snorted. "The hound's name is Tracker, and his paw is supposed to strengthen the Locate spell. The only reason we have his paw is because it was caught in a trap and needed to be amputated anyway. Theo regularly ensures that Tracker's the happiest three-legged pup in Novel."

Dunstan rolled his eyes. "Of course he does, the bullbe—"

A loud whirring of an engine broke the static of sludge rain. I jumped around, expecting a masked psycho with a chainsaw. How was it not right behind us? No, the sound came from around the street corner and grew louder. Another whirring joined it and my freakout doubled.

Two chainsaw murderers?

"There isn't time, Theo! We need to go!"

I pulled him by the arm and he stumbled from breaking his spell. We turned and ran the other direction as a third and fourth engine joined.

"Pansy!" Dunstan shouted from behind. Too far behind. I looked back where he stood, unmoved from the corner.

"Run!" I shouted in a frail attempt to be heard over the rain and roars.

"Why?" he asked. "They're only motorcycles!"

My adrenaline stuttered. They sounded so similar. Sure enough, the first motorcyclist rounded the corner. My brother's advice shouted in my head, feeble against the roar.

Hauntings who loudly announce their arrival and the chase are just as dangerous as the sneakers! They're just more cocky about killing you!

A second motorcyclist came into view and I analyzed their morbid attire. What I thought were zippers and chains on their black leather jackets were instead rows of teeth and tiny knives. Their machines spewed black smoke that didn't dissipate or diffuse. There was something ominous and almost alive about that smoke.

The dark eyes of the motorcyclists landed on the nearest target: Dunstan. Then they whipped out handguns that glinted in the sewage rain.

"Dunstan!" Theo and I yelled.

All light disappeared on the street corner as Dunstan used his ability. Tires screeched, then the first motorcyclist drove out of the dark corner on the wrong side of the road. He looked behind himself, back into the blackness, probably wondering what in horror just happened. The motorcycle bumped over the curb and he dropped his gun to frantically veer back to the road. His overcorrection smashed him into the second motorcyclist.

Poor Theo didn't wince away fast enough. He watched with wide, gaping eyes and mouth at the bloody results. Even though I looked away in time, memories of similar crashes plagued my mind. I didn't need to see the machines skid across the pavement that suddenly acted like a cheese grater. I didn't need to see the marring of faces that would curse them for the rest of their pitiful lives.

I recognized the sounds and the images that went with them.

Behind the black wall, the other engines screeched to a halt with extra sounds of metal crashing against metal, metal against skin, skin against pavement.

The static of rain and distant munching felt deafeningly silent after the death of the engines' roars.

Then came the screams.

The wall of black shifted toward us. Every inch of my body wanted to run away as it enveloped the buildings and crept closer.

"Dunstan, will you stop?" Theo called out. "It unnerves Pansy."

The darkness collapsed to reveal the street as normal again. Well, as normal as any street in the ninth circle of Inferno. Screams of confusion, anger, and pain echoed from around the corner. Dunstan strolled down the sidewalk like he was only there to window shop.

"I think I like this place," he mused.

"Of course you do," Theo muttered.

"Let's get out of here," I said. "Aeron's not here. Tracker's paw should have pointed the way before I pulled Theo out."

Theo sighed. "I know not whether to be frustrated or relieved that we cannot find Aeron here. Let us look elsewhere."

I agreed. As much as I wanted to find Aeron, I didn't want to find him in the ninth circle. We didn't speak again until we reentered the eighth circle. The three of us relaxed again on the simple black pavement where strangers wandered in cloaks lined with lead. The constant chewing disappeared and the sun shined a little brighter behind the overcast.

"And that," I said, "was during the day."

All the same, Theo shuddered. "Why does a place such as Horror even exist? Fantasy has our monsters and wicked witches, though that is in part because we have multiple gods with various alignments. You say Horror has *one* God who is just and merciful. If this is true, why does He allow these terrible things to happen?"

To my surprise, Dunstan answered first.

"Because He allows life to happen."

Theo and I turned to him. He shrugged.

"Don't look so surprised, Theo. You're the one who sent me to the abbey, and magic isn't the only thing they teach us there. Especially while studying the God of Fire, I've learned how life is a hazard to itself. To survive, we must destroy— whether it's the food we consume from other plants or animals, or the shelters we build from trees or quarried stone. Because all life is different, we all have different beliefs on what de- struction is necessary. I once believed it was necessary to destroy an entire town because I thought they were enemies to our family. I can empathize with the people of Horror. Everyone's just doing what they need to survive and protect what they believe in."

"Thanks," I said, feeling understood for the first time in too long. By Dunstan? Weird.

"Also," I added, "I think the other lands need Horror for examples. They can read about Horror and learn from our experiences. Many Hauntings are psychological, so people in other lands have similar experiences. Only their monsters look different."

Theo's eyes met mine, and something snapped into place between the two of us. I sensed an inkling of his confusion, his loss, and his yearning to make things right. In turn, his eyes widened like he felt my sorrow for him and anxiety for Aeron. It was the subtle sensation of Sean's connection. Condemnation, it felt like eons since the last time we used that bond between us.

I reached out and he took my hand as Dunstan pulled out the map to analyze our next move.

"Where should we go next?" Theo asked. "Suppose we move in this direction?" He traced his finger from our location and curved it away from the city center.

"What about farther in the ninth circle?" Dunstan asked. "There's a lot of ground in there where the two circles overlapped."

"I don't want to go back in there unless we have to," I said.

Dunstan asked, "Wouldn't the ninth circle be the best place to hide your son?"

"No," I said. "Even if Abadda is evil enough, Aeron's other two kidnappers looked mortal, and the ninth circle would be equally dangerous to them. Hauntings don't harbor other Hauntings. They're incredibly territorial and wouldn't allow some foreigners to invade their hard-earned space."

"What if we split up?" Dunstan asked.

I scoffed. "Bad idea. I thought you read my brother's book?"

Dunstan responded with a pointed stare. "We have over fifty kilometers to cover. Either we enlist the Virgils to help, or we split up."

"Then we ask the Virgils for help," I said.

"Remind me," Theo interjected, "who are the Virgils?"

"A group of Haunting hunters," I said. "I don't know whether to commend them for their bravery or start digging their graves."

Dunstan folded his arms. "You want to involve everyday citizens in a covert search for your son and likely battle against an immortal fire-breathing wind master? Involving others could destroy our secrecy and tip off Aeron's kidnappers that we're on their trail."

I grunted, frustrated by his logic. "Maybe we can ask for their help when we know Aeron's location and plan an ambush, but for now, the smaller our party, the more stealth we have."

Theo frowned. "How are we supposed to search fifty kilometers by ourselves?"

"We can't," I groaned.

At the same time, Dunstan said, "We divide and conquer." He raised a hand to pause my argument. "Your notes say that in every Haunting, you need to break some rules. Whether it's to lure the Haunting to your trap or to gain more information."

To my surprise, Theo backed his brother. "When we fought Sean's poltergeist, we split up twice. Once to set off the fire alarms, and again when you came to rescue me while the others put together a weapon to weaken it. If we separate, Dunstan can focus on research and intel while we try to locate Aeron. That way, as soon as we know where Aeron is, we will save time planning our rescue without falling into their traps."

I chewed on that for a couple seconds. It was two against one, and their arguments made some sense. "It's still a terrible idea," I muttered. "Fine. Do you have your teleportation spell to escape to Fantasy?"

Dunstan turned his jacket open to reveal his teleportation spell in his inside breast pocket. He patted the spot for reassurance. Even if he ran into trouble, he could escape back to Margen.

"Remember," I added, "no side quests to buy an adorable little monster from a mysterious old man."

"No?" Dunstan chuckled. "But Fantastics are particularly talented at training adorable little monsters into friendly giant monsters."

"Don't do it," I commanded.

"Fine." Dunstan shrugged. "Then, let's divide and conquer!"

I moaned, already anticipating trouble.

Chapter 11

FRIENDS

-   *Oz's Haunting Survival Book,*
    with notes by Pansy Fromm

BERWYNA

Little could stop my smile when I walked into the convenience store. The break away from the hideout was truly a blessing.

The day had started with misery. I spent the whole morning coughing, sneezing, and wheezing until my sickness bothered Abadda enough to heal me with a potion. She'd been furious that Aeron's ability hadn't worked. She gave up on all attempts to calm him. She struck him with her fire and wind abilities, then used a truth-telling potion. But he refused to talk. Only to me did he admit that his bracelet kept him from dreaming.

Unfortunately, Abadda overheard.

She immediately yanked off his bracelet and burned it. Even her sleeping potions weren't enough to calm his cries after that. He refused to nap or sleep, claiming to be too scared to rest without his bracelet, and became incredibly cranky.

I breathed with relief to be away from his tears, yet inside from the screaming streets of the eighth circle. Thankfully, those men in black leathers didn't loiter in the store today. I had a couple hours before sunset to shop and wait for a tall man with emerald green eyes.

I checked the door every time it chimed with a new customer. As soon as Douglas stepped through the doors, I hid behind a shelf.

Great Merlin, he actually came.

I didn't want to appear too eager even as my heart raced with anticipation. Calm down. It was just our second meeting. He was only a handsome man…a very handsome man…who I kissed.

Moving a couple items on the shelf, I spied on Douglas as he looked around, then leaned against the checkout counter. He spoke quietly to the cashier, but I caught words like "new," "rumors," and "wicked." The cashier responded with a shrug and words too quiet for me to hear.

What was Douglas's interest in rumors? Was that how he traveled like a local? At least they weren't talking about me.

Douglas thanked the cashier with a small nod, then wandered down the pharmacy aisle before heading to the cold drinks section. He hadn't noticed me yet, so I grabbed a basket and snuck through the aisles. I entered his peripheral range at the far end of the drinks aisle and trained my eyes forward.

A small smile teased his lips, though he kept his concentration on the door before him.

Of course, a Romantic would play this game. I smirked.

I pretended to lose interest in the section of food before me and moved to the next one, taking two steps closer to Douglas.

He opened his door and pulled out a water bottle. Placing it in his basket, he turned around to stare at the fruit stand. He stole a glance at me and his smug smile grew.

Oh? He wanted to play hard to get?

I crossed down the aisle of refrigerator doors until I put my back directly to him. Then I opened the door extra wide to bump into him. Some sadistic side of me was pleased to hear his grunt of surprise.

"Oh! I'm sorry, I didn't see you!" I dripped with sarcasm.

"Really, Berwyna? A second witness would probably say otherwise."

I smiled, flattered that he remembered my name. I leaned over to peek in his basket. "What are you picking up today?"

"Small items I forgot yesterday." He shrugged. He had the water bottle, a bag of jerky, and a box of sleeping pills.

"Why, Douglas, if I didn't know better, I'd guess the only reason you came today was to see me again."

He shrugged again and smiled. "Guilty as charged."

I blushed, surprised that he accepted the accusation.

"Well," I said, "now that you see me, what's your plan?"

"To enchant you," he said, green eyes meeting my blue, "as you have enchanted me."

My breath caught in my throat, and I had to turn away to gather it again. How could anyone be so blunt and honest? And here I deceived him left and right by pretending to be innocent.

I distracted myself by adding fruit to my basket. "How could I enchant you? I don't know magic like some Fantastic."

"Who said you needed magic? Besides," he said, "everyone knows feelings created by magic aren't true."

"Is that so?" I asked. "Too bad. Supernaturals know, this world could use more love, fabricated or not. Instead, we're stuck waiting for childhood crushes to become the heroes you know they should be, or making desperate decisions because we really don't know what we're doing. They say, 'Be careful who you date,' and 'Respect and loyalty are key,' but is that enough to find true happiness?"

"Oz's book also says to help others around you to remain calm, or they might become Hauntings."

"The exact phrasing actually says—"

Douglas grabbed my hand while I reached for another fruit. I turned to ask about his sudden touch, but his expression made me pause. He eyed me warily before his eyes dropped down to my basket. It nearly overflowed with fruit.

I hadn't meant to grab so many. When I ran out of one variety on the stand, I went to the next, even if they had worm holes. Releasing a heavy breath, I set down my basket.

"Are you alright?" he asked, his voice tender.

No. I wasn't. I was a frayed string, pretending that if I wound myself tighter and tighter, I could be whole again. Not wanting to burden him with my problems, I simply said, "It's been a rough day."

He gave an empathetic nod, then asked, "How many of which fruit did you want?"

"I only wanted three orange apples," I sighed.

"Appropriate for Halloween," he said. A small attempt to lighten the mood.

He reached down to help return the fruit to the stand. His hands bumped into mine as we reached for the same fruit. We pulled back and waited for the other to go first. He didn't move, so I reached in again at the same time he did. Our hands collided and everything became jittery—our nervous laughter, our fidgeting hands…my heart.

"Here, allow me," he said.

"No, it's my mistake."

"It's a gentleman's duty to assist a lady."

"Obviously you don't know me well enough if you think I'm a lady."

"I'd like to change that." He smoldered.

My breath caught again as I wondered, change what? How well he knew me or the fact that I wasn't a lady?

Likely the former as a request to become better acquainted. I scolded my forward thinking, yet my mind wandered and fantasized about his status, replacing Urien with Douglas in my dream future.

I blinked away the shallow daydreams and tried to focus on reality…of Douglas beside me, calling me charming and a lady. Curses, how could I be realistic when this man made my dreams of love and travels feel possible?

I dared to meet his gaze for a whole second before turning to the other items on my list. I had enough money to buy food to last us a week. But if I bought everything now, what would be my excuse to leave the hideout and meet with Douglas?

We emptied my basket of fruit and walked slowly among the aisles.

"Tell me about Romance?" I asked. "All I know is from books and—films." I almost slipped with "theater."

Douglas balanced his shoulders, as if debating how much to say. "It's, er, home, I guess. Not all Romantics are brainless flirts as many outsiders expect. It's not my favorite place in the world though. I traveled a lot as a teenager."

"Oh?" I asked. "Where's your favorite place then?"

"Urban, Fantasy," he said without hesitation. "Though I'm warming up to Inferno."

"Really?" I gave him a side glance. "You *like* Inferno?"

"Certain parts of it," he said with a little wink.

I turned away. Surely he didn't mean that in the way I hoped. Keeping the conversation on topic, I said, "I've never been to Urban before. What's it like?"

He described the cities, comparing them to his limited experience in Inferno as if that would help me understand. In return, he asked me about the city, the Virgils, and different circles as if he planned to explore every street and alley. If only I knew. I struggled to sidestep his questions with vague answers and distractions about the food.

We continued to wander around the store. I asked about places he saw or wanted to see, while he asked about Inferno and what rumors I might know of new Hauntings. We shifted from topic to topic, pulling items off the shelf that struck our interest and humor. We may have discussed anything, everything, and absolutely nothing. I only remembered smiling through it all.

As we waited in the checkout line, he rested a gentle hand on my arm. "May I walk you home?"

I glanced out the store windows to the sinking sunset. I had stayed longer than planned, caught up in our conversations. The ninth circle was frightening enough during the day. I definitely didn't want to walk alone, but I had to think of an excuse for Douglas to drop me off at an office building crowded with Hauntings. Maybe I could say that I lived in the house nearby?

"I would really appreciate that."

Douglas smiled. "Then the feeling's mutual."

Why weren't all men like this? Not even Urien was this sweet to me.

We completed our purchases, then I took his hand to lead us down the path.

The clouds loomed darker and lower as we neared the city center. As much as I enjoyed Douglas's company, I was grateful that we didn't have far to go. We entered the ninth circle and our black path became extra murky.

Douglas's warm hand wrapped around mine. His tender touch sent my mind in a million hopeful directions. I consciously cleared my thoughts, then stilled my heart. With that eventually accomplished, I was surprised how natural it felt to walk beside Douglas, despite the frozen rain that threatened to numb any skin it touched and the constant ominous crunching of the ninth circle.

"You live in the ninth circle?" he asked.

"Only temporarily," I said in a rush. "Only until I find a way to stop my Haunting." As if I could stop Abadda and her growing army of death.

"I see why you didn't want me to join you yesterday. But if I may ease your mind, I've already entered the ninth circle and found it…unwelcoming and lacking services."

"Really?" I asked, dubious. "That's all you have to say about it?"

"All of the shops were closed or abandoned," he said, then leaned close, a mischievous glint in his eye. "There must be stories or rumors about why they're closed. Spare me no details, I want to know them all."

Before I could panic about how to answer, we turned a corner. Down the block was my office hideout…and Abadda's newest recruits. A mix of a dozen zombies, mummies, and ghouls overflowed from the office entrance.

"Whoa." Douglas stopped and stared at the collection of Hauntings. "I thought Hauntings didn't intermingle?"

"It's a—uh," I slurred, mentally scrambling for a lie, "Halloween party."

"They look so real."

I shrugged. "We take Halloween pretty seriously in Horror."

"I'll say."

My next mental scramble was to find a reason to say goodbye to Douglas. I didn't want him to leave, but I couldn't take Douglas too close to the office with those monsters surrounding the entrance. I couldn't let him recognize them as real Hauntings or let them aim their haunts on him.

I slowed our walk and headed down a different street. As much as I wanted to prolong my time with Douglas, wandering lost in the ninth circle was never a good idea. Maybe I could pretend the house behind the office building was mine. But were there starved moans coming from the basement? Never mind that. I took a deep breath and planned my goodbye.

"Thank you," I said.

"For what?"

"For walking me home and being so kind to me. Your sweetness is the brightest light I see all day."

Douglas chuckled. "If only you knew how ironic that was."

"What do you mean?"

A cacophonous scream of a machine and crossing blades whirred behind us. I jumped around to find a lanky man wearing a carved pumpkin over his head. He carried a strange knife with a serrated blade. The blade vibrated with sparks of electricity.

"Run!" Douglas shouted and angled himself to stand between me and the stranger.

The pumpkin man raised his electric knife above his head and charged at us. Lights dimmed around us as if the city didn't want to witness what came next. Douglas stepped forward.

"No! Doug—"

The stranger swung his deadly weapon at Douglas. I stood in terror as the scene seemed to pass in slow motion.

What could a Romantic do against a raged killer?

Time caught up with itself and became a blur as Douglas sidestepped the blade's teeth, swung his elbow into the stranger's arms, then pushed him hard to the side with his other hand. The man with the pumpkin head tumbled to the ground with his blade.

Was his side smoking? From what? Douglas's hands were empty and warm as he grabbed for me.

"*Run!*"

"Wha—"

He yanked me away from the stranger who struggled to regain his footing and control of his weapon.

We ran down the street, back the way we came, with Douglas pulling me along.

"I don't know where we are," he said, panting. "Do you know a good hiding place?"

I didn't. I didn't know Inferno outside of the path between my office hideout and the convenience store. We passed a couple alleys that I considered turning down. No, the first one was too dark with too many hiding places for other monsters, and the second alley was too light with no hiding places at all.

Douglas stopped and his hand jerked in mine. "Here!"

He pulled me back to an alleyway between two abandoned businesses. I could have sworn it was bright with flickering street lights when we first passed it. It was completely dark as Douglas pulled me in. I couldn't see how deep it went and lost sight of Douglas with outstretched hands. I lined myself against the wall, secured by its boundary. I pulled Douglas closer until I could outline his worried face. That brought him very, very close. His eyes met mine for a long second. Then, he turned away to watch the entrance from where we came. At least he couldn't see my cheeks redden in the darkness.

Douglas steadied his breathing. "I haven't fought that way in a long time. It wears me out more than it used to."

"It was incredible," I whispered. "Where did you learn to fight like that?"

He paused. "I grew up privileged to have a personal trainer. I was self-taught for a few years, then joined a club of sorts to practice with a different style and technique."

"No wonder you're so good," I said. "Do you think you could teach me?"

"Er…" He shuffled in the darkness and his leg brushed against mine. It took some serious effort to keep my mind on the conversation.

"You've probably guessed," I said, "that I was kept hidden away for most of my life. That's why I have this regrettable Haunting. I wanted to explore and see new places. Do you think I could learn to be a cultured traveler like you?"

He chuckled. "If my sister-in-law could learn, perhaps anyone could."

"Maybe…" I hesitated. "If I could escape Horror, you could guide me through Urban. Or I could meet you in Romance. You speak like you grew up in a nice home."

He sighed softly and rested his forehead against mine. So close. He whispered, "I was born privileged, sure, but I dishonored my family name. Forgive me if my flirtations gave you dreams of ladyship and honor. I have nothing to offer in a courtship."

He pulled back and I felt our connection tug. Dishonored. What had he done to betray his family?

Who was I to judge after kidnapping a prince?

The space between us felt empty like a void. I slid my hands up his back to bring him closer again and rested against his chest. I breathed in his strength, his warmth, his sweetness.

I lost track of how long we held onto one another as if it was our last goodbye. The time was plenty long enough for the electric knife pumpkin-head to lose our trail. The clouds drifted, revealing the twilit sky and first-quarter moon at the zenith. Somehow, our alleyway remained in the shadows.

I sensed Douglas's propriety when he eventually stepped back. He held my hand as we walked back towards my office hideout. I directed us so we wouldn't cross sight of the office entrance and windows.

Fortunately, there was a small house that looked only recently abandoned right behind my hideout. Its walls were lined with rulers and every measuring tool imaginable. There was a gap on one corner as if the house had expanded since the last time it was measured. I stopped in front of its gate.

"Well, this is my stop." I rummaged through my purse as though looking for my house keys.

He lingered and shuffled his feet. "May I see you to-morrow?"

"I hope so," I said. "I can't promise anything in the future with this Haunting, but I would like to see you again."

"Then I'll wait for you at the store." He smiled. "I'd sooner give up my occupation than these hours with you."

I looked up to ask what he meant, but my breath caught in my throat and stuck there as he leaned in.

Great Merlin! He wanted to kiss me!

My heart hammered with excitement, anticipation, and nerves. He paused a couple centimeters away and hovered for a whole second. Meanwhile, my mind whirled like one of Abadda's windstorms.

Curses of Great Merlin! It was one thing for me to pull him into a quick kiss to save myself from leerers. It was something else entirely when he approached me slowly with honest desire. Did this mean he loved me? Why did he hesitate?

Douglas shifted to kiss my cheek instead. When he pulled away, we were both red with blush.

Did my breath stink? Or had he expected me to make the final move? Or did he somehow know I had terrible secrets?

His expression was conflicted as he said a husky goodnight. The city seemed to grow darker as he turned and darted away. Did heavier clouds block the moon? No, but it was almost pitch black down the street where Douglas had disappeared.

Chapter 12

OTHER PEOPLE

Never approach people if you can't see their faces
A person's outward appearance does not always
reflect their inner personality
The more pitiful a stranger seems, the more
dangerous they can be.

- *Oz's Haunting Survival Book,*
with notes by Pansy Fromm

AERON

I dreamed as I always did without my bracelet. I dreamed of dying. I cried myself to sleep, and then I cried in my sleep, floating above my body as a spirit. These dreams of being dead and seeing ghosts scared me. They haunted me for as long as I could remember. I needed my bracelet back to stop them.

I floated through my locked door to the other side. The voice of my mister kidnapper echoed from below as he spoke funny words like a made up language. Missus reclined in front of a small television that discussed the news, but her eyes stared at nothing as she smiled with a little secret. Another screen showed my room, where my physical body lay crumpled in the corner, not moving. On the table was the key to my dungeon.

Maybe I could take it while they were distracted. I grabbed at the key, but my clear hands waved through. I hated being dead.

There were other ghosts in the room. Lots of them. I pointed at my door, the window, and around Missus and counted to twelve. Normally, I only saw five or six in these dreams. Maybe nightmares were stronger in Horror. At least none of them were scary and powerful gods and goddesses of Fantasy. These see-through people were strangers.

Except one. He had a skinny face and spikey hair. My Uncle Oz floated near the window, talking with another ghost.

"I tried contacting my sister while she was at the park. I think she only heard my singing. If only they weren't staying at the Pinnacle Hotel."

The other floater scoffed. "The one place that does everything they can to block any spiritual influences, Haunting or Supernatural."

Uncle Oz shook his head. "I trained her too well. It's where I'd stay if I was still living. Either way, we've established a presence here, despite the growing Hauntings and that soulless immortal."

The other floater grimaced. "These idiots are literally inviting Hauntings. We can thank God for the little boy's innocence and faith. Otherwise, we'd have no grounds to be here. It takes every one of us to ward off the growing pack of monsters who want to join Abadda's cause."

"I'll try to contact Pansy again, but she needs to relax. Crap, she's almost as anxious as I was. You'd think it would help that she has two gifts from the Supernaturals, but a bond with her husband and magic speed don't help her hear us. Anyway, one of her companions has a limited connection to our zone, and I convinced him to buy some sleeping pills. Hopefully those will help."

I floated towards my uncle, trying to squeeze between the stranger ghosts as they murmured quietly to each other.

Squeezing between people was different as a ghost. I drifted through a lady, embarrassed and surprised that I actually could. She and her friend spared me a glance then did a double take.

"The prince?" she asked.

Others looked and gasped.

"How is the prince here?"

"Oh no, his poor parents."

"How? He was healthy when she forced him to sleep."

I hurried past them to approach the men at the window. "Uncle Oz?"

He jerked around then jumped back.

"Gagh! Aeron? No! You can't be dead, you—"

He zipped off to my room. He appeared a moment later to stick his head through my door. His expression was completely bewildered.

"But you're still breathing?"

I was?

The other translucent people gathered around me again, but looked to Uncle Oz.

"Is he in a coma?" one asked.

I shivered. "I am having a nightmare."

Oz disappeared behind the door then reappeared to check me. "He's alive, everyone. I think. That's not natural." He floated over then paused before me. He offered his hand.

My hand slipped through his, but I felt something. It was the faint memory of a hand in mine as our hands slipped into one another. He pulled on me as if by a string to my room. It was a bit of a relief to be away from the many strangers, but I didn't like to see my sleeping body. As if I wasn't me. My uncle's eyes darted between my two selves.

"This is *not* natural. You're having a literal out-of-body experience? Has this happened before? I definitely need to hire new Fantasy informants if they knew about this and didn't tell me."

I shuddered. "This is only a nightmare. I need my bracelet back to make it stop."

"Aeron." Uncle Oz crouched in his levitating to see me eye-to-eye. "This is real. You're dead, but you're alive. How is this possible?"

"I don't know." I started to cry. "I want to wake up and make it stop. I don't want to be dead!"

I wailed and a chill crept through me.

Oz froze and snarled at something beyond me. "The immortal witch is back. I'd rather have you surrounded by my friends." He put his hand to my shoulder. Again, I felt the strange tug as he pulled me through the locked door like it wasn't there. The room of ghosts stood guard at the stairway. Buttchess Abadda and Mister walked up, surrounded by ghostly monsters. While all the ghosts wore simple robes or cloaks, the nice ghosts had lights like stars or fireflies behind their eyes and genuine smiles. The ghosts around Abadda had pits of darkness or fire brewing under their sneers. Oz's friends helped me feel better, but the bad ghosts frightened me and made me feel gross inside.

"Stay away from the immortal witch," Uncle Oz commanded his friends. "She can't see or interact with us unless we interact with her. It isn't time to fight yet."

A couple of the nice ghosts grumbled, then turned unfriendly against the scary ghosts.

"Get back, you foul creatures," one said.

One of the monster ghosts laughed rudely. "They invited us. They listen to us. Whisper all you want about repentance in their ears, but they chose us."

Mister talked with Missus, like he couldn't hear the argument between the dead. He touched her shoulder with a small smile, then headed towards my room. More of the nice ghosts huddled around Missus, trying to out-whisper the mean comments made by the monster ghosts.

"You know this is wrong," a nice spirit said. "You can still make the right choice. You've been good to the prince."

"You can help Urien. He'll listen to you."

"No, he won't," a mean spirit growled in Missus's ear. "He grows more determined after each ritual. He doesn't care about you anymore. You've done nothing to help him, you little traitor."

Berwyna's face saddened. Good spirits rallied around her again, saying nice things like, "You can be the good woman that you think Douglas deserves."

I poked a finger into Uncle Oz for his attention. "Can they hear us?"

"Bits and pieces to their subconscious," my uncle said. "We can influence their thoughts if they're praying, meditating, or spiritually in tune with us."

Most of the spirits that followed and whispered around Mister were of the scary sort.

One scary ghost growled in his ear, "You grow stronger with each ritual. You summon more demons each time. They obey your command."

"They obey no one," a good spirit called from the back of the group. "You're strongest when you're true to yourself!"

A female scary ghost spoke with smooth and flirty tones to Mister. "Berwyna's blind if she can't see your new strength. You don't need her help. You should show her how strong you've become by taking her like you always wanted."

The scary ghost slid her fingers down Mister's arms and he shivered before he unlocked the door to my prison. Some nice spirits guarded my door, holding back the bad spirits.

"You have no sway here," one of the nice spirit guards said. The bad spirits gnashed their teeth and called their nasty words to Mister as he entered my room.

Something shoved my shoulder.

"Ow!"

Oz turned to me, concerned.

An unseen hand jostled my spirit and my consciousness slipped.

"What's going on? Aeron?"

"Someone is waking me," I said, squeezing my eyes shut. I opened them to find myself waking in my cell with Mister shaking my shoulder. I had a strange thought that I preferred my nightmare over reality. That had never happened before. The thought grew as Wicked Buttchess Abadda hovered over me.

"Did thou sssee the dead?"

I whimpered, but said nothing as I remembered my nightmare bits at a time. I had seen…Oz! Uncle Oz was there! And nice ghosts. They kept me safe from mean ghosts.

"Did thou talk to them?" Abadda demanded. "Thou must convinccce them to join me!"

I huddled farther back to the corner. I did not want to work for Abadda, the Wicked.

She snarled like an angry dog. "Ssspeak!"

"No!" I said.

"No, thou did not talk to them?"

"No!"

"Exxxplain thyself, child!" The Wicked Buttchess growled until her frustration grew into a fiery scream. She swiped her hand at me, sending a sharp slap of air across my face. I fell to the floor, bruising my knees and scraping my hands. I cried.

"Thisss is thy parent'sss fault. If they had not cut me with that cur16 sword, I would steal thy ability and do it myssself."

"I will not help you," I wailed, then used the argument winner that I learned from Cousin Farris. "I will not-not-not times infinity! I want my mom and father. I want to go home."

She snarled. "Then thou art ussseless to me. Even worssse, thou might grow into the one to fulfill that other prophecccy."

PANSY

"Pansy!"

A voice from my past jolted me awake. My eyes scoped our hotel room. We were alone in silence.

"Did you feel that?" Dunstan asked from the corner near the door.

"What?" I asked, my mind still hazy. I grabbed the clock beside the bed. Only three hours of sleep? I grumbled to myself. Not like I expected to sleep much while Aeron was out there somewhere. Theo and I spent the evening wandering the eighth circle, casting his Location spell, failing, walking three blocks, casting Location, nothing. Three blocks more. Location. Nothing.

We returned to the hotel disappointed, frustrated, and exhausted, mentally and physically. Theo was especially cranky. Probably from using so much magic. My worries for Aeron compounded with anxiety for Dunstan until he returned an hour later. He mentioned a brief encounter with a pumpkin-headed attacker and a crowded Halloween party.

"You should have seen some of the mummy costumes," he said. "I didn't see them up close, but from a block away, the zombies looked convincing."

I stared at him wide-eyed. "There's a Halloween costume party in the ninth circle? I can't think of a more obvious way to invite Hauntings to come slaughter them. Were they adolescents or adults?"

Dunstan pondered. "I couldn't tell. Adults? As I said, the costumes were convincing and I was a block away. It was in this little office building next to the Twilight Tower."

I scoffed and shook my head. "Idiots."

We ate dinner, then I found myself strangely sleepy. Dunstan seemed oddly pleased with himself and reassured us that he'd take the first night watch. Good thing too. Theo and I barely bothered to change into pajamas before we rolled into bed.

Just after three o'clock in the morning, I woke up with a start.

Dunstan slowly waved his arms before himself.

"There's a god in here," he whispered.

"Wait," I said, forcing my brain to focus, "are you talking about a Fantasy god, a Supernatural, or a Haunting?"

"The real question is its alignment for good or evil."

Condemnation, my brother-in-law was creepy sometimes. He stood like a hunter, searching with senses unknown to me.

"The god's focus is on you."

Chills ran up my arms, despite the blanket around my shoulders. "And its alignment?"

"It seems," he paused, "friendly."

"You don't sound too sure about that."

"That's because it also feels nervous. We ought to make it feel welcome."

Friendly and nervous attributes weighed heavier toward a Supernatural visitor than a Haunting. Still, I didn't help Dunstan rummage through his pack and withdraw several candles. Lighting them with a determined flick of his finger, he placed them on the table and sat down.

"Come, join my hands. It's a rare and honored occasion when the gods make themselves known."

Tired and wary, I joined him at the table.

"To the one who lingers," he hummed, "I sense your need to communicate with us. Please, allow us to help you."

We sat in silence for an uncomfortable amount of time. All the while, my mind freaked out. Were we having a séance?

"He's not responding to me," Dunstan muttered. "You try."

Everything about this screamed like a bad idea, but if I helped it rest in peace, maybe I could too.

"H-hello?"

"*Pansy!*" Dunstan and I jumped. "*What did I tell you about séances!?*"

"Oz? Is that you?" A smile raised my lips despite my nerves. Supernaturals, how I missed my brother!

I didn't see him, but his voice echoed in my mind like the time he spoke after defeating Sean's poltergeist.

"*I should have put a note in my book to never trust people from Fantasy. They're far too weird and curious.*"

"Oz," I said, "I'm from Fantasy now."

"*I know.*" I couldn't see his face, but easily imagined his confused expression. "*You have a touch of the Supernatural. All of you do, including your son.*"

"Aeron?" My heart skipped a beat. "You've seen Aeron? Where is he? Is he alright?"

"*He's held captive in an office building beside the Twilight Tower. Did you know he has literal out-of-body experiences when he sleeps?*"

"His nightmares," I gasped. His captors must have removed his bracelet.

"*They aren't nightmares,*" Oz said. "*He was like a spirit next to me, literally in two places at once.*"

"That's awesome!" Dunstan gaped.

I shot a glare at him and he flustered.

"Don't you see? That's his ability! He enters the spirit realm in his sleep!"

I gasped. His ability? After all these years…and we suppressed it, thinking the dreams frightened him.

"Oz, can you help him escape?" I asked. There was no reply. "Oz?"

"He's gone," Dunstan said. "I've never been good at keeping the connection. Wake Theo. Your brother gave us our first big break to find Aeron. Though, now it won't surprise me if he gets out on his own."

Then the fire alarm went off.

Theo popped out of bed like a toaster. "Curses!"

"Ow!" Dunstan clapped his hands to his ears. "Is that from the candles?"

"The alarms must be extra sensitive," I shouted over the screeches. "We need to stop it! Fast! Before we find out their fire department's response time! And clean this up! If they find out we had a séance, they'll run us out!"

Dunstan and Theo scrambled to put out the candles. Dunstan absorbed the candle light as Theo sent a tight wind tunnel to smoke them out.

Not helping, guys.

"I could make a blackout," Dunstan shouted as the alarm still screamed. "People can't witness what they can't see."

"No, that would—"

I was cut off as someone pounded on our door.

"Are you alright in there?"

"How do you turn these things off?" Theo shouted back.

"Don't worry! Help is on the way!"

More muffled shouts sounded from behind the door. I commended their fire response. It seemed their fire department across the street actually helped.

"Quick," I hissed, "we need to make it look like a harmless accident. We burnt something in a portable cooker—anything but a séance!"

Theo and Dunstan worked on our alibi while I ran to open the high window. I switched on the bathroom fan when urgent banging on our door insisted we open up or they'd barge it down.

"No! There's no need!" I shouted. I strapped my emergency pack around my leg and ran to the door. I opened it wide, hoping Theo and Dunstan had our alibi ready. A maid and a small team of firemen stood at our door.

"We only wanted a small midnight snack." I waved to my husband and brother-in-law behind me.

Theo and Dunstan crouched around a small smoking cauldron. They dropped in a piece of our jerky that looked remarkably like a withered rat tail…

"Witches!" one of the firemen gasped.

I facepalmed, and Dunstan absorbed all light.

The maid screamed.

Chapter 13

HOTELS

Their thresholds are weaker than loved homes
Calling a floor Level 14 doesn't mean it's not Level 13
Research your hotel for its past Hauntings
Unless you're in Thriller, don't plan on a fire escape
or helicopter to save you from balconies or roof tops.

- *Oz's Haunting Survival Book,*
with notes by Pansy Fromm

THEO

"We need to leave," Pansy said.

Although I failed to see the problem, I did see our auras darken in the moment before Dunstan absorbed the light. Trusting my wife's survival instincts, I grabbed her and Dunstan's hands. We were unable to pack in the dark, though my auras ability let us brush past the firemen at the door. From their stances, I assumed they brandished weapons. They circled around the maid as she screamed hysterically.

I led my wife and brother away from the auras of strangers before whispering, "Why are they screaming?"

"They think we're witches," Pansy said. "Can you lead us out?"

"I can see people, not the hallways," I said. "Where are the stairs?"

Dunstan faded on some of the lights ahead. They flashed red with alarms.

"Our little candle lights caused this much of an alarm?" I asked. "Should we not go back and explain the misunderstanding?"

"No," my wife said, running us towards the "Exit" sign. "Horrors are 'shoot first, ask questions later' types of people. The only time they want to get chummy with a threat is when they're incapacitated, or trying to stall their deaths."

"We mean no harm," I said.

"It doesn't matter. We learned where Aeron is. We can rescue him now and return to Fantasy."

Dunstan's voice came from my side, asking, "How can we stealthily rescue him when we're on the run? These people will see us and give chase as soon as we leave my shadows."

My brother had a good point, and Pansy gave no response. We stepped into the light that illuminated the exit.

"There they are!" someone shouted behind.

"Get them!"

Pansy urged, "Let's go!"

"Halt!" a voice called from the hallway. "I'll shoot!"

We continued to run and Dunstan blackened the whole hallway again. A gun fired. Pansy's aura blurred as she tapped into her speed. Dunstan and I grunted as she shoved us to the ground. The bullet broke through the window behind us, shattering the glass. My wife solidified at the stairwell entrance with the door open and waiting for us.

"Come on!" She waved us to run faster.

I was last to go through the door with one more glance down the hallway as Dunstan released the light. The firemen and maid stared after us, mouths gaping or pinched tight with anger, eyes wide with fear or determination.

What did they think of us? The fireman's accusation echoed in my mind. *Witches.* Yes, as a matter of fact, I had the magics of a wizard with my wand. Were good witches or wizards an impossibility in Horror?

We stumbled down the stairwell as red lights flashed. Pansy could have used her speed to run ahead, though she remained with us.

She mumbled to herself, "This was exactly what I was trying to avoid! We don't need another Haunting right now. Isn't our search for Aeron enough?" Her voice rose and echoed through the stairwell. "I asked for an alibi! What in Horror were you thinking?"

"You said 'portable cooker,'" I said.

"And you thought of a *cauldron?*"

"Can we shout about this later?" Dunstan hissed. "I can make it dark, I can't make us silent! It defeats the purpose of hiding in the dark if you give away our location with your voices."

To confirm his point, a shout overhead announced, "They're headed downstairs! Cut them off!"

Pansy cursed and burst through the exit to the well-lit first floor. Across the lobby, people hastened to block the main doors of entry and exit. The manager stood in front, trembling with a walkie talkie and an emergency hatchet in hand.

"Stop right there!"

We did. I put my hands up, then Pansy and Dunstan followed suit.

"This is just a misunderstanding," I said.

"We heard a report that you are witches!" an employee shouted.

Another one said, "They cut the power on the second floor, which is a criminal act of vandalism!"

"Inspect your cords," I replied in an even voice. "You will find them untouched."

The manager asked, "Then how do you explain the witness accounts upstairs, and why did you run?"

Another employee added, "We accused you of witchcraft! What do you say to that?"

"Not all magic is evil," I argued.

"Theo, that's—"

"You confess then?" A security officer cut off Pansy's retort. He and his partner stepped in front of the employees and pointed steady guns at us.

I wanted to clarify their accusations, to clear the misunderstandings, except the crowd of employees shouted.

"They're witches!"

"Burn them! Kill them all!"

"They broke our Haunt-Free record!"

Behind us, footsteps tumbled down the stairwell. We would be surrounded soon.

I lowered my hand to reach for the wand sleeve in my pocket.

"He's reaching for something!" An employee pointed. The policeman aimed his gun at me and his aura lengthened.

"Keep your hands where I can see them!"

I spoke slowly. "We mean you no harm."

The policeman kept his gun trained on me and Pansy crouched, ready to tap into her speed.

"Dunstan," I whispered. We shared a look and silent nod. The back of my mind acknowledged the odd moment of having the same plan as my wayward brother.

Blackness.

Screams.

Hands shoved me to the ground.

A gunshot.

More screams.

I slipped on my wand sleeve as the auras of the police and employees ducked down. Pansy's short aura hunched over me as Dunstan's crouched.

"Pansy!"

"Stupid guns. Stupid Hauntings. Stupid magic!"

I accepted her grumbled accusations without screams of pain as a sign that she was fine. I grabbed her hand and Dunstan's arm to direct us around the crowd at the door. We had to nudge a few people out of the way.

"Sorry. Excuse us. We meant not to harm anyone."

Pansy shushed at me as one of the employees swung his arm at my face. I reacted with the first spell that came to mind, *"Rodegad!"*

The arm dropped like lead. I could only imagine the shield encasing that I gave it. The confused person screamed in terror.

"They did something to my arm!"

We burst through the doors and ran into the night. The light of the first quarter moon filtered through the clouds though Dunstan kept a five-meter radius of black around us. That way, we could mostly see what came ahead. Dunstan took the lead since his late night excursions gave him a proper knowledge of where we were.

"Crap," Pansy muttered as we ran. "Crap, crap, crap! What supplies do we have with us? I have my emergency pack, but left everything else behind. How can we enter the ninth circle and fight Abadda like this?"

I was in no hurry to admit that I only had my wand and the clothes on my back. Dunstan likewise answered with silence and running faster.

Two blocks later, Dunstan groaned, "I need to release the light from the hotel. It's too far away."

"I am surprised that you held it this long," I said, puffing.

Pansy grumbled from behind, "We need to run faster then. They'll come after us as soon as they can, and I've never faced a mob Haunting before."

We ran a couple more blocks before turning in a different direction. I had no idea where we were headed, other than it was downhill. I found myself grateful that Dunstan had explored the town each evening. My gratitude turned into unease when I recognized the icy black pavement ahead. One block away from the border of the ninth circle, Dunstan told us to turn again, running parallel to the border.

"Okay," Pansy said, moving to the front, "slow down to boredom. Dunstan, put away your shadows. Magic will make us stand out more than if we walk normally."

Dunstan released the light, allowing us what limited visibility the nighttime overcast provided between the lights of orange decorations and jack-o-lanterns that lined each building. Pansy pulled us aside to catch our breath beneath a store canopy.

"Is it normal," I asked, "for people to stroll the city at this late hour?"

Pansy grumbled, "Not at three in the morning. We're a night early to pretend we're trick-or-treating."

Curses, today was Halloween? That meant that I missed Pansy's birthday. Was there a worse time to celebrate and wish her happiness?

"Can we hide inside?" Dunstan asked, peering in the dark store windows.

"It's after hours," Pansy said. "It won't be open."

"Theo can unlock doors," he scoffed.

"That's breaking and entering and we've done enough damage with magic!" Pansy hissed.

"Pansy," I said, "although you are originally from here, you cannot expect Dunstan and me to pretend we have no abilities *nor* magics. They are part of who we are as Fantastics."

Pansy turned on me, deadly serious. "Yes, I do expect it. We're on the hunt for Aeron, which means we need stealth. Otherwise we'll become the hunted."

"I think we're too late for that," Dunstan said. He pointed down the street where we came. "Look. They called in the Virgils."

A mob of twenty or so people marched down the street. They lit the road with torch fires, flashlights, and flip-phone screens as if they were unable to decide which era of tools to use against a witch hunt. The firemen carried their axes and handguns while others wielded rifles and even pitchforks.

"They're watching each other's backs," Pansy said. "They won't be easy to sneak around."

"Pansy," Dunstan said dryly, "did you forget my ability? I can sneak past anyone."

"I have my ability too," she said, "but using them will only confirm their suspicions that we don't belong here. Look at their faces. We embarrassed them by breaking their 'no Haunting' streak. Those people are out for blood. If they catch us, we'll be lucky if they burn us at the stake. They might torture us for information about our witchy friends, and since we don't have any, they'll imprison us until we're on the brink of death. *Then* they'll burn us at the stake."

I risked another glance around the corner at the mob. Pansy was right. Their auras shone several centimeters long, proving their intent to kill. This was not a mob to simply rid their town of evils. This mob was livid.

"Now, we're running through Horror in the middle of the night," Pansy grumbled. "Fine, do what you need to do to get us back inside. It'll be better to break and enter a building that looks lived in. If it's abandoned, it's more than likely to be haunted."

The building we rested against was dusty and blocked with boards, so we went two doors down to a small bookshop. I magicked open the front door's heavy bolt lock. Holding the door open, I let Pansy step through first. Our eyes locked for a second as she passed me, her tension radiating from her like her short aura. She stepped over the threshold and we discovered the motion detection system. A blaring alarm announced our location. The Latin translation of "silence" entered my mind before I could ask, and I threw a jab of "*Zilendium!*" at the sound.

Down the street, voices of the mob shouted.

"There's an alarm!"

"It came from this way!"

"I think they're in Brian's bookshop!"

Pansy, Dunstan, and I shared wide eyes of worry before Dunstan blacked out the store.

The Virgils shouted, "Did you see that?"

"We've got them now!"

"It's pitch black inside. Do you see_anything?"

The mob gathered around the entrance, pounding on the door and windows. My breathing quickened, praying they stayed outside. They frowned with anger, determination, and in an attempt to hide their fears.

"Careful," one warned another. "Don't put your face right up to the window, or they'll suddenly appear and scream."

"Windows make faint reflections. Treat them like mirrors."

Pansy's aura tilted. "Are they quoting my brother's book?"

"Sounds like it," Dunstan said. Despite his calm voice, his aura silhouette revealed his quick rising and falling breath. "What if I black out the whole block? We might sneak past them through the front door."

"And run into a waiting mob?" I asked.

"It's the last thing they'll expect."

Glass shattered and people clambered inside with battle cries.

"Run!" Pansy hissed, pulling me away from the windows, towards the back. We stumbled into bookshelves and walls as the mob raced inside. Our hands fumbled in Dunstan's darkness until we found a door handle. We yanked it open and staggered out. The back door led to a small cement patio with a plastic chair and smoking station littered with cigarette butts. Gravel, dirt, and weeds paved a wide road to an industrial-sized dumpster and a long, dark ditch.

"Down there!" I pointed at the ditch. We ran down the path to the gulley of dark stones, as if a dried stream once flowed there. Pansy and I slid into the ditch, falling the last meter to the bottom. The stones were as hard as iron. "Dunstan, can you—"

Where was Dunstan?

I started back up the trench. "Dunstan?"

Pansy pulled me back down. "Shh!" Her grip on my arm tightened as her eyes darted about. "Crap," she whispered. "Condemnation, we're in a malebolge. This is no place to hide, but where did Dunstan go? Did we get separated, or did they catch him?"

Voices shouted above as the mob tore through the store.

"Did you find them?" someone shouted.

"They must be hiding somewhere!"

"Maybe they transformed into books?"

I exhaled with relief. "It does not sound as though they caught Dunstan. Perhaps he is still inside?"

"Burn it all!" a Virgil shouted.

"But it's Brian's Bookstore?"

"The witches used it as a sanctuary! It's haunted now! Burn it!"

A small cry escaped Pansy's lips. I understood her pain without asking why. The same thoughts raced through my head.

Such meaningless destruction! Why? All those books! All that knowledge! What lengths would they take to destroy us? Were we safe in our hiding place?

I turned to give my wife a consoling touch only to see the true cause for her cry.

A dozen red eyes stared at us. I might have missed their auras—dark as they were in this pit of night—except their lengths gave them away. Horned demons.

"Run!" I said, while Pansy urged, "Climb!"

Pansy's aura was lighter than mine, so I took her lead. Pansy blurred as she struggled to climb out of the trench with her speed ability. The incline was steep, and for every two steps upward, the rocks slid her back one. I cast a shield wall between us and the horned demons. They brandished wicked scourges embedded with bones and glass.

I attempted to climb the loose stones of iron, though I slid twice as often as Pansy.

The horned demons whipped and lashed their scourges at my shield. It shattered after only five hits.

Curses, what was the magic word for "soil?" I pointed my wand arm at the ground and shouted, "*Derra!*" then scooped it upward. Pansy yelped as the rocks rose beneath our feet and carried us to the top of the trench.

A *Whop!* broke the air as stinging pain scratched around my left ankle. I cried out. One of the scourges lashed around my foot. I followed the snare's line back to a grinning demon with burning eyes. He yanked back on his scourge. The tug slipped my foot out from under me, threatening to pull me back down to the bottom of that black pit. Pansy blurred, metal glinting in her hands.

She cut the whip and helped me back to my feet. Just in time for the Virgils to sound the alarm.

"There they are!"

"Curses." Would this night never end?

"Run!" Pansy grabbed my hand. To my surprise, she pulled me towards the burning building. Towards the Virgils.

"Pansy?"

"Shield us," she commanded.

It was utter madness. Our auras waved between shades of deadly dangerous and maybe-we-might-possibly-survive-this-if-we-were-fortunate.

"*Rodegad! Aura!*" I cast a shield and column of air around our bodies as we jumped through one of the broken windows of the burning bookstore.

"What the horror?" one of the witnessing Virgils cursed. "They jumped in?"

"Fire might be their power!" another shouted. "Back away, in case they evolve into bigger Hauntings than before!"

Pansy and I crawled on our hands and knees over fallen beams and book piles, breathing and seeing with small air columns that I magicked over our faces. I was unsure whether to be worried or relieved that Dunstan was nowhere in sight. There was, however, a dark room over to the side. I pointed and nodded to Pansy, then we crawled to it. I created another shield around the door before opening it. That kept most of the oxygen from pouring out. We collapsed inside, panting, kicking the door shut behind us.

We lay inside the bookstore office with a large desk, a couple sleeping computers, filing cabinets, and two rolling chairs. Stacks of books and packaging supplies occupied one corner, and a mini fridge occupied another. No Dunstan. There was also no fire in this room. I cast another shielding spell over the door to ensure that it stayed that way.

Pansy and I lay flat on the floor for a few minutes, catching our breath and whispering prayers. Pansy prayed to the Supernaturals that the Hauntings would go away. I prayed to the gods of concealment and silence that the Virgils would leave without a further search.

I still smelled the smoke. Pansy said that they would burn us if they found us. That possibility became all too real as the fire raged around our room. Pansy's worries and the gravity of our situation fell on me. Hard.

Bullbeggar. How could we rescue Aeron with this? Pansy and Dunstan said that they learned Aeron's whereabouts. Fantastic. Except, we were stuck in this room, hiding from a mob and horned demons.

Wood creaked as more bookshelves collapsed and the roof cracked. The mob cheered from the front, their auras regularly passing by our high window.

I prayed harder for our safety. I prayed for Dunstan's safety, wherever he was. I prayed that the Virgils would give up, go home, and feel satisfied. I prayed for the unfortunate owner, and hoped Brian would be compensated for his bookstore. I prayed the hardest for Aeron.

"Please, keep him safe until morning."

Chapter 14

ARE THEY HUMAN?

People with disfigured faces or features
are generally lonely and misunderstood,
but if you offend one, they *will* Haunt you.
Don't trust one sense alone to confirm a person's
or animal's identity.
It's okay to cry. Emotions, like empathy and love,
are part of what separates us from Hauntings.

- *Oz's Haunting Survival Book,*
with notes by Pansy Fromm

PANSY

I barely heard the Virgils over the fire's roar. Pressing my ear to the wall, I heard, "If you don't see them die, then assume they're still alive."

"Condemnation," I swore. "They're not going to leave us alone." How were we supposed to find Dunstan and rescue Aeron with pacing guards? When pulling Theo into the burning building, I'd hoped to regroup with Dunstan. If he hadn't left, perhaps he would come back. "If you lose something, go back to the last place you saw it" was a basic rule of life, not only in Horror. Based on the attitude of the Virgils around us, I assumed he hadn't been taken by them. Maybe he used his teleportation spell to escape? How would we know?

Theo and I huddled in the bookstore office building, one door away from an inferno within Inferno, and one window away from a vigil of Virgils. Beyond the mob was the malebolge pit of sadist demons, and beyond the fire was the terror of the ninth circle.

I analyzed Theo's ankle wound for infections, then wrapped it with supplies from my emergency pack. "Oz said Aeron's in an office building by the Twilight Tower. Condemnation, they took our *child* into the ninth circle! Those monsters! What are they doing to him? How are we supposed to save him? We have no equipment, it's night—so the Hauntings have the upper hand—and to top it all, we're exhausted from limited sleep and a mob chasing us around town."

Supernaturals, my adrenaline faded as I finished wrapping Theo's ankle. My head and body ached with vengeance for rest.

Theo frowned. "Forgive me, how could we pack in Dunstan's blackout? You said we needed to go, and I assumed grappling in the dark for supplies would waste time."

"It would have been, but—" I groaned with frustration. Thank the Supernaturals that the Virgils couldn't hear us over the devouring fire and collapsing bookstore.

"No matter what we should have done. It is done. Now, we move to what is next."

"How?" I flipped my hands in the air. "We have our abilities, your magic, my emergency pack, and the clothes on our backs. We're in our pajamas! They're made for sleeping and comfort, not battling a mob or whatever else we'll face out here! Not only do we need to find Dunstan and save Aeron, but we're stuck in a burning building guarded by a mob!"

I turned away from Theo, ashamed of my emotions even as my face burned and my head ached from holding them in.

This wasn't how a lady was supposed to act, but I was never meant to be a lady.

"Pansy?" Theo shifted to crawl around me. "I understand if you are frustrated. I am also. We are trapped here, away from Aeron, all because of my foolish—"

"Saving Aeron and going back to normal won't fix everything," I snapped.

Theo paused and took another step closer. "What do you mean?"

I shook my head. I didn't want to say it. I didn't want to vocalize and confirm my worries and fears. A tear escaped and Theo stiffened.

"My flower?"

When was the last time he used that term of endearment? I wiped my face and forced out my feelings. "What happens after? Even if we get out of this mess, regroup with Dunstan, save Aeron, and go home. Then what? We go back to living separate lives where we work all day, rush through meals, and maybe share a quick kiss for the columnists? We've been drifting apart for months, maybe years. Aeron's kidnapping was just a hammer to the wedge."

"What?" His surprise increased my frustration.

"You haven't even noticed? Of course not," I scoffed. "You're too busy being marquis. You're always looking at the big picture, at some far off future that might never happen. I just want to be appreciated for being *here now*."

"You want to appreciate being trapped in a burning building in Horror?" he asked, rubbing the back of his neck.

"No," I groaned and glanced up for Supernatural help. "Before this whole misadventure. I needed you to appreciate me, that I was always there for you, for the people, even though it drained the life out of me."

I hung my head and cried. I didn't want Theo to see how much I hurt.

It's okay to cry, my brother's long lost voice returned to me. *Emotions make us human, and that separates us from Hauntings.*

Theo wrapped his hands around mine. He still had no words for me, so I sniffled and continued.

"When was the last time we went on a date? The last time we kissed for our own pleasure? We're not even roommates who share the same bedroom. Are we simply political partners? I need a husband, Theo. I need *you*. I need you to be human with me, with all your flaws and vulnerabilities. Can we take a day off from being marquis and marchioness? We dropped everything to save Aeron. Can we drop everything again to save our marriage?"

His hands tightened around mine like my words froze him. I looked up and our eyes met. Theo's consciousness nudged mine.

Supernaturals, I didn't want to use Sean's bond between us with these messy emotions. The bond opened us to each other's knowledge, experiences, thoughts, and even muscle memory if it was on our minds. I tried to block out my emotions, but I was too late. Theo's eyes widened and blinked back tears as he gained a true understanding. "Pansy, forgive me. I had no idea you felt neglected. Please, I—let me—"

In return, I felt his desperation to make things right. I felt his mental exhaustion as he played the game of politics every single day. Every conversation was a battle to please the lords and ladies while also obligating them to share their wealth with their employees and tenants. I felt his deepest fear of dis-satisfying any citizen who might revolutionize the duchy, take away our home, livelihoods, honor, and even our lives. I had no idea he shouldered so much. I also felt his new fears of losing Aeron to his wicked stepmom…and losing me because of his bargain and ignorance of my pain.

He was determined though. Theo was a fighter, after all.

He stood with his good leg and pulled on my hand to help me stand in front of him. Then, he bent low in a lavish bow that sent my mind into déjà vu. All he needed was his gallant cloak to swing behind him.

"Please," he said, "allow me the opportunity to become better acquainted with you. May we start by belatedly celebrating your birthday? I hoped to celebrate properly after we returned home with Aeron."

I squeezed his hand and a smile tugged at my lips. "You remembered my birthday? With everything else going on?"

"Of course," he said, straightening. "After we find Aeron and take him back home, we will take a holiday. We will go somewhere with just the three of us. Then the two of us will go somewhere for as long as you want. Also, I have appreciated eating our meals together lately. Perhaps we can make it a daily habit. I may need reminders to break away from my duties, though you are my number one priority. You always have been, always will be."

My heart soared with hope from his words. He confirmed them as he met my smile with his own. He kissed me with a tender passion that was only known between lovers. Our thoughts and feelings became one. We would make things right. We would rescue Aeron so we could be a family together.

As for Dunstan…well, he was a grown man who previously proved himself in the nights of Horror. He'd find us here eventually, or (if worse came to worst) he had his spell to escape directly to Fantasy.

DUNSTAN

I could have sworn that Theo and Pansy were right behind me. I couldn't see auras in the dark as Theo could, but my blackout training was usually enough for me to sense my surroundings in the dark. I blamed the chaos of the Virgils and the bookstore burning.

When Pansy said, "Run," I blacked out the block for us to slip through the front door. Only when I released the light again, did I realize that I was alone. Bullbeggar.

I darkened and hid in an architectural alcove of an old bank across the street. I watched for Pansy and Theo to come out of the bookstore. I waited even as the Virgils broke inside. Where were Pansy and Theo? Did they escape from a back way?

If Theo ever asked me, I'd never admit that I was truly worried for him. I'd smirk and tease him about being incompetent even as I knew his ability was more reliable than mine, his magic was stronger than mine, and his way of convincing people to do what he wanted was more effective. He was Margen's best option for a future duke. I couldn't let him die.

Beads of sweat gathered on my forehead as the Virgils set fire to the bookstore. The absorbed light of my crevice burned within me. Heat coursed through my veins and sweat rolled down my face.

Alright, think, I mentally mumbled. *Theo and Pansy are smart and skilled. They probably escaped from the bookstore.* I inserted a prayer to my God of Fire, *Don't let my brother die from your gift given to man. They must have escaped. That means they're probably looking for me or looking for Aeron.*

Who was I kidding? They'd look for their son. Pansy knew that Aeron was near the Twilight Tower. I could meet them there. Except, that meant leaving the burning bookstore. I'd never forgive myself if I left and they were still inside… burning, needing me, waiting for me.

Please, let him find a way out. Let them escape to safety.

I turned out of my little alcove and headed towards the Twilight Tower.

Even as I prayed, guilt stung me. I'd promised to serve the gods of Adventurers, yet my relationship with Berwyna cracked that promise. My feelings for her were inconvenient, to say the least. I was supposed to help my brother find his son, not start a Romance.

Bullbegging heart.

If she lived in the opposite direction then she'd be easier to leave behind. No, life was too ironic for that. She had to live near the Twilight Tower, near my destination for Aeron. At least Oz said that Aeron was in an office building, not a house like Berwyna's.

Maybe I could swing by to say hello…and goodbye. The thought of never seeing Berwyna again twisted my insides. Very inconvenient, indeed. As if I could abandon everything and everyone to settle in a little house in bullbegging Horror. All for a woman who barely knew me…a beautiful woman with eyes like the freshest water, hair like refined silver, and an attitude that both challenged and enlightened me.

Inconvenient bullbegging heart.

I neared the looming Twilight Tower, remaining on the fringe of the eighth circle, darting from shadow to shadow. I searched hiding places and intersections for any signs of Pansy or Theo.

As soon as Pansy and Theo had Aeron in hand, they'd have no reason to stay in Horror. I still wanted to pick up my copper shortsword, which the craftswoman promised to finish this morning. I really hoped to have it with me before facing my wicked stepmother. I'd sure like to gut her with it. As if I could even touch her immortality; as if I was the "royal bridge between life and death." Or whatever that prophecy said.

I turned in to the ninth circle a block early from the Twilight Tower. Even if it was my third time, the unnerving munching grated against my consciousness. The fat droplets of sewage rain splattered to the ground and globbed on my rain jacket. As much as I wanted to stop by Berwyna's house, I knew Theo would never forgive me for neglecting the search for his son.

I turned the corner to spot the Twilight Tower a couple blocks away…and the office building next to it. Either the bouncer to the Halloween party was truly as skinny as a skeleton, or it wasn't a costume. A figure moved before a window, cloaked and *translucent*. It was followed by a sickly woman with blood-red hair and the posture of a royal.

Bullbeggar.

Fear clenched my heart, and I ducked back around the corner. That Halloween party was no ordinary costume party. They were Hauntings. True, undead, and cursed Hauntings. As if facing Abadda wasn't scary enough, she surrounded herself with monsters?

No way was I going in there alone.

My magic was under a different school than Theo's, so I couldn't cast Locate or Search as he did. I was also no good in the search for Aeron since I wasn't familiar enough with my nephew. If we survived this, I was determined to remedy that. For now, all I had was the skill level for a small fire light to direct me towards my familiar person within three hundred meters.

I closed my eyes, slowed my breathing—which was a feat of its own after my sprints between buildings and fear of so many Hauntings nearby—then concentrated on a mental image of my brother. If he and Pansy had escaped the burning building and came to the Twilight Tower, I would find them.

I whispered my prayer for magic and focused on locating Theo…on locating my brother…on locating…Berwyna's house was so close.

Whatever pathetic flicker of flame I summoned then vanished. I groaned and wanted to punch something. Why did nothing work?

I absorbed the light around me and converted the light, ready to melt the closest—

Whoa, I wasn't *that* angry. Where had that come from?

I released the heat and light with a long, meditative breath.

If I couldn't find Pansy and Theo, maybe I could learn more information about the "Halloween party" before we crashed it.

Who was I kidding? I just wanted to see Berwyna again. I wanted it so badly that my heart ached. Who cared if it was past midnight? I was already separated from Pansy and Theo, and the damage was already done to my priest magic. If my magic was lost, apparently, so was my heart.

Bullbegging heart.

Chapter 15

SIGNIFICANT OTHERS

> -   *Oz's Haunting Survival Book,*
> with notes by Pansy Fromm

BERWYNA

I paced the upper room of our office hideout. The noises downstairs made me restless, but entertaining the princeling all night exhausted me. According to Abadda, he failed his duty to help her, so instead of trying to help him calm down and sleep, my new orders were to keep him awake. None of this made sense.

The best way to keep him awake was to stay awake with him. A few hours after Abadda's new commandment we were both too tired and grumpy to care. Aeron refused to eat or play, voicing all my mental complaints against Abadda, her commandments, and our situation. I daydreamed about Douglas and how he'd sweep me into his arms to take me away from this awful place.

Anytime I thought about dozing off, the growls below frightened me back awake. I tried and failed to preoccupy my thoughts by encouraging Aeron to play. He was equally unsettled by the noises downstairs.

Monsters of various types hunkered below, snarling quietly like they plotted our deaths. They whispered among themselves, restless from the shouts outside. Rumors of a riot floated through the streets like ghosts. They said three witches infiltrated the safest hotel in the city. We saw the smoke plumes of their fiery deaths, but the city was still on edge.

I peeked through the broken blinds of our window to spy any commotion. What I saw nearly stopped my heart.

Douglas surveyed my office hideout while hiding around the corner of the abandoned house that I said was mine.

Curses, did he see me? What was he doing here at this time of night?

As much as I wanted to run out to him, my circumstances required caution. I turned on the television to a child-friendly show (at least, I was fairly certain it was child-friendly between the static and light flickers), then stepped out of the toy filled dungeon when Aeron was distracted.

Wiping sweaty palms on my skirts, I went downstairs. Abadda stood in the middle of a room with monsters and demons chanting around her, fire burning within her mouth, the air still as death, yet a strange current pulled everyone towards her. Just one of those skeletons or zombies could be a Haunting to murder and kill dozens of people. Yet twenty of them thronged about Abadda, happy to serve her, happy that she spared them and allowed them to bask in her majesty. I slipped past, hoping she wouldn't notice my absence. I didn't want to imagine what would happen if she did.

In another room, Urien finished his own summoning spell as a ghoul crawled from a bloody pentagram on the floor. It moaned at its master, who cracked his whip to his side. I stayed an extra second at Urien's room, wondering how that could be the same boy who innocently asked me to join him for an Adventure only three days ago. He'd collapsed and griped after Abadda forced him through his first summoning. This time, he stood with confidence and dark power. Was it the lighting or did his once-baggy clothes now strain over bulky muscles?

He turned and caught me staring. I couldn't run without causing suspicion, so I stayed and scrambled for an excuse to leave as Urien approached me.

Stepping closer, Urien's new strength definitely wasn't a trick of lighting. He grinned down at me. "Berwyna. Did you come to welcome the newest recruits?"

I shuffled and hoped my childhood friend wouldn't catch my lie. "I need to step out for a bit. One of the prince's toys ran out of batteries, so I need to buy more. Will you watch him while I'm out?"

"Right. Be careful," he said, his eyes distracted by the newly recruited monsters. "The word is there are strange folk about."

"I won't go far," I said, and stepped out the back door. I ran to our neighbor's lot to appear like I came from their back door instead. The weird house had an open window, which emitted a distant growl as I walked past.

"Douglas?" I hissed. He jumped, then a huge grin of joy and relief spread over his face. It was so sincere. My heart broke to think of the lies I'd told.

He joined my side, and I pulled him by the hand to hide inside a landscaper's tool shed. Made of metal slats, the shed was barely tall enough for Douglas and crowded with lawn and gardening tools. A single bald bulb hung in the center, but thankfully, a string of lights also lined the top perimeter. Crisis averted, according to Oz's guide. The shed was hardly a sanctuary, but at least it was out of sight, out of the rain, and had lots of possible weapons. Not my first choice for a romantic secret meeting place, but Douglas held onto my hand after I closed the door and plugged in the decorative lighting.

"Safe enough," I said. "What are you doing here?"

"I'm sorry, I know it's late, but I had to see you. Especially when you didn't answer your door right away. I was worried that you went to that Halloween party."

His eyes glanced in the direction of the horde of Hauntings who guarded the office building.

"Sorry," I said, "I had to explain to my Haunting partner why I should go outside the night before Halloween. You shouldn't have—"

Douglas pulled me into an embrace and I inhaled his scent of fire and smoke. It was better than cologne. His strong arms wrapped around me, more tender and earnest than any of Urien's touches. He held me close enough to feel every heavy rise and fall of his chest.

"Please forgive my forwardness," he whispered in my ear. "Where I'm from, people fall in love faster than the rain falls from the sky."

"You love me?" I asked, surprised.

"I—" He pulled away to look me in the eyes. "I care about you…deeply. More than any woman I've ever known. So much that it tore my heart to think that I may never see you again."

"I care about you too, Douglas. Why might you never see me again?" I knew several reasons: I lied to him, I didn't really live here, I was a Fantastic on a terrible Adventure, I was a kidnapper. Douglas couldn't know any of those reasons. What would he say if I told him? I wouldn't blame him for fleeing from me like I was a monster.

He struggled with his words. "The family reunion hasn't gone as planned. We'll make another attempt to unite the family, but we're unwanted here. I'll need to return to my homeland soon."

"To Romance?" I gasped.

Douglas winced and caressed my cheek with a tender hand. "How I wish I could stay to be with you."

"You want to stay in Horror?" I laughed. How I wished to *leave* to be with him. If only I didn't have a conscience that begged me to remain with Urien and Aeron as a final thought of humanity and kindness. If only I didn't need Abadda's tears every morning to feel halfway healthy again. Then, I'd leave with Douglas between two of my pounding heartbeats.

He shook his head. "But you hardly know who I am. Berwyna, I have a dark past and current occupation that forbids romantic relationships, even with someone as wonderful as you. I must say goodbye."

If his farewell didn't clench my heart, I might have laughed at the irony. I hardly knew him? He hardly knew *me*! Even if he had a dark past, it was better than a dark present. He didn't have a kidnapped princeling locked in a room.

A dark past. Psh. I'd have one too if I managed to escape Abadda.

I realized, "I don't need to know about your past, because who you are now is enough." He opened his mouth to argue, but I continued, "I know you are a traveler with a keen understanding of other cultures. I know you prefer Contemporary lands because you have a sweet tooth and an appreciation for conveniences. I also know you like whole milk, barbeque-flavored snacks, and soap that smells of pine trees."

He laughed a little, though his eyes spoke of a deeper, mental conversation that considered my words. If this was goodbye, I wanted him to know how much I appreciated his friendship and the hope he gave my heart.

"Douglas," I said, "I know you as a true gentleman who offered to help me from the moment we met. You showed me more tenderness than I could hope to deserve. You've become more dear to me than even my closest of friends. If only I could run away with you and start fresh in Romance—" I stopped myself. Did I just suggest we elope? Or worse, run away without commitment? What a fool I could be!

Fears of my forwardness vanished as he swooped down to press his lips against mine. He was timid at first, ready to pull back at any sign of discomfort from me. Once I overcame my shock, I pulled him closer. He held me tighter and opened the kiss. His lips explored mine, strong and confident. Yet his passion seemed equally surprised by True Love's Kiss.

It had to be. What else could fill my heart with such desire? What else could feel so natural, so right, so perfect as this moment?

I opened my eyes to make sure it wasn't all a dream. No, even my wildest of dreams wouldn't have imagined a kiss like this in a tool shed in Horror. Monsters snarled a block away and some ghostly wind howled nearby, but I felt safe in Douglas's arms. One of his hands slid up my back and into my hair, sending shivers back down. I closed my eyes again to become enveloped in his kiss, relieved that our intimacy was private.

If it wasn't? Supernaturals help us if Abadda found me prioritizing someone else. I couldn't let her know about Douglas. She'd hurt him or use him against me. The way I felt with him, about him, and for him swallowed my every desire. We met only a couple days ago, but I felt as if I'd known him all my life.

Douglas broke the kiss all too soon. I cradled myself against his chest and palmed his pounding heartbeat. He was so warm.

"Don't leave," I sighed. "Don't tell me that we can't be together, or say that kiss was our last."

"We shouldn't have even had a first. But I'm glad we did."

I pulled away just enough to see the joy on his face.

"Must you leave? Let me go with you." Curses to my health and Urien and…Aeron. No, curse it all, I had to stay for Aeron.

Douglas released a heavy breath. "It would be better if I come to you, but…there is a way." He reached into one of his pockets and pulled out a piece of parchment. On it was a poem written in calligraphy.

He stared at it, as if mentally debating with himself. With a blink and a little shake of his head, he pressed the paper into my hand. "Burn this tomorrow," he said. "Last time I was in Fantasy, I asked a priest to write a teleportation spell. If you burn this paper, it'll transport you to the location where it was created. I'll find another way off Horror and meet you there. No matter how far apart we are, I'll find you."

"No matter how far?" I asked.

"No matter how far," Douglas reassured me, and met my lips with another unforgettable kiss.

My mind swirled with dreams of traveling the world with Douglas. Who knew what the future held for a Fantasy seamstress/kidnapper and a disinherited Regency Romantic?

Even with the promise of tomorrow, we loathed the thought of saying goodbye. We hesitated, lingered, shared sweet whispers and blissful kisses, wishing life was simple. But a feverish cold grew in my bones and my morning sneezes began. I couldn't let Douglas see me like that. I needed Abadda's healing potion.

It was almost sunrise by the time I returned to our hideout. My mind was everywhere but inside the horrible office building. Hauntings of all sorts leered and jeered at me as I passed them upstairs. I hardly noticed. My face couldn't stop smiling, despite my sniffles and coughing. My mood was shocked back to reality when confronted with the looming dominance of the wicked duchess.

She hovered over me with her stolen wind ability. Light and heat emanated from her throat, begging to scorch my face. She glared at me with her black, soulless eyes. Curses, her stare froze my blood.

"Where didssst thou go?" she demanded.

I barely managed to whimper, "Out."

"To be 'out' can mean anywhere in Novel. Where didssst thou go when I commanded thee to keep the child awake?" she repeated louder.

"I-I" —I stuttered like a kid trying to make excuses— "But I asked Urien to watch Aeron."

"He," the duchess hissed, "has other dutiesss."

She moved in a flash, too fast for my eyes. She spun me around to shove my face against a wall. I cried out. Nearby monsters took interest. A couple liches hooted with anticipation, calling bets on how long I'd last. A vampire shied away as if he couldn't watch for the memories it stirred.

With only one of her hands, Abadda held my right arm behind my back and kept me pressed against the wall. Her other hand was clasped around my left wrist, extending my arm outward. She leaned close to hiss in my ear, "Have you been in exxxchange with spiesss?"

I had half a breath to panic. Then, she released an inferno from her throat, aimed directly at my extended arm.

I screamed.

Werewolves howled, ghouls cheered, the one vampire cringed and humbly bowed his head.

My skin burned until it boiled, but Abadda wasn't done. She was immortal. She didn't need to pause to breathe even as my screams stuttered with coughs. The heat became unbearable as it seared to my nerves.

She finally stopped to demand, "Ssspeak!"

I couldn't breathe, let alone talk. My screams and coughing fit gave way to sobs. My arm. I couldn't feel it outside of the pain.

"Why did you abandon your dutiesss?" Abadda snarled.

I had no excuse. Only the truth. "Douglas," I cried. "I went to see Douglas."

"Who is Douglasss?"

"A—" I almost said friend, but that was a lie. He was more than that, but I couldn't let Abadda know. "He's a Romantic," I said. "A traveler. He's just—" I paused as a thought for my possible salvation came to mind. "He's nobody compared to you. I don't know why you care, because even if he wanted to, there's nothing he can do against you. Your plans are inevitable, Your Highness."

"Is that Berwyna?" Urien's voice entered the scene. I cried out, unsure what to feel about him witnessing my torture. Again. "Hey—wait! What's going on?"

"Dissscipline," Abadda snapped at him, then returned to hiss in my ear. "You are right about one thing. No one can hinder my plansss. Especccially you."

She finally released me from the wall. I collapsed to the floor and cradled my burnt arm. Whether the top layer was skin, tissue, or muscles, I couldn't tell. From my elbow to my fingertips, it all looked like molten lava. Urien came to crouch beside me, and I cried, sniffled, and coughed for breath. Abadda, the Wicked, turned away, mildly irritated.

Urien helped me to stand and slowly walk up the stairs to the monitoring room. Even if I no longer dreamed about a Romance with Urien, I appreciated his companionship. We'd known each other for so long, and it was a small relief to have a friendly face in the middle of this disaster.

If I ran away with Douglas, who would watch over Aeron and Urien?

"You need one of her phoenix tears," he said. "It's about time for your healing potion anyway."

"No. I'd rather suffer the pain than have her attention on me for one more second." I shuddered from the mere thought. A glance at the camera screen showed Aeron sleeping in his toy-filled prison. The young prince was huddled to the side and barely moved. He slept with a small smile and seemed to enjoy his dreams. It tore at my heartstrings to see him so peaceful and content. "Has the prince made any trouble?"

"He's sleeping." Urien shrugged. "I don't get why it's a problem. Whatever his ability does, the queen says it's wasted on him. A couple Hauntings are transporting him at sunrise."

"To where?"

"The Valley of the Shadows of Death."

Chapter 16

LOCATION

Leave when your new house is a good deal and
neighbors are scared of you
Fix any faulty floors, plumbing, door locks,
and other fixtures
Know what's inside the walls of your home
Never try to escape upstairs. You'll only get trapped
Update lights every year, so if they flicker or fuse,
you know it's a direct Haunting alert

- *Oz's Haunting Survival Book,*
with notes by Pansy Fromm

AERON

I fell asleep again as soon as Missus left me alone. In my dream, I was surrounded by the dead. My new way to get to know people was to ask, "How did you die?" This was Horror, so the answers were never pretty. Axe to the head, wire around the neck, chainsaw…anywhere. Then there were the monster deaths. Eaten for werewolf breakfast, soul sucked out by mummies for lunch, drained for vampire dinner. The list grew with each person I asked.

I struggled to remember all of them since they did not look mangled or broken. They smiled at me and promised to help me. I grew comfortable in the presence of my new ghostly friends.

"Hey, look! Watch this!" I waited until Uncle Oz turned my way before rising a foot from the floor. "I can go higher! Want to see me go higher?"

I liked floating higher than everyone else. It made me feel tall, like a grownup. I floated high enough to see the scary ghosts behind the line of friendly spirits.

"Why are there monsters in Heaven?" I asked.

Uncle Oz turned to briefly acknowledge the scaries. "This isn't Heaven. Not yet. It's like a middle ground for Supernaturals and Hauntings. This area of the city is already prone to lots of Hauntings, and your kidnappers are stupidly inviting more. It's only because of you" —he pointed to me— "that my friends and I are here. Your innocence and purity protects you from them."

He used a couple confusing words that adults liked to say, so I said, "I guess."

Uncle Oz smiled. "I just realized why it's strange to see you here. Normally, we only see children in the Spirit Zone if they were sacrificed over the Moloch Altar."

"Why?" I asked again.

"I'm not sure." He squished his face thoughtfully. "Because the Moloch Altar is broken and demonic? I'd have to ask Paul. He knows that kind of stuff. Normally, when children die, they're taken straight to Heaven."

"Why do they go straight to Heaven?" I asked.

"Because kids are too young to fight as Supernaturals or Hauntings. They're subject to their parents, and don't understand the fight for good or evil yet."

"So if I die, I will go to Heaven? What if I make mistakes?"

"Everybody makes mistakes." Uncle Oz shrugged. "I sure did, but more depends on which side you fight for."

I thought of the Heroes and their Adventures of fighting off big scary monsters. "What if I do not want to fight?"

"We must fight or we allow the devil to win. Don't they teach that in Fantasy churches too? Those who do nothing are the easiest for the devil to take over."

"Why?"

"Not sure. Maybe because slothfulness is one of the deadly sins."

"Why?" I asked again.

Uncle Oz paused and frowned at me. "You're just going to keep asking why, aren't you?"

"Why?" I grinned.

Uncle Oz sighed and shook his head. "I think that's enough questions. I'm just glad that even though you're here, you'll get to grow up."

"But why are you here? Are you supposed to be in Heaven? Or did you make a mistake and this is the naughty place?"

Uncle Oz laughed. "This isn't Heaven or Hell. Middle ground, remember? When Horrors die, we become either Hauntings or Supernaturals. Most people who become Supernaturals stay here only until they've accepted their deaths, then move on to Heaven. Hauntings can of course choose to continue on to Hell, but…it's not the kind of place most people are excited to go. A lot of Hauntings stay to torment the people or places they knew in life until they're forced to 'retire,' so to speak. Some of the Supernaturals stay to help the living to fight the Hauntings. We can interact with the living based on our gifts."

"Oh, alright."

"You're not going to ask why?"

"Why?"

Uncle Oz paused. "Naw, you'll find out soon enough. Actually, if you visit us every time you sleep, we should give you orientation."

"What is or-in-ta-shun?"

"It's your welcome to the afterlife." He reached his clear hand into my chest, which looked weird, but felt a little ticklish. "Concentrate on our connection. I'm going to take us somewhere, and I don't want to lose you on the way."

"Alright," I said, and concentrated real hard on his hand inside me.

"Aeron?"

I raised my eyes, and Uncle Oz smiled at me. Only a second had passed, but we were not in the dark office building anymore. We were outside, on the path up to an old church of dark stone. Two ugly creatures stood beside the door. I huddled down closer to my uncle and whimpered.

"It's okay, they won't hurt you. They're gargoyles. They guard the church from demons. This is our Headquarters."

He removed his hand and gestured for me to follow him. I wished I could hold his hand while we drifted past the winged beasts and through the door. I braced myself as we hit, but felt nothing as we glided inside.

The church was bigger and brighter on the inside. The dark stone glowed a bit, as if it too was a ghost. The windows showed an outside that was different from the one we came from. It did not look at all like Horror. It actually reminded me of the Faenor side of Fairy, with green grass hills and wildflowers of every color. I spotted one or two spirits through the windows, walking calmly among the hills. It was like a painting of peace.

Inside the expanded church building, it was more like organized chaos. Spirits surrounded us. They studied at desks, chatted with one another, reviewed maps and papers, or focused hard with their eyes closed.

"What are they doing?" I asked.

Oz jumped at my exclamation. The thought that I scared a ghost made me laugh a little.

"Shh." He put a finger to his lips. "We speak softly in the house of God."

"No one else is whispering," I said.

"You don't need to whisper, but—what do they call it?—use your 'inside' voice."

"Yes, Uncle Oz," I said with a strained whisper and pointed at the ghosts floating about in a flurry. "What are they doing?"

"They're working."

"Why? Do they need money?"

Uncle Oz chuckled. "No, the dead don't need money. But we have a lot of work to do for God and the living."

"You work for the living? Does that mean I am your boss?"

"No," my uncle said with stern eyes, though he still smiled. "Our boss is God."

"Which god?

"What?"

"Which god?" I repeated. "The God of Spirits or God of Death?"

"Um…" My uncle blinked. "There's only one God. Didn't your mom teach you that?"

"Oh, yes. Mom says there is only one God, but Father and Tutor White teached me the names of all the gods. I try real hard to remember them all."

My uncle groaned and muttered, "Fantastics. I heard the Spirit Zone's a little different over there. Let's see, if I remember right, all Fantasy 'gods' are like Supernaturals. As long as you're in Horror, all you need to know is the one true God."

"That is easy," I said. "Oh, I remember! Mom says he is the God of Everything. How can he do everything though?"

Uncle Oz motioned to the spirits all around us. "That's what we're for. God knows everything and lets us help. He gives us duties to help the living, improve ourselves, and to develop our abilities."

"Ghosts have abilities?" I asked in awe. "Like my ability to be like you when I sleep?"

"Ah, well," Uncle Oz fumbled, "I guess abilities was the wrong word. They're different from Fantastic abilities. They're more like gifts. We're just *more* of what we were when we lived."

Still confused, I said, "I guess."

"Here." Uncle Oz led me to a separate room where a few spirits waited. The room was like a painting of my great-grandfather's war tent. Instead of a tent, we stood in a stone room of a church. Instead of a general, a spirit hovered over the map sprawled across a table in the middle. Instead of knights practicing sword fights on the sides, one spirit breathed with concentration as he prayed, while another multiplied herself a dozen times before transforming into various animals. Instead of my great-grandfather, the Valiant King Fromm, the spirits looked up with hopeful eagerness to my Uncle Oz.

"How's it going?" he asked.

"Still waiting for Dante's return," said the spirit by the map.

"Which should be any moment," said the female animal spirit.

Uncle Oz nodded. "Good. Don't stop what you're doing. I'm just giving my nephew the tour since dying every night is apparently normal for him." The spirits gave me wide-eyed stares before smiling in welcome then returning to their activities.

"Now, about those gifts," Uncle Oz said to me, and pointed at the meditating spirit. "That's Paul. He was a bishop in life, so now he's more aware of the thoughts and emotions of others and also has a strong communication link to God to give our reports. And over there's Francine. She was a veterinarian and worked with animal control, so she has gifts to multiply herself and transform into animals that can be visible to the living."

"Fantastic! What about you?"

166

"Me?" Uncle Oz asked. "Well, I was a Haunting analyst and researcher. So I have a greater sense of awareness for Hauntings' strengths and weaknesses."

"Oh, that is neat, I guess."

He leaned in. "I'm also especially gifted at dispelling Hauntings. As a fighter in life, God granted me the gift to condemn their souls. It's irrevocable and requires me to go head-to-head against some scary Hauntings, so there are only a few of us who can do it."

"Fantastic!"

The spirit from the map floated over. I thought he wanted to talk to Oz, but then he stopped in front of me with a friendly smile.

"So, you're Pansy's little boy?"

"My name is Aeron Fromm, Earl of Margen, and I am not little," I said proudly. Did he not see how high I floated, like a tall person? "I am five years old."

The spirit raised his eyebrows. "Fromm, right. Hard to believe it's been over five years."

Uncle Oz smirked at the other spirit. "You know my sister's safer where she is. And don't tell me there's nothing going on between you and Francine. I've seen the way you two look at each other."

The other spirit flustered and Uncle Oz laughed.

"Aeron, this is my buddy, Sean. We didn't know each other in life, but he—uh, dated your mom."

Sean shrugged with a sign of relief. "Sure, we can skip the details."

"You wanted to marry my mom?" I asked. "That is what dated means, right?"

The two men tensed with discomfort.

The meditating Paul muttered, "Your awkwardness is distracting."

Sean laughed a little. "He's not wrong. We were engaged, but I became impatient. We hunted a Haunting and got in too deep. Or technically, it got too deep into me. I was abducted and infused with a poltergeist. We took care of him though." He grinned at my uncle. "His was the first soul you dispelled."

"Just doing God's work," Oz said, and they passed their arms through each other in a spiritual high five.

His confusing explanation sent my mind drifting to another thought. "You could have been my father?"

Sean froze again, and Uncle Oz coughed.

"Are you sick?" I asked. "Can spirits get sick?"

"No," he said with another little cough. "Habit from life. No, I'm just trying to change the subject. So, um, Sean here has the gift of healing since he had an interest in the medical field and the gift of tangibility due to his connection with a poltergeist."

"Fantastic!" I said. "You would be a neat father."

"Some change of subject," Sean muttered, and nervously glanced at the spirit named Francine. "Oz, you were able to contact Pansy?"

"Yeah," Uncle Oz said. "We lost connection before I could give details, but they know Aeron's location."

"Good. With any luck, they'll grab Aeron and get out of Horror before that witch's army becomes a Mass Haunting."

"We might be too late for that. Ah, here's Dante." Oz gestured to a spirit who entered through the wall. My uncle said to me, "You'll probably read his book when you're older. He also has a greater sense for Hauntings, but as one of Horror's first explorers, he's especially gifted at navigating."

Dante waved over to Oz and the others came to listen. Francine's many animal selves snapped back into a single woman.

"Dante! What did you find? Were you able to follow the immortal Haunting?"

"I was. I followed her to the shadow side of the Valley of Death."

Francine gasped.

"What was she doing there?"

"Recruiting."

Paul laughed. "Like she could ever convince that Hell hole to obey someone."

"She has," Dante said. Everyone went silent. The dead were good at that. Dante continued, "More than forty Hauntings follow her from the city. I was unable to determine how many will join her in the valley. Creatures of darkness and demons alike flock to her. She asks them to serve her and fight by her side. In return, she promises them a world where the sun never shines from her storms, where Hauntings can travel and rule the lands outside of Horror."

"We need more help," Sean said. Somehow he managed to become extra pale—for a ghost.

"What do you think you are?" Oz said flatly. "This is why I asked you three to join me in the first place. But I agree. We need more support. Paul, can you petition God for more help?"

Paul shook his head. "All others are called away for Halloween. God gives us His confidence."

Uncle Oz sighed. "Sure, I'm confident in our capabilities, but our enemies grow stronger. We need time then."

"You do not have it," Dante said. "They plan to collect their horde by the nightfall. She returned to the city to gather more cursed souls. At sunrise, they will relocate the prince and head to the Valley of Death. Now, if you will excuse me, I must find a Virgil willing to listen to my promptings about their 'unknown trio of witches.' If I can convince the Virgils to leave the prince's parents alone, perhaps they can escape Horror before it is lost to that immortal witch's army."

He left the room by floating through a wall, leaving the five of us.

"Sunrise," Uncle Oz grumbled at the peeping sunlight. "That could be any minute now."

"What does relocate mean?" I asked.

They all turned to me as if just remembering that I was there.

Uncle Oz reached for my hand to pull me down to his eye level. "They're taking you somewhere else."

"Will I get a bed there?" I asked. "I do not like sleeping on the floor."

Uncle Oz smiled kindly, though his eyes looked sad. "I don't know, Aeron. I hope so. They'll likely take you somewhere to make it harder for your parents to find you, but they can't take us away from you. I promise I won't leave you."

"I thought your book says you die if you make promises."

Uncle Oz chuckled. "Only during Hauntings. Plus, I'm already dead. Nothing can force me to leave you."

Chapter 17

Never watch a horror movie
Stay away from screens in general
The more innocent something appears,
the more likely it is to become haunted
Treat any reflective surface as a mirror:
windows, water, silverware...etc.

- *Oz's Haunting Survival Book,*
with notes by Pansy Fromm

PANSY

For the first time since Aeron's kidnapping, I slept well. Ironic, considering how Aeron was still in enemy hands, a mob waited outside for our heads, and we were lost somewhere in Inferno's eighth circle. There was only one reason I slept so well against every reason I should have rested fitfully: pure exhaustion.

After Theo and I expressed our concerns, he openly performed spells to turn our little bookstore office into a place of refuge. We practiced linking through Sean's bond as I mentally relayed the Latin words for shield, invisibility, and avoidance to ward off the spreading fire and the Virgils.

Linked with Theo, I felt the darkness that burdened his mind with every spell. Even the most innocent spells encouraged Theo toward malicious intent. To my surprise, Theo said the magic was kinder during our link.

We decided to wait for Haunting powers to weaken at sunrise before searching for Aeron in buildings near the Twilight Tower. We also hoped Dunstan would rejoin us before then. Theo transformed the mailing supplies into a pile of pillows and blankets. With a couple hours before sunrise and the Virgils still circling like vultures, my husband took me in his arms and loved me. Pure exhaustion.

The first morning rays shone through the window blinds to tease my eyes open. Theo was already awake, hunched over our map. At the sound of my rustling, he turned to bless me with one of his perfect smiles.

"Good morning, my flower."

"Morning," I moaned like a zombie. "Dunstan's not back? We'll have to rescue Aeron without him then."

Theo shook his head with a little frown. "His help would be preferred. However, we waited long enough. I think that the Virgils are finally heading home."

"It's about time," I said. I couldn't wait to have Aeron safe and sound, but I'd really hoped Dunstan would come back. "Sunrise. Most Hauntings are crawling back into their holes now. Do you have a plan?"

Theo pointed at a building on the map. "The Twilight Tower is here. You said that Aeron is kept in a business building nearby?" He pointed at a third drawn circle. "I did another searching spell this morning and sensed Aeron between two and three seconds. It intercepts here with the previous two circles." He pointed to a spot where the three circles met. "Aeron must be here. It is near the Twilight Tower, as Oz said. We can sneak in using invisibility spells and your speed. I am positive Aeron spent time here, and we should at least find some clues."

I met his determined stare and nodded. Today was the day we'd find our son and take him home. I was sure of it. Confidence grew from my gut, but dread came with it.

We were going into the ninth circle again. We'd face his kidnappers and Duchess Abadda. We had to rescue him before nightfall, or the power of Halloween would make Hauntings impossibly stronger. Considering the motorcycle gang from last time, the pumpkin-head killer Dunstan mentioned, and the idiotic Halloween party, who knew what other Hauntings we'd run into while in the ninth circle?

"The other part of the plan," Theo said, "is to embrace the image that the Virgils set on us."

"What?"

"They called us witches because we have magics and abilities. What makes us Heroes in Fantasy makes us Hauntings in Horror. If those are the facts, then so be it. Let us go haunt the living daylights out of Aeron's captors. May I see your brother's book?"

"I—what? You want to *become* a Haunting?" I frowned, but pulled *Oz's Haunting Survival Book* from my emergency pack and handed it to him.

My husband leafed through my brother's book, muttering to himself, "This book is everything we know about Hauntings."

"About how to avoid and survive them," I clarified.

"Also," he said, raising his eyes from the pages to look at me, "how to act like one."

"What?" I leaned closer to read over his shoulder, as if I'd missed something through all my years of studying, memorizing, and utilizing my brother's book.

Theo read, "'Number One Rule: Stay away from drugs, sex, and violence.' Why is that?"

"Because," I said, "Hauntings are lured to those who lose control of themselves." Then, it dawned on me. "Oh. So, we'll prey on those with weakest self-control? How will that work if we prey on Hauntings?"

Theo flipped through the book to another section. "We do not need to kill them, just clear a path to Aeron. With magic and our abilities, we can create the situations and illusions of a Haunting. 'Run Away When: lights flicker, there is no cell phone service, it is always raining, or when you see the reflection of anyone or anything that is not supposed to be there.' If you know the Latin, I can translate how to magically create these scenarios."

"What are we reflecting?"

Theo pinched his lips and his eyes glimmered with concern. "I have an idea that I dislike. However, it makes the most sense. We will reflect *you*."

"What?"

"If there is a problem, you are our best escape artist with your speed."

I gestured to my simple sleeping clothes. "I'm not that frightening."

A mischievous smile crept up Theo's lips. "There are easy illusion spells that can change your appearance."

Ten minutes later, Theo and I stepped out of the burnt bookstore, covered with shield and invisibility spells. I didn't notice any Virgils or people who specifically watched the store, but there were some cars on the streets and early business workers who could call us out. Theo and I stepped lightly, holding hands. Theo could still see my aura, but I needed to hold him and look carefully to catch the warping of light around his form.

We moved silently and slowly for the first block. As soon as we turned a corner away from Brian's Bookshop, we ran. The Twilight Tower was two miles away, but only a couple blocks away from the border of the eighth circle. We passed a convenience store when Theo tugged me to a stop.

"That alleyway is pitch black, and there is an aura in there."

"Dunstan?"

"Probably. The person's aura is laying down, alive, not in danger and not a danger to us."

We stepped into the edge of the blackened area when Theo removed our concealing spells. The crispness of the unnatural darkness definitely seemed like Dunstan's ability. Theo whispered into the alley, "Dunstan?"

A waking snort echoed in the alley. Light returned, revealing Theo in his sleeping wear, and me with my Hauntings costume of Theo's illusion spells.

I appeared in an old fashioned black mourning dress. Its ends frayed and shredded with decay. Dark blood stains blotched my bosom and down my side. Dirt and grime created a second layer, like I'd climbed from my own grave. I wore heavy eyeliner and smudged makeup while the extended length of my black hair hung loose. My clothes and hair drifted in a ghostly manner, and black smoke seeped from my skin.

Dunstan shot up with a shout of, "Bullbeggar!"

I tapped into my speed and tapped out again to reappear beside Dunstan. I rasped with my best imitation of a dead soul, "Never split up."

For the first time I'd ever known, Dunstan screamed. The light disappeared from the alley again.

"Whoa, hey," I said in my normal voice. "It's me. They're only illusions."

Dunstan released the light, revealing a two-foot copper sword in his hands. Theo laughed from the mouth of the alley, hugging his stomach with heavy breaths. Dunstan glowered at us.

I smiled back and mimicked a robotic voice, "We thank you for participating in this test regarding the Haunting status of my costume." Theo caught his breath and reached to help his brother stand. I gestured to the strange sword. "What's that?"

Dunstan's expression went bashful. "I, er, commissioned a weapon to alleviate the dangers of my ability. It can store and transfer the heat that I convert from light. I've yet to test its limits, but your little test confirmed its usefulness."

"Fantastic." Theo grinned, surprisingly pleased that his dangerous brother found a way to become even more dangerous.

"Really?" Dunstan asked, also surprised. "You're not mad?"

"Should I be mad?" my husband asked. "Do you plan to use it against us or for us?"

"For," Dunstan answered eagerly.

"Then I see no problem." Theo shrugged. "We lost all of our other equipment. I will accept any advantage and weapons to fight Abadda."

I wasn't sure if I trusted Dunstan with his new weapon, but I trusted Theo. If Theo trusted his brother, I would too. I met my husband's eyes, and he nodded. "His aura is short and light, despite his separation in the night."

I still demanded an "alive and human" test before explaining our plan to haunt the Hauntings.

"Finally" —Dunstan grinned— "a plan I can support."

Theo scoffed. "Of course you do. My biggest worry is the amount of magic I need to use."

Dunstan likewise filled us in for the details on the office building near the Twilight Tower. "I couldn't get inside," he said, "though I think I saw Abadda in one of the windows. It looks like she gathered an army of Hauntings. They seemed restless last night, like they were preparing to go somewhere."

"Theo," I asked, "can you cast Locate to make sure Aeron's still in there?"

He pulled out his hound's foot and whispered the spell. The longer it took, the deeper he frowned. The foot remained still.

"He's not here," I said, my heart plummeting.

Theo pocketed the foot and rested a comforting hand on my shoulder. "Perhaps the Hauntings know where he is. I say we continue with our plan to intimidate them, except alter our goal for information."

"I see that Pansy's dressed for the occasion," Dunstan said. "How else do you plan to scare those who usually do the scaring?"

Theo turned to me. "What kills them?"

I gestured to my emergency pack. "Certain tools and metals in specific parts of their bodies, usually their hearts, brains, or spinal cords. Incorporeal Hauntings are a bit more difficult to destroy and generally require religious prayers, symbols, or personnel."

My brother-in-law tapped his sword against his palm. "So, they'd be afraid of a priest like me?"

"Basically," Theo chuckled.

"Sure," I added, "but it's more about attitude. Hauntings prey on the vulnerable and selfish because the strong willed are those who vanquish them."

Theo nodded again, writing notes on the other side of our map. "The Virgils might frighten a Haunting. I can make an illusion of a couple dozen people."

"What about," Dunstan offered, "illusions of their own kind who have been slaughtered? That could create a mental destabilization."

It was my turn to nod with agreement. "Make them consider their own weaknesses and mortality. It would also suggest that someone was nearby who had the skills and strength to kill their kind. It would be unnerving for the other Hauntings too. I don't imagine even a wraith smiling over a crumpled vampire on the floor with a wooden stake in its heart, neck slit open, and garlic shoved down its throat."

"Thank you for that visual." Theo gagged.

Dunstan grinned. "Theo, that visual you're choking on, do you think you could create it?"

"And solidify it? I think not!"

"Is that a no because you don't want to, or because you can't?"

"Just because I have the capability to do something does not mean I have the desire."

Dunstan leaned over to whisper loudly to me, "I don't think he can do it."

I jumped back with a yelp as a bald corpse in ratted black clothing gaped open before us. Blood spewed from his chest like a mini fountain around a carved stick. More blood drained from its severed head and its emerald eyes gazed sightlessly upward with its gaping mouth stuffed with garlic cloves.

Dunstan narrowed his eyes at the illusion. "Seriously, Theo? You made me the corpse?"

Theo shrugged. "You provoked me."

"It's a decent illusion though," I said. "We could leave a couple similar corpses down certain streets to steer them where we want. It's time to spook the rats out of their nest."

"Down the street and around the corner" —Dunstan traced a path on the map— "is a gym and public pool that looks like it closed down a couple of years ago."

"This," I said, grinning with vengeful ideas, "will be too easy."

Chapter 18

SNEAKING

Never spy through small holes (peep holes,
cracks, small spaces between doors)
Never listen for killers through doors
(especially when it's quiet)
Assume that Hauntings know where you are
at all times and will stab you through doors/walls

- *Oz's Haunting Survival Book,*
with notes by Pansy Fromm

BERWYNA

I sat with the office's security screens as I applied a cooling cream to my burnt left arm. A loud tumbling sound behind the wall indicated the electric heater kicking on. Every time, the noise freaked me out a little, but I appreciated the invention in this cold and dark building that somehow grew colder with every new body that entered. Hauntings were cold and heartless…unlike Douglas.

Footsteps on the stairs announced someone's approach.

I stilled and watched, holding back my sniffles to stay quiet. Oz's book said that calling out after hearing strange noises only alerted the Hauntings of your location. Then, Urien's face appeared from the stairwell. I breathed with relief (though it sounded like a cough) and he grinned when he found me.

"There you are."

"Here I am," I said.

"Why won't you come ask the queen for your healing potion? You need it more than ever with that arm, and there's no reason to watch the camera feeds."

I didn't answer. I sniffled and struggled to wrap a long bandage around my injured arm.

"Here." Urien took my hand to help me with the wrap. "You won't need this if you have your healing potion."

"I can't," I said. I didn't want to see Abadda. I didn't want to ask her for anything, indebting myself even deeper to her.

I stared mindlessly at the collage of our security cameras. The hordes of monsters gathered downstairs. They crowded inside from the daylight and the brewing thunderstorm. Their snarls, growls, and howls echoed up to us and made me nauseated.

My eyes wandered to the feed of the prince's room. It was empty. An hour ago, a skeleton and vampire came by with a nondescript white van to transport the prince someplace else. I wished to go with him, if anything to get away from this place, but also to give the unfortunate child some friendly company.

With Aeron taken away, I remained for Urien. I couldn't abandon Urien. Even if I no longer dreamed about him romantically, he was my friend, and I worried about him.

He finished tying the wrap around my arm, and he gave me an encouraging smile. "It's Halloween. The queen's plans will be fulfilled tonight." He took my hands to pull me up beside him. "We're taking every Haunting we've recruited to join those that the queen gathered in the valley. She and our Hauntings will be unstoppable with the power of Halloween, and we'll be at her side as rulers of her nation. We'll have everything we ever wanted: riches, prestige, and respect."

"And this horrible Adventure will be over?" I asked. "We'll finally get to go home?"

Urien's smile hesitated. "Sure, if that's what you want. And we'll do it all together."

Our monitor screens flickered. I leaned in, concerned.

"What was that?" Urien asked over my shoulder.

"I'm not sure," I said. Some mental warning said it was a problem though. "I've heard about things like this happening in Mystery. What do they call it when someone takes over the viewing screens with their own?"

"Um, hacking, I think." Urien reached up to scratch his head, then decided to rub his chin instead. A more dignified pose. "But why? The prince is no longer here."

They flickered again.

"What's going on?" Urien asked. "I thought technology was more advanced in Contemporary?"

They flickered a third time, but this time they fuzzed with static. Urien smacked the side as if a beating could make it function the way he wanted. Then he jumped back with a yelp. I screamed.

A woman stared back at us. Her black hair waved past her shoulders and she wore a black tattered dress. Her dark eyes burned with hate. She looked familiar, but she disappeared before I could place her tormented face.

The screen returned to the Prince's empty room, but her expression remained in my mind.

"That was freaky," Urien muttered.

"Was that a Haunting?" I gasped.

"Not one I've met. Maybe she came to join our trek."

"Trek?"

He pulled me into his arms as the heater rumbled on. Wait—

"What was that?" I asked.

"It was just the heater turning on," he said, his voice distant as if distracted. He stared at me, his expression unreadable.

"But the heater's already on."

The sound of the heater kickstarting repeated, but the currents remained the same.

"Is it broken?" Urien scowled at the heater.

I shivered and sneezed, despite the warmer air. "Can we go somewhere else?"

"But we're alone here."

"No, we're not." I shuddered from the memory of the woman from the screen.

"Fine," he sighed. "Let's go downstairs for the queen's healing potion."

Normally, I dreaded the idea of surrounding myself with monsters. With the odd circumstances of the last few minutes, however, I was ready to surround myself with lots and lots of people, even if they were terrifying. I hadn't met any of the Hauntings, but from what I saw and heard from upstairs, they didn't seem friendly. They reminded me of the pumpkin-headed man from the night before, and I wasn't eager to become acquainted.

We went down the creaking stairs as white light flashed through the windows and open door. A crash of thunder quickly followed.

Urien and I stayed on the stairs as monsters of every variety crowded into the little office lobby. A drenched mummy slunk across the threshold.

"Disgusting." A vampire beside the mummy grimaced and took a stiff step away. "You are soaking vet."

The mummy moaned back, "I could take these rags off and dehydrate your organs. Then we could have a beauty contest."

The vampire hissed, but cut off as Urien called for their attention.

"Alright," he said. "As soon as the thunderstorm covers the sun, Queen Abadda will lead us to the valley. Until then, please make room for everyone."

He stepped down the stairs and the monsters made way for him. I followed closely behind, surprised by the respect these powerful creatures and beasts gave to Urien. I dared to look some in the eyes and instantly regretted it. Maybe "respect" was too hopeful. More likely, they tolerated him. I kept close to the walls as we headed towards the manager's office. Just outside the door, I tugged Urien to a stop.

"I don't want to see her. I'd rather be sick and injured than face her again."

Urien chuckled. "You'll need to get over your intimidation of royalty when we become kings and queens. Fine, you stay here. I'll talk with the queen."

"Oh." I tried to hide my irritation at his pride. He glowed like a teacher's pet about to get a gold star. My heart clenched at the thought of staying among the crowd of monsters. I forced myself to be brave and said, "Fine."

He offered me a small smile and gave my hand a squeeze before going into the office. With the door shut behind him, I put my back to the wall for a small measure of security. My back hit something and I turned around to find a framed piece of art hanging on the wall. It seemed empty, like a portrait background with no subject.

A witch nearby noticed my focus on the painting and pointed. "What do you suppose that's a picture of?"

A vampire joined our studious staring. "It looks like a portrait vhere ze muse stood up ze painter."

"I could'a sworn it was a portrait earlier," a lich said. "But the person couldn't'a walked off."

"Why not?" I asked. "They do it all the time in Fantasy."

The monsters slowly turned dead stares on me. Me and my big mouth. These weren't the type of people to tease.

"This," a werewolf snarled, "ain't Fantasy."

Another werewolf snickered and added, "This is Horror. When a portrait is missing its person, it ain't out for a tea party."

The manager's office door creaked open, and Urien exited. I almost didn't recognize him. He wore a new black cloak that emanated authority. Underneath, he wore a combat suit of black leather, held together with straps and buckles. Its designs emphasized strong curves, but ended with sharp points. It screamed the allure of mystery and danger.

Seeing my examination, Urien chuckled and showed off with a puff of his muscled chest.

"Do you like it? I'd say Queen Abadda's tastes are quite regal. She has one for you too—"

"Please, no," I said a little too fast. "I mean, um, I'm sure this style looks much better on you than it would on me."

"I don't know." He stepped closer then looked up and down my frame. "Some new leathers could present you better as a princess than that tattered dress."

My cheeks reddened, embarrassed to think of how filthy I must have looked to Douglas. He'd kissed me anyway, so did it matter?

Urien said, "Be careful, Berwyna. Queen Abadda said the boy's parents are here, and they found our hideout."

"Marquis and Marchioness Fromm? They're here?" I whimpered. Everyone in Eimad knew of their powers and the Adventures they accomplished together. Lady Fromm was renowned for her upbringing and survival in Horror. I suddenly felt like a trespasser behind enemy lines.

This was her territory, her homeland. What were we doing here?

Urien's smile didn't waver. "It was perfect timing for us to leave. The gods smile upon us and our Adventure."

I didn't notice Urien step closer until Abadda called his name, and we both looked up.

"Thy presssence is better suited up front," she rasped, "that thou might lead thy followersss."

"Yes, Your Highness." Urien snapped a quick salute. He spared one more smile at me before disappearing through the crowd. Was it my imagination, or had there been a hint of leering in his smile?

A nearby chortle grabbed my attention as a ghoul sneered at me. A spider crawled from her sleeve and she took it by its hairy legs. She chortled again as she pulled its legs off, counting them like flower petals.

"He loves you, he loves you not…He loves you, he loves you not…"

The spider squirmed with each forceful removal of its limbs. The ghoul didn't notice, but kept her shadowed eyes on mine. "He loves you…He loves you not?" she cried with the eighth leg. "I'm so sorry, child! Maybe next time?"

My stomach churned as the legless spider rolled in her palm. I struggled to keep my lunch down.

"Maybe," a giant spider clicked, "if you didn't use insects with even-numbered limbs, you'd have a different result."

The ghoul snapped her fist closed to squish the legless spider. "Hmm, perhaps. Humans have odd-numbered limbs if you include the head." They both looked at me and laughed.

The chill air curled around me and I shivered. The lights cut out. I was the only one to yelp with surprise. Some of the monsters grunted in amusement.

Abadda rasped, "It isss time!"

The room became a cacophonous roar of howls and battle charges.

I wanted to find Urien, but the crowd pressed against me towards the exit. I thought it was still late morning, but the overcast sky brought an early nightfall. Perhaps there was something else that made the world around us darker. It seemed lighter around the house next door, as if the sun peeped out for that spot alone.

Otherwise, the ninth circle of Inferno looked the same as night: dark, overcast, rainy, smelly, and oily. In the distance, that constant munching sound echoed from the unknown.

Monsters at the head of the group shouted, "Haunting Hunters to the north!"

"No, it's the Virgils from the east!"

I craned my neck to see around them, but only caught a glimpse as Abadda's army of Hauntings buzzed with anxiety. The woman from the security screen stood behind a mob of people with various weapons. Did she glance to the side, as if instructing someone out of sight?

"Priests guard the south!" some other Haunting whimpered.

"This way!" Urien shouted from somewhere ahead.

The Hauntings burst into a mad dash. I struggled to follow, hiking up my skirts to not trip, coughing to breathe. The monsters around me snarled with anger and frustration at the change of pace.

Many of them quickly passed me as their powerful legs outmatched mine. I wasn't sure why we ran, so I didn't mind lingering behind. I just didn't want to be last. Our group of monsters shifted by creatures and their speed. Led by Abadda, the ghosts, skeletons, vampires, werewolves, and giant spiders went quickly ahead. Urien led the middle with the demons, ghouls, goblins, liches, witches, and monsters of scales and blobs. At the tail end, I ran with the mummies and zombies. I was actually fast compared to them, and I didn't dare look back for the sight of monsters chasing me.

They moaned behind me, wordless and tuneless. There was something else unrecognizable in the city. I strained my ears to hear it over the rain and mysterious munching.

Shhhh-k…Shhhh-k…

The sound shifted between sliding and dragging, and I couldn't determine what that click noise was at the end.

"What's that sound?" I whispered to no one, but hoped someone nearby would answer. The zombies and mummies around me only moaned louder.

Shhhh-k…

My heart jumped as the sound gained on us. I struggled to quicken my speed to hopefully join the middle group.

Shhhh-k! Shhhh-k!

I glanced to my sides, unsure where the sound came from. It sounded close! In my glancing, I saw why we ran. Mobs of people ran at us from the left side. They brandished weapons and shouted obscenities at us. From the right, a truck flickered into sight between the buildings. A guillotine was set up in the back. Its blade fell.

SHHHH-K!

A zombie's head rolled off the back. I fought the urge to puke and ran harder. Despite the burning in my legs and lungs, I moved faster. My stuffy nose forced me to breathe through my mouth, drying my throat. I coughed with every step, sounding just as ill as the undead around me.

Shhhh-k!

The sound faded and I dared to look back. The guillotine truck was nowhere in sight, but fewer mummies and zombies followed.

SHHHH-K! SHHHH-K! SHHHH-K!

The sound of death was everywhere! There was no escape! How could I not see it? It echoed in my own mind! Where was it? Was the sound *inside* me?

At last, the Hauntings ran into the safety of a building. Urien stood at the door and held it open, ushering everyone inside. Ripped posters on the side of the building advertised shapely bodies with far too little clothing.

A gymnasium?

I stumbled through the doorway and smelled mold and chlorine. The rest of the Hauntings huffed and puffed except those of the first group. They barely looked winded as they argued about who was first through the door. The last zombie waddled through and Urien closed the door behind.

"Curse them, we lost half the group," he muttered. He climbed to the top of the register desk at the front of the foyer. It creaked under his weight. He spread his arms out for an announcement, but the Hauntings didn't notice.

"Can I have your attention?" he shouted. Only a few turned. Abadda floated behind him. She fingered his neck fondly and whispered something in his ear. Her seductions sickened me and increased my disappointment in Urien.

"Beasts of the underworld!" he shouted. Abadda's touch amplified his voice, and his tone became more commanding. "The Haunting hunters will not come for us here. Prepare yourselves. This is our last stop before our march to the valley where we join our forces. Any who stand in our way will be terminated! You needn't be scared of the common people. They will lay at our feet in death or obedience. After tonight, we will rule all of Horror!"

The monsters cheered and yelled with eagerness. Urien accepted a bundle from Abadda and stepped down from the desk. He joined my side and smiled as he took my arm.

"Once we rule Horror," he said, "we'll live like kings. No one will order us around again."

Once we ruled Horror? I panicked. I didn't want to rule Horror, I wanted to leave it!

Urien either didn't notice my inner turmoil or he ignored it as he offered his bundle to me. "Some new clothes for you. Queen Abadda is pleased you didn't fall behind. Go, change, and wash up. It's a big day."

Chapter 19

NEIGHBORS

Don't trust anyone. Neighbors are never looking out
for your best interests.
Be wary of kids, twins, and old people (especially
when they wear a lot of red or makeup)

- *Oz's Haunting Survival Book,*
with notes by Pansy Fromm

BERWYNA

I used a stall to change into the dress Urien gave me—correction, the dress Abadda, the Wicked, gave him to give to me. That way, I felt less guilty about despising it. Similar to Urien's new outfit, it was made of black leather and followed swirling patterns that ended in sharp points. It was thick and strong like armor, but looked like a whore's dress. It pressed up against my bodice and opened up for a fair amount of cleavage. It spared no covering for my shoulders or arms. At least the skirts reached down to my ankles and boots.

I stepped out of the stall with my arms crossing over my bodice to cover my nakedness. I dreaded leaving the bathroom to the peeping eyes of the male monsters and Urien. Half of me was tempted to change back into my filthy set of Horror clothes.

My stall was immediately taken by a lich.

More monsters crowded the wall of sinks and mirrors. Succubuses fluffed their hair from the run, practicing their hypnotic smiles in the mirror, as werewolves stretched and demons sharpened their claws.

I tried to sneak by unnoticed, stepping lightly and pressing my back to the stalls. I still failed.

"Scared?" a lich sneered at me, using a sinister knife to pick at her teeth.

"You're one to talk," a witch crowed. "I saw how your body quivered from that mob in the street."

"Nothing could scare me." The lich puffed her chest out. "I once had an entire town on the run."

"Really?" a vampire scoffed. "It must have been ze town vhere I drained every citizen, save for one old man."

"What happens when you run out of organs to steal?" a skeleton snapped. "They all come to me in the end. Dry sticks and bones are all we are, even you."

"Garrraaghhh!" a zombie moaned.

"Shut up, Walker!"

What was I doing here?

A small moan escaped my lips and a few of the monsters turned back towards me. I didn't meet their hungry eyes. I couldn't. Despite my efforts to calm down, my breathing quickened.

Breathe. In-out, in-out. Too fast.

"I-I can't handle this," I whimpered.

"Let me bite her," the vampire said. "She vouldn't be nearly so scared if only a certain tool could kill her."

"No," a werewolf growled, "your transformation would take too long. Let me bite her!"

"You vouldn't know vhen to stop chewing, you mutt."

"What did you call me?"

"You heard."

"Say it again!"

Skeletons brandished ivory knives. Giant spiders clicked their pincers. Ghosts drifted closer. The thick black blobs oozed around my feet.

With a whoosh, all the cabinet doors swung wildly open. I jumped back, and a couple others yelped. When I moved to close a cabinet door, a large spider crawled out. My turn to yelp. I made it a good one, even as a ghoul snatched up the spider and tossed it into its mouth. The juicy crunch threatened the firmness of my stomach.

"I felt an unknown presence," a ghost said. "It felt human, but it was too fast. Is the queen testing us?"

"I'm not a queen," a voice echoed in the steam. "I'm a marchioness."

By the heavens, was it Marchioness Pansy Fromm? Was she right behind me?

I jumped around, twisted and turned, but saw nobody. Then someone screamed.

"There!" someone else shouted, pointing at the large bathroom mirror.

I turned back around. There was a reflection of a woman I couldn't see. It was the woman from the camera screens, but this time I recognized her as Pansy the Haunting survivor. Her long hair was black as a stormy night. Her mourning dress may have been beautiful for the old fashioned time it was made. It frayed, stiff with dark red stains. She didn't say another word but her eyes screamed of anger and hate for us.

I heard she was Unsettled, but this was beyond anything I imagined! The powers and achievements that I once adored and honored about her now terrified me. This was the mother of the child I kidnapped.

The bathroom lights flickered. On-off-on, off-on, off, on.

Each flicker revealed Lady Fromm glaring at us from a new position. I heard about her ability for speed, but she was in multiple places at once! Her lightning speed zipped her around the bathroom to appear like she was everywhere at once. One thing was clear, there was no running away from her. There was no escape.

She lifted her arms and black smoke streamed from her body. She spoke with a whisper that gradually grew louder until she screamed.

"Et non morieris in peccatis vestris!"

The lights cut out.

One of the ghosts screeched. "She knows the language of the dead?" The lights returned.

"What did she say?" a lich asked.

"She said we will die in our sins!"

The lights flickered off-on-off. A werewolf howled and its pack joined the eerie song. It did not help to settle my nerves. It rang and echoed as if twice as many wolves howled.

"Ire in gehennam!"

"She commands us to Hell!"

Lights on, but the marchioness was nowhere in sight. All the faucets turned on full blast. They poured thick red liquid that bubbled and oozed. I shoved my way behind the limited security of a shower door. A metallic scent filled my nostrils while the plumbing screamed.

"I smell," a vampire hissed, "blood!"

The three vampires' nostrils flared, eyes widened with ravenous hunger. They bore their pointed teeth and hissed. The vampires launched for the nearest blood vessel—me, with no more than a glass shower door to protect me. The rest of the Hauntings launched back, wanting my blood for themselves. The lights cut out, leaving my ears to explain what followed.

Scratching, biting, howls, and hisses. Weapons flashed, teeth snarled, and claws ripped. The light returned to reveal a bloody massacre. Inhuman blood splattered and dripped over the doorway. Half of the Hauntings moaned on the floor, clutching their hands to their hearts. Their life source oozed past their fingers and puddled beneath them.

I simply stood there in my little shower stall, too terrified to move. But I needed movement. My instincts shouted, *Run!*

The dark presence of the marchioness faded, but the destruction continued. The remaining Hauntings continued to fight. Ghouls scampered, werewolves clawed, a lich brandished her tools, mummies absorbed organs, and vampires grabbed for sharp bites.

My feet refused to move while my mind screamed at me. *Run!*

"Hey!" Urien stood outside the doorway with a vicious whip. He'd replaced his simple cattle whip with a scourge. Made of the blackest leather, it was splintered with shards of wood, bone, silver, gold, and other materials known to kill monsters. "What in horror is going on here? Where's Berwyna?"

My legs finally obeyed my need to run. I scrambled out of the shower stall and latched onto Urien like a leech.

Many of the monsters snarled and glared fire at Urien, but somehow he managed to stare right back. "The queen put me in charge so that means you do what I say. If you can't play nice, I'll make you work hard. You want me to use this on you?" he asked, lifting the scourge. "Huh? It has a piece for each of you, so don't think you're above the queen's powers. You want me to treat you like animals or beasts? No? Then obey!" He turned to me and softened his voice. "Berwyna, come with me."

He escorted me back to the main lobby then turned into the office behind the sign-in desk. As we passed the masculine monsters, the reaction for my new dress was as bad as I feared. They whistled, catcalled, and jeered with crude jokes. Urien opened the door for me and glared at the monsters before stepping through. As soon as the door closed behind him, I broke down.

"I can't do this, Urien! I can't! I quit! I'm done! I can't do this anymore!"

"Hey, hey." Urien took me in his arms and held me. I sobbed into his chest as he stroked my hair. "It's okay, the nightmares won't get you, I'm here."

I lifted my head away. "For how long?"

"What?"

"Until Abadda comes back? Then you leave me alone with those monsters!"

His eyebrows furrowed with defense. "What do you mean? That's not how it is. Queen Abadda has a lot of duties for me. I've asked you to help, but you—"

"Don't turn this back on me," I said. "This is all Abadda's fault. We only came to Horror because of her. We never should have left Eimad. Everything had been perfect. We used to be friends, remember? Now, I can't even trust you with my happiest of moments. We shouldn't be this way, we shouldn't be here."

"You can't trust me? What are you talking about?"

"It's too late, Urien. I'm leaving. I'm going home."

"Fine," he said, disappointed. "I'll meet you back at the office hideout. You'll miss the best part because you were too scared."

"No," I snapped. "Since when was the hideout ever considered home? I'm going *home*, to Fantasy." Curses to Abadda and her healing potion. I struggled to breathe between wheezes and sniffles, and my arm was still horribly mangled. I'd sacrifice my health and use of my arm to get away from this place. This whole time, I thought Abadda was more frightening than Pansy Fromm. I was wrong.

Urien rocked back. "You can't leave, we're at the peak of our Adventure! I know things look dark right now, but that's right when we win! Believe me, the queen has—"

I exploded. "You don't get it, Urien! I'm done! I'm done with this horrific 'Adventure!' I'm done with this place! I'm done with us! I'm done with this conversation! I'm leaving!"

At last, he didn't come back with some eager and overly hopeful reply. He blinked, taking a moment to register my words. He could chew on them while I snacked on pastries in Fantasy. I hesitated at the door, hearing chaos beyond. The monsters snarled and roared, probably in another fight as they howled and shouted. I didn't hear Urien growl behind me.

"No, you don't—"

He grabbed my arm and yanked me back. I yelped as he wrapped his other hand around my back and trapped me in his arms. He covered my mouth with his own, kissing me with determination…and anger.

Before I met Douglas, I imagined Urien would be my first tender kiss. I imagined it would be sweet, innocent, and loving. Not this. Nothing like this. Douglas's kisses had been far more sweet, far more loving. They hadn't exactly been innocent, but Urien forgot all sense of propriety. He shoved me against the wall so his hands were free to shuffle up my skirts. Urien took my favorite daydream and turned it into a nightmare.

In my mind, this wasn't Urien. This was Oswald. I was back in that terrible room of blood and torture.

But I was no longer the hypnotized twelve-year-old.

I wedged my hands between us and pried us apart. Then I slapped him with all I had.

"Berw—"

"Don't!" I shouted, balling my hands into fists and scrambling from his embrace. "Don't you dare come near me again!"

He stepped closer. "But I—"

"No, stop!" I kept my eyes on him while I backed away to the side exit. I clutched onto the poem from Douglas and planned to read it as soon as I was away. Maybe if I left now, Abadda wouldn't notice, and the Fromms wouldn't know that I took their child. Either way, any punishment would be better than continuing this Haunting with Urien. Maybe I could put this all behind me and flee with Douglas to Romance.

Forget the fact that it was pitch black outside with a raging storm and the night screeched with scattering Hauntings; the ninth circle of Inferno welcomed me.

Chapter 20

MAGIC

- *Oz's Haunting Survival Book,*
with notes by Pansy Fromm

THEO

Dunstan and I listened to the chaos of the gymnasium from outside and around the corner. As much as I wanted Aeron close by, I was glad he was nowhere near the frightened Hauntings. We snickered over the mayhem that we created as if we were kids pulling a prank. Except our victims were monsters who fought to kill. They deserved to be terrorized… right? They imprisoned my son and plotted with my wicked stepmother. They were already a centimeter away from slaughtering each other. Did they deserve our nudge?

Pansy blurred back to us, then tapped out of her speed. She was truly a phantasm, beautiful and frightening. A dark desire swelled within me, urging me to take my wife, claim her, tame her dangerous nature.

Curses, my magic was twisting my mind.

I forced myself to consider Pansy's short aura. She was not dangerous, and people were only tamed by themselves. As she neared, I released my spells on her. The black smoke faded from her skin, her hair fell with natural gravity, and her haunted dress returned to rumpled sleeping clothes. I likewise felt the malicious pressure leave me. Fortunately for Dunstan, his magic was unnecessary as he just used his ability to scare the Hauntings inside, creating blackouts and heating the pipes to create steam.

"They're tearing each other apart," Pansy said, "but I don't know if they'll talk."

"If they are fighting each other," I said, "then they are fighting Abadda's orders to work together and serve her. We have them questioning their loyalties. If we can catch one alone, it should break."

Pansy scoffed. "I think I saw some near-humans who might talk. Supposing they're not catatonic. Zombies can hardly talk even when they're coherent, then goblins and ghouls are too tricky to tell the truth. We'd need to catch one, so the ghosts and globs aren't options either."

I considered what remained. "I could spell-duel a witch into talking with us." Yes, I wanted to fight one of those wenches and teach them a lesson for their wicked deeds.

"Maybe," she said, "but I worry about you using so much magic. We could also threaten a werewolf, vampire, skeleton, or mummy with their weaknesses. They're either fighting inside or scattering. If we want to catch one, we need to act fast."

Dunstan grunted. "They can't run if they can't see where they're going. I blacked out the whole block."

"Fantastic." I grinned and reached for their auras in the darkness. "I will lead the way and say when I see an aura."

I walked slowly in the darkness, feeling my way around the building by the walls. As we rounded the corner, I spotted several long auras leaving the gymnasium. Some wandered in the darkness with their hands outstretched. A couple, probably werewolves, bent over on all fours and smelled the ground. Separated from the rest, a solitary person with a shorter aura heaved with emotion. Her cries reached our ears.

"Do you hear that?" Pansy asked me.

"Yes. At 10 o'clock."

The woman sobbed without shame. Pansy nodded towards the sounds. "That's a broken woman if I ever heard one."

As much as I wanted to console her, I realized she was exactly the type of person to tell us about Aeron. One of the werewolves turned in her direction and growled. The woman's aura darkened.

"Grab her!" I hissed. "Dunstan, she is on your side."

I led our charge and cast a silencing spell on her screams as Dunstan grabbed her. We ran with her struggling in tow until her aura lightened and the other auras wandered elsewhere. We released her in the dark. With *"Avigo,"* I froze her limbs before unsilencing her voice.

She openly sobbed.

Some dark part of me took pleasure in her anguish. I growled in the darkness, "Where is the Earl of Margen?"

The woman's sobs clarified into words. "I just...want to go...home."

"Berwyna?"

Dunstan released the light to create a single spotlight around the woman. The woman blinked hard in the light with red eyes. Her left arm was wrapped as a mummy, though her open fingers showed burn marks. To my surprise, my brother returned all light and revealed us. The woman squinted at my brother.

"Douglas? Wha—"

"You know each other?" Pansy asked.

Except, she had called him Douglas. I asked, "Is she from the abbey?"

Her mouth dropped as she stared from my brother to me, back to Dunstan, to Pansy, then back to Dunstan.

Her breathing gathered speed as she cried, "You're *Dunstan Fromm*? The *Night Terror*?"

She swayed as if to faint and my brother reached for her.

"I'm sorry, I hid my past identity," he said, "but how do you know that name? I didn't think my old Wanted posters made it to Horror. And what happened to your arm?"

"You said you were from Romance," she whimpered.

Pansy tapped her foot impatiently. "What's going on here? How do you know each other?"

"We—" The woman coughed. "We really don't know anything about each other."

My brother sagged. "I'm sorry I didn't tell you the whole truth, but barring my identity I never lied. I love you. You're the most fascinating and beautiful woman I've ever met."

Those were words I never thought to hear from my brother's mouth. Merlin's beard, he was a priest sworn to Fantasy! No Romances, no Hauntings, no Cases—only Adventures until he finished his training. I cared little for the whole conversation as my fingers twitched for action and my blood boiled for movement. Pansy, likewise, shifted back and forth on her feet, ready for answers.

"You may have been honest in a few things, but I wasn't," she said. "I'm not from Horror, I'm a Fantastic. I helped kidnap Prince Aeron. Dear heavens—your *nephew!*"

She broke into more tears and Dunstan rocked back.

"You—what?"

Pansy went aghast. "You fraternized with the enemy?"

"More like courted," Dunstan mumbled. Fool, that made it worse.

The young woman sobbed harder. "I never should have fixed up that sickly queen! I never should have helped kidnap the earl! I never should have come to Horror!" She sniffled, then dared a blushing glance at Dunstan. "I thought it was true love, but even that was a lie."

How long would they *talk*? We needed answers, solutions, and objectives. This woman confessed to kidnapping my son, to stealing him away to Horror, and tricking Dunstan out of his magic! No more talking. "You bullbegging curses of Merlin!"

"Language, Theo—"

I ignored Pansy as I rushed on the woman named Berwyna. I grabbed her from behind with my wand hand aimed at her throat.

"Where is Aeron?" I hissed. "What did you do to him?"

"Theo!" Pansy and Dunstan shouted.

"She's already terrified!" Dunstan added.

True, Berwyna cried as a babe, though her cries only fed my fury.

I growled, "Tell us!"

"I don't remember!" she wailed. "They said something about a valley. They took him away this morning. The poor child, he didn't do anything wrong!"

"The Valley of Death? Did they talk of shadows?" Pansy asked. She reached towards me as if approaching a wild animal. "Theo, back off."

"I don't know!" Berwyna cried. "I guess that sounds familiar?"

My arm tensed and a growl grew in my throat. Pansy appeared beside me. She grabbed my fingers and bent them backward, forcing my hand away. She then shoved the woman's shoulder to break her free. As soon as she was away, Dunstan shouted for the god of protection, placing the woman behind a thin shield. Curses, his magic truly was blunted. My own, however, felt strong, surging with power, and on the brink of explosion.

"Theo!" Pansy grabbed my arms. "Look at me."

Her eyes met mine and she palmed my heart. I stumbled as if she had pushed me. A light broke through my vision and the screaming power within me snuffed out. I slid my hand over her heart in return. Our bond. My fury faded and my unconscious sneer relaxed into a sorry terror of my own self.

"Curses—I…" Utter shame welled within me. What had I done? The mere memory of my malicious thoughts terrified me.

Pansy bit her bottom lip and worried her eyes. I felt her concern for me through our bond, and I realized that she had likewise felt my shame. "We got the information we wanted," she said. "Our plan to scare them worked. Now, we need a new plan of extraction. You understand? We are not Hauntings," she ended with emphasis.

I let out a slow and uneasy breath, shivering, as if releasing my tension.

"I am sorry," I whispered. "Please, forgive me. I was just… angry…and scared."

She held me close. "I know. I am too. We don't need to be possessed or hypnotized to lose control of ourselves. Good people can do bad things." She turned to gesture to Dunstan and the woman behind the chipping shield. "Especially when labeled as bad people. I never thought I'd be the one to tell *you* to calm down."

I felt her sincerity more than heard it as she slipped her hand into mine. "I—forgive me. I know not what came over me."

"Magic of Horror," she said. "I didn't know exactly what would happen if we overused magic, but that was worse than what I expected. I know you, Theo. That wasn't you. That wasn't even an angry you."

"Thank heavens," Dunstan chuckled. "You weren't that angry even when I tried to kill you for the duchy."

I gave my brother a pointed look, then asked Pansy, "You know where they took our son?"

"The Valley of the Shadows of Death."

"Then we will follow," I said. Turning back to the woman in the crumbling shield, I asked, "Do you know Duchess Abadda's plans?"

She coughed and nodded. "Abadda's whole purpose of coming to Horror was to gather an unstoppable army. She tried to make your son work for her. He didn't use his ability like she wanted, so she sent him ahead to the valley. She had half of her army here and planned to join forces with the other half of monsters she gathered in the valley. I don't know what she plans to do with Prince Aeron, but their conquest begins with Halloween night."

Pansy's eyes grew wide. "She's right. They'll be unstoppable during Halloween. We have to rescue Aeron before the sun sets."

"What about her?" I asked, gesturing to Berwyna.

"She should leave," Dunstan said. We all turned to him, though he refused to look our way, especially the woman's. "Leave us, leave this place, and run as far away as she can."

She choked on a sob and her shield broke completely. That got his attention. He looked directly at her. Maybe it was the lighting, though my brother's eyes appeared to glisten with moisture.

"Because no matter how far..." he whispered.

I waited for him to say more. Instead, Berwyna gasped and clutched her hand to her heart. She nodded with heavy breaths, then turned and ran.

She was lost in the chaos of the city before Pansy broke the silence.

"Can we go now? The Hauntings have a head start, and we'll need to go back to the eighth circle to find a cab. The Valley of Death's about an hour away. We can talk on the way" —she glared at Dunstan— "but what the horror was that? Hauntings are for killing, not dating! You could have sabotaged everything! Our element of surprise, our plans, and our hopes to ever find Aeron!"

"Not to mention your priest magic," I said. "I made stronger shields than that as a novice. Not that I advise using magic after what just happened."

"I'm sorry," Dunstan whispered. "I didn't think she was capable of such wickedness. I thought the only risk was to my sad attempt at magic. I was ready to sacrifice it for her."

"At least we have our abilities," I said. "Aeron still needs us, and we need our wits about us in the Valley of the Shadows of Death."

Chapter 21

EXPLETIVES

Don't swear to anything if it's not true
Choose your expletives wisely. God commands not to
use His name in vain in the same list as His
commandment not to kill anyone.
Cursing by a Haunting is the beginner's version
of demon summoning.

- *Oz's Haunting Survival Book,*
with notes by Pansy Fromm

AERON

I slept in the back of a van and watched the scenery wave by as a spirit. Never before had I seen a red river, or lake of fire, or smoking ground. Horror was a strange place. Uncle Oz floated beside me. It was an awfully long journey because we went awfully slow. I probably could have run faster. I asked them before falling asleep why we went so slow and the vampire sneered at me.

"So zat ve don't make noise, so shut up."

I asked more questions until they ignored me. Then I cried. Finally, I slept.

The skeleton glanced back at my body then mumbled in its toneless rasp, "I know the queen said not to let him sleep, but I can't stand his whining. We'll wake him when we're almost to the valley."

"Not yet," the vampire replied. "My bats are near vith ze report. If he hears about his parents' death, his crying vill be insufferable."

A swarm of bats flew past, whispering screeches in the vampire's ear.

The vampire glowered.

"What did they say?" the skeleton asked.

"Ze rest of ze Inferno group has been crippled."

"What! How?"

"Zey caught a traitor. I figured zat little Fantasy wench was no good. She confessed zat ze child's parents were behind ze attack. Zey make fearsome Hauntings vith zeir Fantasy powers."

"Pansy," Uncle Oz groaned, though they didn't hear him. "What are you doing?"

The skeleton cursed and grumbled. "All the more important then that we get this brat to his final resting place."

"Is something wrong with Mom?" I asked.

"I thought she knew better than to use magic in Horror. She's acting like a Haunting…against Hauntings. Hauntings aren't meant to succeed, so who can win this battle?"

"The Heroes will win," I said. "And we are the Heroes."

"Are we sure about that?" Uncle Oz asked, troubled.

"Of course," I said. "They kidnapped me. I am the victim, Mister and Missus are villains, and Mom and Father are Heroes."

"I doubt that's the way the Mister and Missus see things."

"Why not?" I asked.

"It's hard to explain," Oz muttered, "but Paul's been watching them. They didn't kidnap you out of anger or hate. They're just confused. Most 'villains' are. With Pansy scaring them, they'll consider themselves the victims and your parents the villains."

"But that is wrong."

Uncle Oz smiled, but he seemed sad. "Someday you'll understand the world's not so simple."

I frowned, unhappy with that answer. Thinking about that unknown, distant someday, I asked, "Uncle Oz, when I die, will I be like this forever?"

"I don't know," he said. "I've never met a Fantastic spirit, especially one with abilities."

The van slowed to a stop. Our destination was a large circle of rocks in the middle of nowhere. Sheer canyon walls cut off the horizon in every direction. There wasn't a stream or lake anywhere. The ground was dusty yellow with sparse bushes and thin trees. It looked dead. I missed the giant trees in Fairy, the green grass, and colorful plants, even the funny looking mushrooms that Mom would not let me touch.

"Where are we?" I asked.

Uncle Oz grumbled, "This is The Valley of the Shadows of Death. They brought you to the Altar of Moloch, ruins of an ancient temple known for sacrificing children. It's evil. You need to be careful here. Paul said I only have permission to dispel Abadda, no one else, but she can't interact with us unless we engage her first. Don't step into the shadow. I can't stop it from consuming you."

I asked, "What shadow?" but my uncle's attention was on the skeleton and vampire.

They stepped out of their front seats and rounded the back to me.

"Wake up!" the skeleton shouted.

My consciousness drifted. An invisible force pulled me towards my body. The vampire grabbed one of the back doors and shook the whole vehicle with it.

I opened my eyes to find myself back inside the van, trapped in the limits of my body.

"Get out," the skeleton commanded.

I huddled more into the corner of my cage. I had a dim memory of driving here from my "dream," but I could not remember the details. Uncle Oz said something…about shadows?

The skeleton sneered and grabbed me faster than I could move away. He snatched my arm and yanked me from the van. "Get out!"

I stumbled to the ground and skinned my knee against the hard ground of red rocks. It tore at my skin, but did not bleed. I started to cry, and the vampire hissed at me.

We stood outside a strange ring of boulders. I tried to go limp, but the skeleton dragged me inside the ring of boulders. Inside was another ring with larger rocks that stacked closer together. In the center of the rings was a large statue of a bull and a pile of stones with a flat slab on top, like a table.

"Ah, here zey come," the vampire grinned with pointed teeth.

Dead trees creaked and swayed like they were in a storm. The sky was dark with heavy clouds, muffling any light. Still, a darker shadow crept from the valley cliff towards the circle of boulders. Rats and large bugs fled before the moving shadow. Compared to the creaks of the trees, the silence of the shadow scared me. The darkness swallowed everything it passed. Jagged rocks, scraggly bushes, all absorbed in the blackness that swallowed all light.

Wicked Buttchess Abadda flew over our heads to the center of the stones. She spread her arms wide, then slowly brought them in.

"Come, my sssycophants," she hissed. "It isss time."

A sound grew from the distance. A quiet wave of high pitches. Were they screams? They cried over each other, hundreds, maybe thousands of voices screaming and growing louder, growing closer from the other side of the stone ring. The wind surged around the circle of stones, vibrating in a swirling howl. I screamed. The other screams became louder and separated, but all the more chaotic.

The ground trembled, rumbling dust and pebbles. A line of monsters marched from the direction we came.

Mister led an army of monsters, so many I could not count them all. I knew many types of cursed people in Fantasy, but never did they look as angry as these. They stopped outside of the ring of stones.

Above me, Abadda gathered her winds and terrors. Behind me, the screeching sounds overwhelmed my ears. A black cloud of birds flew overhead. More monsters joined from that side. Abadda had her army of death, and I stood in the middle of it.

A woman with black hair and a determined face flickered into sight, running through the Hauntings.

"Mom?" I cried. "Mom!" I wanted to run to her, but the skeleton yanked me away, farther into the circle. Mom's path to me was cut off as some Hauntings blurred around her.

Father and a bald man were close behind Mom, but stayed on the other side of the Hauntings. How could they save me?

"You won't come any closer," Mister said, stepping forward from the line of monsters, "if you value this woman's life."

He held Missus wrapped in a spiky whip that pricked her every time she moved.

"Berwyna!" The bald man stepped closer. Was that my Uncle Dunstan? I sort of recognized him from paintings. How did he know Missus?

The Hauntings slowly moved around my father and uncle or grouped around my mom.

"Then you do know each other," Mister mumbled.

"Did I not warn thee, Urien?" the raspy voice of Abadda echoed through the air. "Ssshe betrayed thee! She tried to abandon thee, excccept the foolish girl ran into my lichesss."

"No!" Missus struggled.

Abadda continued, "Ssshe revealed our hideout to the brat'sss uncle and told him all! She plotted against usss from the beginning."

"No! That's not how it happened!" Missus cried. "I didn't know he was Earl Fromm's uncle!"

"She didn't know!" Uncle Dunstan argued for her. "I lied about my identity!"

Missus whimpered as Mister pulled her closer with his whip. "But you met him? Every night?" Mister snarled.

"I-I did," Missus admitted and sniffled. "I don't want anything to do with this Haunting. Kidnapping Prince Aeron was wrong. I can't stand the way Abadda controls you, Urien. I left because—"

"Save your breath," Urien spat. "You don't have much of it left."

She cried. I watched, unable to move or understand. Father looked for Mom, and Uncle Dunstan drew a strange sword. To the side, a woman screamed. Father spun around.

"Pansy!"

Mom was somehow bound to a rock with a rope as Hauntings blurred around her.

She screamed, "Protect Aeron!"

Abadda hovered above her hideous army.

"Kill them!" she snapped, and all horror broke loose.

PANSY

There wasn't time to warn them further. I tapped back into my speed and struggled against my rope bindings.

Condemned speed demons.

We'd taken a taxi to the mouth of the Valley of Death, but the driver refused to go farther. Theo did a quick Locate spell to confirm that Aeron was nearby. It pointed us toward the Altar of Moloch…toward a crowd of Hauntings only three hundred feet away. Condemnation, they were going to sacrifice my son.

Theo worried at the sight. "Pansy, go. We can try to fight them, though only you are fast enough to grab Aeron and get him out."

I panicked. "You expect me to leave you?"

"I expect you to save our son, now go! We will wait to confirm your safe transportation, then follow."

Dunstan cringed with a confession, but I didn't wait to hear. Abadda's army saw us and were on their way. I tapped into my speed and ran straight for the thick of them.

I didn't expect the speed demons. There hadn't been any in the Inferno group. They were the only creatures faster than my five times speed ability. The only other creature I'd fought that was faster was a goblin with the stolen feet of Tom, the Swift. I'd killed it in a damp dark dungeon, of all places, and wearing my wedding dress, of all things.

This time, however, there were three speed demons. They didn't steal their speed or gain it halfway through their lives. They were born with it, and they were naturals.

I barely managed to stab one in the face as the other two tied my hands. They pulled me to one of the outer stones and spun around until I couldn't move. I growled in frustration and struggled against my bonds. One demon gleefully considered how to slowly slice me into pieces.

He reached for me, but stumbled. "What?" He grabbed for me again, but was pushed back by some invisible force.

"Something's guarding her!" it sneered.

Did Theo cast a shield over me? No, I could barely see him between the masses of Hauntings between us.

The two demons argued about what to do as one kept striking the air around me.

A flicker of light caught my eye. The faint image of a person, translucent and powerful, stood between the demon and me.

I whispered a confused prayer of thanks to the Supernaturals.

"*You're welcome,*" a voice whispered in my mind. Oz's voice.

I gasped.

My brother was here! He protected me!

"*He's not the only one,*" another voice whispered.

Who was that?

I remembered stories of angelic armies, and I prayed that my eyes would open to them, if only for a moment.

I blinked. Movement to my right startled me. A translucent bear floated between me and the demons. I was about to ask her to protect Aeron instead, but when I turned toward my son in the middle of the stone circles, my heart stopped. Oz guarded Aeron's side. I almost cried for the love I felt for both of them.

A translucent eagle soared above Theo, Dunstan, and— Sean! Sean's spirit slapped back the group of Hauntings that rushed on my husband. The Hauntings yelped with surprise, like they couldn't see the spirit who struck them.

Abadda's eyes glared fire at the Supernaturals. They were her equals in power, though on the opposite spectrum.

I blinked and they disappeared. It was enough.

We weren't fighting alone. The Supernaturals allowed certain Hauntings to come after us because they knew we could defeat them. We were meant to win this.

With that encouragement, I finagled my knife to saw at my ropes. The vampires and skeletons circled around me. Behind them was the largest pack of werewolves I'd ever seen. Their hot eyes zeroed on me. The two speed demons turned their attention to Aeron.

They were first on my list.

Chapter 22

EATING

Cook with garlic
Be suspicious of red sauces
Eat with genuine silverware
Spike drinks with holy water

- *Oz's Haunting Survival Book,*
with notes by Pansy Fromm

THEO

After casting a shield spell on myself, I looked for Pansy. I caught glimpses of her between the monoliths and groups of monsters. Zombies and mummies separated me from my wife and child. The Valley of Death became an arena as monsters charged for us, ahead and behind. The place would soon earn its name. There was already a dead imp-like demon from Pansy's fight. One moment she was tied to one of the stones of the outer circle. The next, she was gone. Before I could worry about her, a wretched and garbled scream erupted and another demon became a corpse.

I spotted Dunstan's aura in a blob of darkness a few paces to my left. His shadows moved quickly around him, disguising his true position. Only with my auras ability did I see him standing in the center, analyzing the young man in black leathers and the woman named Berwyna.

Abadda's henchman shoved Berwyna behind him to a group of liches. She screamed as the liches pulled her back with hateful snickers. Then the man in leather stepped forward to meet Dunstan's challenge. He commanded the other Hauntings to "Leave this one to me," then loosened his shredded whip with crackling snaps.

The zombies and mummies slowly turned towards me. They moved with a lot of strain, as if pushing against some invisible force. They still advanced if just for one agonized step every second. Three witches and a black flock of birds circled overhead and devoured any hopes for retreat.

My shield sizzled from damage near my stomach. I had to put my back to the zombies and mummies to watch the three witches sneering at me.

"I advise you to keep your eyes on us, little copycat," one cackled.

"I am no copycat," I muttered and swirled my wand arm above my head. I snapped it at the witches, shouting, "*Aura imbeduz!*"

The two on my sides cackled with laughter even as I struck the one in front with a wind lashing.

"*Utthozh vzhush!*" they all shouted, waving their hands in the same fashion over their heads then snapping towards me.

Their words were unfamiliar, though the effect was similar as air sliced at me. Similar, yet stronger. I rushed forward, barely dodging the currents that whipped past my shoulders.

"Who copies whom?" I jeered.

"Mom!" Aeron cried from within the ring of boulders. Running to him meant running straight into the wall of zombies and mummies. Then, beyond them, Pansy fought the fastest Hauntings. I prayed for Aeron's safety, except Abadda was somewhere within the circle. There was nowhere to run, nowhere to hide. A battleground was no place for a child.

I ground my teeth in frustration as a spell zipped passed my arm again.

A witch jeered, "We told you to keep your eyes on us."

"Really now," another cackled, "you wouldn't want to make us jealous, pretty boy."

The witch who spoke winked at me with a knowing smile. She was beautiful, especially compared to the other haggard and mole-poxed witches. The magic inside of me…desired. Disgusting. My jaw began to hurt from my clenching. Magic was my only weapon to fight back. I had to use it to survive, though what would I become by using Horror's dark version of magic?

I forced myself to concentrate. The witch's smile was pointed, and her eyes spoke of hate. There was also her aura. It was almost as long as my wicked stepmother's.

I retracted my earlier thought on her beauty. Her evil intentions made her just as hideous as the other two.

"Theo! A little help?"

Beyond the witches, Dunstan struggled to avoid the man's scourge and its jagged cords that whipped like snakes. The birds could sense him and snatched at him from overhead, revealing his position to Abadda's henchman. Dunstan's aura frantically waved them away and quickly moved before the man's scourge caught him.

"Don't look away, pretty boy! *Utthozh oren!*"

I barely cast a shield in time to block the fire spell from the witches. Behind me, zombies and mummies stepped closer. Overhead, birds blackened the already darkened sky. They would overwhelm us within the minute.

Holding back every monster was impossible.

BERWYNA

The liches pulled me back from Urien, towards the stone circle. They grabbed me with callous hands, squeezing the burn wounds from my left arm. They forced me to watch helplessly as Douglas—no, *Dunstan*—and Urien fought. It tore my heart apart. Urien, my childhood friend and crush, had turned evil by Abadda, the Wicked. Douglas, my gentleman protector and recently found love, was Dunstan, the Night Terror.

These two men I loved were no longer the men I loved.

It begged the question—did I truly love them, or only the idea of the men they pretended to be? Douglas was not some humbled gentleman from Regency, Romance. He was a man I knew of from rumors. He was the third son of the Duke of Margen with the ability to create darkness. The Night Terror had been a terrorist in Fantasy until he fought Marquis Fromm for the title of future duke. Then, the craziest rumors said he became a priest.

It didn't match the man I came to know at the convenience store. Who was he really?

He hid somewhere within a changing shadow as it shifted left then right, expanding and shrinking so his exact location was only determined by the crows that attacked from above. Urien lashed his scourge at the darkness, its multiple tails flying with minds of their own.

Dunstan's voice cried out from his darkness. Then, his blackened spots expanded to envelop everyone outside of the stone circle. The liches yelped and grabbed me tighter.

I struggled against their hands, confused, frustrated, and scared.

PANSY

Even tapped into my speed, I barely kept up with the speed demons. Only one remained as the second had its stomach sliced open and lay lifeless where it tried to dissect me. One wouldn't be a problem, but it wasn't alone. Abadda knew about my speed ability and sent her fastest Hauntings after me while she called other Hauntings around her and Aeron.

I wanted to run to my son and snatch him away, but even if I managed to go around the pack of werewolves, I couldn't burn the teleportation spells without them attacking us. The second fastest Hauntings surrounded me. The skeletons and vampires weren't up to my speed, but there were so many of them! There were easily as many Hauntings before me as the entire Inferno group. Plus, we were unsheltered in the Valley of Death. This wasn't the streets or hallways we cornered them into. This was their domain.

A skeleton rushed in at the same time as a vampire. They came at me from opposite sides. I waited for the last millisecond as the skeleton reached for me with its boney fingers and the vampire gnashed its nasty teeth. I rolled my back to narrowly scrape by the skeleton's reach, then grabbed its humerus to direct its charge right into the vampire. It tumbled around, spine wrapping around the vampire's neck until the bones severed from each other. Still gripping the upper arm bone, I smashed it into the vampire's skull with a sickening crack.

Remembering an old anatomy joke, I smirked. "I don't know about you, but I found that humerus."

I traded out the funny bone for one of the skeleton's femurs. An odd thought recognized my dance lessons coming into play as I fought the Hauntings. I did free spins to smash my improvised bone club into those sneaking behind me, chassés to dodge, and even ganchos to hook their legs and pull them off balance. Surprise. Being a noble helped me be a better survivor.

After smashing the next dozen skeletons and a couple more vampires, my arms ached with strain. I stopped to breathe and a new vampire latched onto me. Its nails dug into my skin and its hungry eyes leered at my neck. Saliva dripped from its pointed teeth.

I dropped my bone club to switch out my wooden stake. By the time I had it firmly gripped in my hand, its teeth were far too close for comfort. Then again, a hundred feet away would have been too close for comfort.

I slashed my wooden stake across its face then jabbed into its chest.

"Supernaturals," I called in half curse, half prayer, "could you hold them back long enough to let me breathe?"

I held still for too long. A new skeleton scratched at my side with another vampire right behind it. Something sharp bit into my ankles. A skeleton had burrowed through the ground to pop up beneath me.

Sorry, a woman's voice answered in the wind, *it takes all I have to hold them back. Or would you like to fight them all at once?*

Gritting my teeth, I yanked one foot free, simultaneously throwing my knee into the skeleton in front of me. It buckled into itself, and I punched my elbow into its left scapula. It went down, jumbling into the one below. I tried to kick my other foot free, but their bones locked into position.

Clawed hands grabbed my arm as the vampire reached me. No time to stop. I ducked down and jabbed my wooden stake upward to its heart. Blood showered over me until I shoved the carcass off of me.

"Three at once is plenty enough," I growled.

I picked up another separated femur from nearby and smashed it at the skeleton hand that still grasped my left ankle. I smacked my own talus a little as I broke the fingers that tethered me. Mobile again, I chucked the bone to pull out my silver stake and stare down the werewolves that separated me from Aeron. Abadda struggled against some unseen foe, but spared a moment to smirk at me from over the werewolves.

"What is the phrassse they use? Oh yes; sssic 'em."

The hairy group of people began to change. Extra hairs sprouted long and thick from their arms and neck. They hunched over as fifth limbs erupted as tails. Nails thickened and spiked into claws. Eyes turned yellow and noses lengthened into carnivorous snouts. Their clothes shredded off their backs and massive legs. With the final transformation they arched their necks to the sky and screamed. I clapped my hands over my ears as their screams morphed into howls. They landed on all fours and panted.

Wolves were already some of the largest dogs, but these were gigantic like bears! Two dozen pairs of yellow, orange, and blood red eyes focused on mine.

Condemnation! These were the same type of werewolf that killed Oz. They didn't need the full moon to change, and they retained their human intellect. They were the oldest and largest form of werewolves, who hunted for sport instead of a mad need for meat.

"*Pansy!*" Oz cried, his voice filled with pure terror for my soul.

The werewolves charged.

Chapter 23

TESTING OTHERS

- *Oz's Haunting Survival Book,*
with notes by Pansy Fromm

AERON

I did not understand what was happening. My father and Uncle Dunstan fought somewhere in the blackness outside of the circle of rocks. Mom was a blur as she fought all sorts of monsters between the two rings.

"Mom!" I cried.

"Sssilence him," Abadda hissed as she flew above the scary bull statue in the middle of the circles. She jabbed her hands outward, blocked, and dodged as if she was fighting someone invisible. Looking hard, I thought I saw Oz's light flash around Abadda.

Two of the witches flew on broomsticks above the darkness. They circled a small spot and cackled with laughter.

One of them sent a spell at me. I cried out as it struck me, but my voice cut off! I tried to shout, yell, or scream. My voice was gone!

I could not call for help. Mom and Father could not hear me!

Abadda called again to her monsters, "Tie him to the altar!"

Mom's blur came closer, but was blocked by the gross little demon who was somehow faster. I thought Mom was the fastest in the world? She also fought huge, hairy animals.

I tried again to call for my mom, but my voice made no noise.

A rumbling under my feet drew my focus to the ground. The rocks cracked and bulged beneath me, and I stumbled away. A scaled, worm-like monster broke free of the ground and snarled at me. I stepped back as it snapped at my face then burrowed into the ground again. The rocks shook beneath me, returning for another attack. I turned and ran. I went to the right, but it raced ahead to steer me left. I turned left, but a second worm monster blocked my way. They boxed me in until I was at the stone table in front of the bull statue. I climbed on top, hoping to go above their reach.

The scaled monsters circled around my little table and did not come any closer. I thought I was safe until the black birds swooped down to nip at me. I ducked and put my arms over my head for safety. They bit at my arms, drawing blood, and pulled on my hair. I crouched down into a ball and covered my face. That seemed to stop them.

I peeked when they did not attack again. They remained close, perched on the tall stones of the inner circle. I barely had time to look up as a witch flew over me. She dropped something on me, heavy and long.

Rope?

It moved.

Snakes!

I squirmed as they tied around my ankles and arms. Others lay on top of my body, pinning me to the stone. A long skinny one curled around my neck, again and again. I tried to reach up and pull at it, but my arms were too heavy with the snakes wrapped around.

I froze as Abadda hovered over me. She grabbed one of the snakes, then, using one of her long nails, sliced it open. Like an artist with her pallet, she painted the snake's blood on the altar around me. She drew circles and triangles, whispering funny words. Finishing, she floated away from my sight, still whispering. Before I could wonder what happened, the bull statue breathed out a thick shadow that rolled toward me.

THEO

The witches with long auras gave me no time to rest. I barely blocked their spells with my cast shield or counter spells. The auras of zombies and mummies were mere meters away, still blocking my view of Aeron and Pansy. I concentrated on my link with Pansy and caught quick impressions of her frantic fighting. At least she was alive. As long as she lived, she fought to reach Aeron. Dunstan still struggled against the unkindness of ravens and murder of crows, swiping at them with his shortsword while trying to avoid the lashes from the young man who served Abadda. Dunstan's attention kept glancing at Berwyna, who struggled against a group of liches, keeping her just outside of Dunstan's blackout.

I could not help them all, though maybe I could help Dunstan enough for him to finish the rest.

I thrust my wand arm towards the birds.

"*Aura imbeduz!*"

My body heaved as my strength surged outward. A tidal wave of air smacked into the oncoming flocks. They tumbled in their flight and squawked as I pushed them back. They collided with slaps and crunches. I doubted the first couple rows would ever fly again. The simple creatures in the back decided the fight was not worth the hassle and turned back.

A small smile escaped my lips before the witch's spells hit. They attacked all at once. Their strange language of spells cracked at my body shield with sharp slashes of fire.

I collapsed as pain stabbed into me from all sides.

"Theo! No!"

Dunstan? He swiped at a few more ravens as his aura stumbled in my direction. I smiled between the pain. He was a good man.

In Dunstan's darkness, the witches wandered towards my general direction. They were unable to see me, though I saw their auras.

Perfect.

I pointed my wand at one, then the other. "*Ajua! Ajua!*"

I struck them with jets of pure water. They screamed as their auras sank to the ground, melting in the darkness.

"Theo?" Dunstan shouted in confusion. He returned the light directly around me. The witches boiled into the ground with their final squeals. Their clothes remained in a murky pile of slop. I enjoyed the sound of their deaths far too much for my liking. Just a few more spells, and perhaps we could grab Aeron and escape this place of distorted magic.

The zombies and mummies moaned close enough to enter Dunstan's spotlight. I groaned back. I needed more than just a *few* more spells.

"Pansy's survival book warns about celebrating too early. Back to work, Dunstan."

PANSY

Memories of facing, fighting, and killing the werewolf who killed Oz raced through my mind. It was of the oldest, strongest, and purest packs of werewolves. They could control common wolves, and they healed from everything except silver to the heart. Even with my speed, taking care of one of them was tricky enough. A whole dozen pack was another story. They charged for me. With my ability, they appeared to run at a fifth of their normal speed, but they were still fast.

I recalled everything I knew about werewolves. Once human, they'd been bitten, but not killed at some point. They had supernatural strength, speed, and sense of smell. This particular breed could transform at will. I knew of a pack in Fantasy who gathered every full moon for hunting, but in Horror, werewolves were generally lone wolves. I wondered if I could make them fight each other in their efforts to get me?

The pack of werewolves and that condemned final speed demon blocked me from Aeron. Terror gripped me as I caught a glimpse of my son tied to the altar and Abadda flying above him with her stolen wind ability.

Where was Oz? Wasn't he protecting Aeron?

A small light flickered around the speed demon, fighting it, distracting it.

This was my chance!

I pulled out my silver stake and vulgur knife, then dashed for the werewolves that blocked me from Aeron. My vulgur knife wasn't silver, but it was a magically charged blade.

They saw me coming and bared their teeth and claws. I dashed between two werewolves, slicing them in their sides as I squeezed through their grasps. The one sliced with my knife snarled while the other howled at the sting of silver.

The speed demon broke away from Oz to rush at me. It reached to shove me to the ground, but I reached back. I grabbed its arm, using its motion to pull it to the rock floor with me. I pulled hard and didn't let go as its face skidded across the hard surface. My knife was buried into its back before it could stand.

"Not fast enough," I snarled.

The last speed demon was down, but I was surrounded by the werewolf pack.

Condemnation, Aeron needed me, but these Hauntings wouldn't leave me alone.

A frustrated growl rolled through the air as Oz's voice returned to fighting Abadda. She grinned wickedly as something dark oozed toward Aeron.

I stowed my knife to pull out my pistol. I hadn't expected to face so many werewolves and only carried six silver bullets. Without a bullet to waste, I prayed to the Supernaturals that my aim would be true. My speed ability didn't influence the bullets, only my speed to aim and shoot. I needed to be close to be sure they couldn't dodge before I shot their hearts. I loaded all six silver bullets into the chambers as the werewolves circled me and closed off any exits. They crouched to guard their cores and prepare to charge. It didn't look good.

My hands tightened around my pistol and silver stake. I stood and dared them to come closer.

Chapter 24

COMBAT 7 DEADLY SINS WITH 7 VIRTUES

Those susceptible to the seven deadly sins will die
The virtuous will live or die as heroes

-   *Oz's Haunting Survival Book,*
    with notes by Pansy Fromm

THEO

I sent another spell of whipping wind at the nearest zombie, decapitating it. My aura lightened slightly, though only for a second before the next zombie reached for my brains.

The inner circle of Pansy's casualties was a graveyard of bones drenched in vampire blood. Growls of a dogfight erupted from her section as she continued to fight the fastest of the beasts.

With the birds no longer revealing his position, Dunstan easily avoided the younger man's whip, though the liches entered Dunstan's darkness to distract him. Dunstan sliced at them with his heated blade, though they were as undead as the zombies and continued to guard Abadda's henchman and Berwyna. Even with his new copper sword, Dunstan was out of practice with his heat conversion and ran a little slower with each strike.

I would have gone to help if the mummies and zombies stopped breathing down my neck. Whatever angels helped me before were apparently preoccupied elsewhere. The auras of mummies and zombies blurred around each other as their endless horde stepped closer.

BERWYNA

Another lich left me to aid Urien inside Dunstan's darkness. A scream returned to us only seconds later. The remaining five liches held me outside the wall of shadow with their backs to one of the monoliths. We all shied back further as a hand emerged from the darkness. The lich crawled out, a burning hole in its gut.

The burnt lich grasped at his stomach, moaning and coughing more than I did. Foam gathered in his mouth until he choked on it. I couldn't look away while the other liches scoffed and muttered their disapproval. They didn't even care that one of their own had fallen.

What a horrible life! What a horrendous death!

It was not how I wanted to die, but my current situation showed little else for a future. Or was it? Burdening my mind and my pocket was a spell to escape. Did Dunstan say to burn it or simply read it? I couldn't remember, but either way, I doubted I'd have enough time. What would happen if a Haunting took it instead? I couldn't let that happen.

Dunstan, the Night Terror, fought Urien's wicked scourge and lich fodder while somewhere in the darkness, the marquis fought against monsters that moaned for organs. Between the rings of stones, the marchioness blurred beyond sight as she fought against the largest werewolves I'd ever seen. At the altar, Abadda wrestled in the air with an unseen being as the child squirmed under a growing mass of darkness.

I couldn't abandon and betray the royal family again. I couldn't leave, but what could I do in this battle of magics, abilities, and supernatural powers? I was a simple seamstress. My skills were sewing and needlework. What good was a needle and thread in this place of monsters and demons?

In the shadow of one of the circle's stones, I had a sinister thought: how evil could it be?

Something about these valley's shadows made me want to be wicked. I felt in my pouch for my pack of needles. I found my largest—almost the size of a quill. Was it wicked if it saved my life? If it could stop Urien and Dunstan's fight?

Be able to turn anything into a weapon.

Words from Lady Fromm's book on survival. Of the many times I'd pricked myself, I never considered my needles to be deadly. I ran my thumb down its smooth frame to the sharp point.

Before I could plan my next move, a man shouted in pain. Dunstan's darkness shrank to reveal Urien holding tightly to his scourge. He bled from deep gashes in his shoulder and side, but held his whip handle with both hands. It stretched into the meter block that remained of Dunstan's shadows. Urien laughed between gasps for air. "Finally! I caught the elusive Night Terror!"

PANSY

Three werewolves went down from my revolver's silver bullets. Not enough. I replaced it in my pack with my silver stake and vulgur knife—even though the magical dagger wouldn't kill them.

I was a flurry of motion as I cut down werewolf after werewolf. Adrenaline raged through me as I stabbed one then another. They kept coming. There was no time to stop. Some of them stood up again when I missed a direct hit to their hearts. I didn't have time to be precise. I had to move!

Even when they were held back by my Supernatural helper, they plotted against me. Unlike the werewolf that killed Oz, these were pack hunters. They planned, lured, trapped, then struck. I had scratches all down my back, my left leg, right arm, and an ugly one along my jaw.

Claw scratches, I reassured myself. They meant to kill me, not transform me.

It was a small reassurance.

My feet dragged from dodging. My legs stung from the scratches. My core suffered from the maneuvers I swung into to bend under their claws and slam my stake into their hearts. My arms…they were the worst. My arms were in agony from scratches and the efforts of stabbing through skin and muscle over and over again. Pulling my stake out was almost as sticky and thick as plunging it in. I was a mess of blood, but I was alive.

I wouldn't be for long unless I finished them all.

Two more werewolves charged at me. After a bit of a struggle, two more went down. Three more scratches lined my left arm and a deep one gauged my left thigh.

I winced with each step. How much more could my body take?

Fighting my desire to collapse from exhaustion was almost as bad as fighting the werewolves themselves. There were few enough that I could probably break through them to Aeron, but then what? The spells of teleportation would burn too slowly for us to escape. I had to kill every last one before Aeron could be safe.

THEO

Unlike Pansy, I was ignorant of the weaknesses to every Haunting. I relied on my aura ability to gage how dangerous a certain spell would be. As soon as their auras went black, I cast. I knew how to protect people, heal, and shield them with my wand. The only offensive word I knew was "attack." After that, "aura" for "air" was always the easiest for me to remember.

I cast "*Imbeduz aura*" like a parrot to send a wave of slicing air at their necks. I did not know their specific weaknesses, though I figured chopping off their heads was a sure declaration of death. Also, it was a distance maneuver for multiple monsters at once.

With the mummies disposed of, I sliced at the zombies. Killing them was easy. The hard part came with their sheer numbers. They advanced on me at just a kilometer per hour yet they advanced all the same. I cut three down and five more crawled over to replace them.

The moans were the worst. All of them moaned. Tuneless yawns of hunger echoed in my ears as they rounded me.

They would overwhelm me if I kept this up. It was time to experiment with something new.

I considered a spell to cast and how to direct it. I smirked as auras went black. With one spell, I beheaded the whole front row of monsters.

I grimaced at my initial emotion. Since when did I take pleasure in taking life? What had Horror done to me? To my mind? Whatever it was, I needed to control it and not let it control me.

Concentrate. I needed a virtuous focus.

A snarl behind me caught my attention. Another werewolf crumpled to the ground in Pansy's massacre. She stilled enough to solidify in my sight, bent over and panting. She was covered in blood. How much of it was her own? She tightened her grips on her weapons and blurred again.

The monsters had thinned enough that I could finally see Aeron between the large stones. Seeing him brought little relief. He struggled on the altar. Above him, my wicked stepmother spoke to the side and pointed at me. That did not bode well. Likewise, the shrinking of Dunstan's darkness and laughter of a corrupted soul clenched my heart.

My family was my focus. Finish this, and I could help my family.

I slashed out my spell and instantly dropped five zombies. Again. Again. Again!

Their numbers tapered. Only a dozen or so remained. I sliced out another spell as something pushed me.

I regained my balance and looked for my new foe. I saw no one. Boney hands pushed me from behind and I spun around. No one. Not even an aura.

Invisible skeletons?

"Forgive us for our late arrival." A deep laugh chortled behind me and I spun back. Still, I saw no one, no aura, nothing. The air coalesced into a faint outline of black—black as a poltergeist. I panicked.

"You do not see us," a deep voice rumbled, "because we do not wish to be seen."

"Who are you?" I shouted as something else pushed my side.

The one I could see solidified as much as a spiritual demon could solidify. It was a floating skeleton, partially translucent. It also wore a long, black, and frayed hooded cloak.

The Haunting grinned at me wickedly. Several other voices joined as it spoke, "We are the wraiths."

The wraith disappeared and suddenly I was pushed in every direction. With each push, they swiped at me with little blades. I yelled from the stinging pain. They were like parchment cuts: thin, deep, and probably infected.

I waved my wand blindly at my foes. I always relied on my sight. My auras let me see everyone always…except these monsters.

Without the sense of sight, I relied on hearing and smell. I almost vomited by concentrating on those senses. I heard every squishing sound of weapons sliding through skin and organs, followed by screams and death moans. Then the smells. Metallic blood and acidic guts wafted through my nostrils. Then we were surrounded by putrid monsters who lived and fed off of rot and grime.

Desperate not to let myself fall into more wicked hands, I sent another air attack at the zombies to finish them off.

Then, the wraiths. How could I fight them? I knew nothing about them. Were they corporeal or incorporeal? Were they cursed or undead? Skeletons or ghosts—how were they so *fast*? Pansy could fight them. What would she do?

I looked for her, reaching for our bond. Every other time we connected, it began with locking eyes, then a touch. How could we connect when she blurred out of sight? Would she even hear me if I shouted her name? I had to try.

I reached for her with my arm, voice, and mind. "Pansy!"

An unseen foe grabbed my outstretched arm. My wand arm. I had a full millisecond to fear the worst before it happened. Opposing forces slammed into me.

Snap—Crack!

Pain exploded from my arm and erupted from my mouth. My forearm bent unnaturally. My source of magic—The Wand of Gandiduz—splintered out of its sheath.

"Ah, yes," an invisible wraith chuckled. "The queen said we would find this on you. And there it is. What are you without your magic?"

Useless.

Chapter 25

COMMON COURTESY

Don't start a relationship when
you're involved in a Haunting
Never cross a pregnant woman
Never get between a mother and her child

- Oz's Haunting Survival Book,
with notes by Pansy Fromm

PANSY

Only one werewolf remained in front of me. She had a slice at her side. I recognized the cut as the first werewolf I sliced to break through to Aeron.

I killed them all? Every muscle in my body ached, but I felt confident...enough. At least to say out loud to my Supernatural helper, "Leave me. Help Aeron and Oz, or whoever needs it more."

No time to celebrate. I wasn't done yet.

The last werewolf sneered at me and stepped to the side. I didn't break her gaze as she paced around me in a circle. Then she stopped and grinned wickedly.

That couldn't be good.

Something bulldozed into my legs and flipped my feet up. I didn't notice one more werewolf sneaking from behind. We launched through the air at his speed. A roar of teeth gaped for my calf. Panicking, I switched gears to spin my torso and slam my stake into his back. The werewolf's body lurched with the impact and went limp, but he still propelled us to the ground. We landed with a tumbling contortion, my legs under his dead body.

I pushed at it to sit myself up again. Horror, my arms! They shook from the strain. I needed to move.

Supernatural condemnation—*move*! There was one more!

BERWYNA

"Dunstan!" I shouted, surprised by the emotion I felt for the man who tricked me into loving him.

Urien spared me a quick look. How could one face hold so many expressions? He looked hurt, betrayed, and furious.

With his eyes on me, he gripped his whip and twisted. Somewhere in the darkness, at the end of the whip, Dunstan shouted in pain. His shadow shrank.

"No!" I tried to step forward, but the liches held me back, squeezing my burnt left arm. Even if I could move, I wasn't sure what to do.

Would I go to the Night Terror's aid in the darkness? No, more likely I'd go to Urien and beg him to stop. Could I threaten him with my needle?

Urien yanked on his whip to bring Dunstan and his shadow closer. The shadow around him shrank until it remained only around his form.

"Urien! What are you doing? Let him go!"

"So he can kill me? I don't think so," Urien snarled, and pulled on his whip again. Dunstan shouted louder than before and his shadow disappeared. His suffering gripped me.

The Night Terror trembled within the grasp of Urien's splintered whip. It wrapped around his arms, legs, and body several times, tight enough to cut through his clothes. Urien twisted his handle a little more. The wicked whip lengthened for another loop around Dunstan and squeezed tighter. Dunstan shouted in agony. Blood leaked from his sides at the edges of the whip, and sweat beaded down his face.

It tore me apart to see him past the point of exhaustion. The back of my mind acknowledged that the only reason he pushed himself was to save me and help his family.

Knowing who I was, and what I did...he still cared for me. Knowing who he was, and what he did...I still cared for him too.

"Stop!" I cried and sniffled. "Don't do this!"

What good did pleading do? Urien refused to look at me. He was too caught up in his anger. I needed him look me in the eyes. I needed to bring him back to his senses.

I clenched my quill-sized needle firmly. It was strong between my fingers, thick and sharp on both ends. A self-made weapon.

I casually raised the needle as much as I could within the grasp of the liches, then swung it down with all my strength. I hit the lich behind me in the thigh. She screamed. I yanked it out and she released me to double over in pain. Before the others could understand what happened, I swung my needle up to my other side and caught the lich on my left in the face. It jabbed into one of his eyes and scraped against his cheek. He also let go of me to flinch back. I was still surrounded by five liches, but only one continued to hold onto me. I scraped my needle across his hand and he snapped back. Then I ran.

They chased after me, but they didn't run with terror coursing through their veins. Urien saw me coming, but didn't dare change his position with his whip. I threw my arms around his shoulders and hugged him from behind. I buried my face into his back and cried.

"Stop, Urien! Please! Don't do this! You were everything I wanted until this misadventure, but I don't know who you are anymore!" I lifted my face and edged around to make him see my tears. "Please, stop! Don't hurt Dunstan, I love him!"

Urien's eyes widened with surprise. His mouth flared into a snarl. "What about *me*? I'm stronger and more powerful than ever, but you pushed me away! The Night Terror is a traitor! He has no home or honor! How could you want him over *me*?"

I sniffled through my tears. "I wanted to love you, Urien, but I never wanted you to become a murderer. Dunstan is my true love and I would die inside if you killed him."

Urien stared back at me, mouth moving up and down without words. Then his eyes caught fire and he snarled, "Then die!"

He elbowed me hard in my chest. I stumbled back, falling into the hands of liches again. Urien took hold of his whip with both hands and yanked it to the side.

Dunstan and I screamed together.

AERON

The snakes that tied me to the stone table were too heavy and thick to move. I tried to scream for help, for my mom and father, but my voice was still gone. I wiggled and squirmed but could not get loose. The shadow of the bull statue crept toward me. It moved on its own and was too thick and bubbled to be a normal shadow. The snakes spat as the black shadow covered my feet. It soaked through my shoes and under my socks to my skin. Its cold touch worked up my legs and I shivered. It left a tingling feeling through my feet and ankles and chilled me to the bone. Reaching my bum and fingertips, I lost control of my feet. I could not kick or even wiggle my toes. It looked like my bottom half was in a bubble of tar. I panicked, wondering if it somehow broke my body.

What are you? I thought. *And what are you doing to my legs?*

A whisper of the darkness spoke directly to my mind without a mouth.

"I'm stealing your life away, I am."

I tried to scream again. It read my mind!

"Such a young life," it continued. "So much to live for. Yours is the tastiest life I've had, yes-yes. Savor you, I should. Lengthen this out and enjoy you, I should, but…it's too much!"

From my wrists, the shadow became darker, then grew to slam over my arms and chest. Only my head remained as the shadow happily moaned.

"Hmm, yes, yes! Hmm-hmm! More!"

I screamed a breathy wheeze as the shadow grew again and covered my face.

With a shiver, I realized the bone chilling feeling I felt earlier was from the shadow sinking into my skin and to my bones, sucking the marrow out of my life. I tried to scream, but opening my mouth only filled it with the darkness. It rushed down my throat and clogged me from the inside. No air. I could not breathe.

PANSY

As I shoved at the dead werewolf on my legs, it suddenly became heavier. A guttural growl revealed the last werewolf. She stood on top of the carcass and sneered down at me. My legs were completely pinned as she dropped down and grabbed my shoulders. I couldn't move.

What was the point of an ability for speed if I was immobile? Being five times faster than time itself only drew out the pain.

I could still think faster. Come on! Think my way out of this! I'd escaped worse situations!

I doubted that as the werewolf dug her claws into my shoulders, breaking skin, drawing blood, causing screams. It was like ten knives twisting themselves deeper and deeper. She yanked her right hand claws from my shoulder. The open wounds were as bad as the initial stabbing. My entire arm twitched from the pain that seared through my nerves.

If I thought it couldn't get worse, I was wrong. She used her free hand to slash at my face. Her claws raked down my left side, from my forehead to my chin.

Condemnation! I couldn't even grit my teeth from the pain as it tensed my bleeding neck muscles. Despite all I'd been through, I kept control of my speed. Until that moment. The pain forced me to tap out of my ability and I screamed. My vision darkened at the edges.

No! I needed to hold on! I needed to save Aeron!

I willed myself to focus. It was all I could do to keep myself from screaming. Focus. There would be time for pain later.

I managed to open my eyes. Aeron no longer struggled within the shadow. Was he dead?

While my motherly instinct wanted to deny even the possibility, my Horror instinct told me it was too late. I didn't even have the strength to cry out for him. After all we did to save him…we failed.

Chapter 26

NEVER SAY:

"I promise..." — lies, or kept to an early grave
"I am invincible!" — famous last words

> - *Oz's Haunting Survival Book,*
> with notes by Pansy Fromm

AERON

My little body tingled with coldness and swelled with the need for air. No one could save me. Did they even know that I needed help? I could not scream for them. There was nothing I could do.

My lungs burned. My whole body ached. But worst of all was the depressing feeling that I truly grasped for the first time: hopelessness. The pain became too much.

Then, it disappeared. My spirit floated from my body as if I had fallen asleep. Except, it felt different this time. I could breathe again, though I realized I no longer needed to.

Was I...dead? Forever? Was I supposed to be sad? Instead, I felt relieved. I saw my parents and then became sad. Mom trembled on the ground. She looked like she was in a lot of pain. I wanted to help her, but how?

Francine and Sean battled the skeleton ghosts around Father. Francine was more of a distraction while Sean made the attacks. I felt their emotions of determination and worry. I did not know their emotions in my dreams like I did now. Was that one of my spiritual gifts?

Uncle Oz zipped around, fighting Abadda, forcing her away from me.

Abadda met my eyes. I thought Uncle Oz said she could not see spirits if we did not interact with her? I felt her anger, hate, confusion, and…fear?

"Death on the Altar of Moloch ssshould have restrained thy spirit from risssing! Be gone!" she shrieked.

"Foolish witch," Francine jeered back. "His spirit rose *because* he was killed on that altar. You misinterpreted the meaning."

In the blink of an eye, Abadda flashed to Francine and threw her hand across her with a fierce swipe. With a puff of smoke, every one of Francine's spirit animals vaporized.

"No!" Sean charged at the wicked buttchess. His hands glowed with a bright light. He flew to her faster than my eyes could watch, but somehow Abadda was faster. She slapped a dark hand at Sean and he too dissipated into smoke. Uncle Oz said nothing, but I felt his astonishment and fear. With mental capacity beyond my young mind, I understood. Abadda gained even more power from sacrificing me to the bull statue. She not only had the power to take the lives of the living, but also to banish the spirits of the dead.

"Stay away from her," Uncle Oz said from beside me. "If she takes me down, don't wait, just run. Think of the church and go there."

"But she cannot take you down, right?" I asked.

He glanced back at me with calm and sad eyes. He knew, then I knew. He only had one thing left to do. "Watch over your mom for me. I'm passing the job as her guardian angel to you. Tell her I love her."

I opened my mouth to say something, but he was already before Abadda, zipping back and forth, up and down, all around her in a blur of motion. He jabbed with his bright light of dispelling. She blocked with her dark expulsion. I sensed his growing frustration as she blocked him again and again. His emotions opposed Abadda's wicked glee of a challenging fight.

Uncle Oz faked left and broke through her defense. He jabbed at her elbow and I felt a momentary leap of success. She jerked, and her left arm went limp. Then she struck back.

She shoved and twisted her entire right hand through his core. She curled her long and pointed fingernails. My own insides twisted by watching it.

I expected to feel his pain. Instead, I felt his peace. A small smile even crept up his lips as he closed his eyes and faded.

"Uncle Oz!" I shouted. There was nothing I could do. He was gone.

The Wicked Buttchess Abadda turned eyes of ice on me.

Uncle Oz said run to the church. I closed my eyes and concentrated on the dark church with the scary guardians. A rushing sound filled my ears as I traveled really fast, even though no wind waved my hair or clothes. I opened my eyes and the little black-stoned church with its hideous gargoyles greeted me. Hundreds of miles away, the evil queen's rage reached my senses. Her fury over my escape flamed against the Hauntings around her. Rather than feel their pain and anger, I turned my attention toward the church.

At least I already knew my gifts. Buttchess Abadda saw me with my gift to become visible to the living, and I felt the feelings of others with the gift of emotional understanding.

Drifting through the church doors, I noticed the spirits in flurry. Ever busy saving the world. I drifted alone to sit in a pew.

"Prince Aeron?"

Paul floated beside me. Right, he was there because of his gift to commune with God.

"Uncle Oz told me to come here."

"Yes," he said, "you should be safe here."

Even still, I sensed his sadness. He knew Oz was gone.

I bowed my head and waited for my tears to fall. They didn't come. Being dead was weird. I felt safe, but my mind was still troubled.

I missed my mom and father. They were fighters and Heroes, even if they were unable to rescue me. They fought and struggled for good. But there were too many monsters. Mom and Father could not beat them all. They would die too. Even if I could not cry, my insides hurt to think of my parents going through so much pain.

What about Uncle Oz? He was a fighter to the end, even in death. He was a Hero. What happened to him? And Sean and Francine? Where were they?

A soft whisper, as if in the wind, drifted into my thoughts. "They are with me."

Though the whisper entered my mind the same way as the voice from the valley's shadow, this voice was gentle. My heart filled with peace like I had never known. Oz, Sean, and Francine fought for good and after all these years, they could rest.

Was there anything I could do? I was unhappy to sit there and wait for my parents to die. I wanted to fight!

"God hears the prayers of the children," the gentle voice said in my mind. I opened my eyes, but no one stood by me. The voice spoke again. "I wait for you beyond the door."

There were a few doors in this church, but somehow I knew the voice meant a specific one on the right. I stood and floated over. Usually it was effortless to drift through walls and doors, but this one I had to push. I staggered through and entered a world that looked nothing like the real outside.

It was the world from the windows. A path stretched before me paved in gold. The grass was as green as back home, and flowers sprouted in every color imaginable. A man sat cross-legged at the top of a hill. He looked solid and I did too. I wondered if this was still the spirit realm. It definitely was not the living realm. The gold path was smooth as water, and the man wore a robe of white fire. His hair was not gray, but silver with light. There was a sense of gravity on me again, though it felt loose. I walked up to the man on the hill.

"Are you God?"

He turned to me with a smile. "Hello, Aeron."

This was the God of Everything. As much as his presence awed me, I was confused. He let me die. He let the monsters hurt my mom, Father, Uncles Oz and Dunstan.

I cried, "Why?"

"Your parents can do hard things, Aeron. You can too. Sometimes, people need reminders of how strong they are so that they can face the future with hope."

With those simple words, He conveyed so much. I felt a wave of emotions from Him—happy satisfaction in me as a person, in my desire to fight for good, in my abilities, and in my questions for truth. There was also sorrow—for my death, for my parents' struggles, for the wickedness of Abadda and those who followed her. There was something else that was a bit unclear, though I somehow understood it. It was a mix of hope, belief, and determination. It said the sorrow would not last. He did not explain how, but He was so sure of it that I believed it too.

"Come, sit with me," He said with a gentle smile. "I want to show you something before you decide your next step."

I joined Him on top of the hill and gained the viewpoint of the city beyond. The streets and buildings were built of the same smooth gold and several spirits wandered around. They did not bustle like those of the Spirit Zone. They walked, chatted, or just rested.

Below, Sean and Francine held hands and waved to me. I waved back, wondering if Uncle Oz was down there somewhere.

"Your uncle is here," God said, knowing my thoughts. "He has worked hard and served me well. He has earned a time of rest."

"Then he is alright?" I asked.

God smiled. "Yes, he is well here."

He pressed a finger to the soil. A beautiful flower with large teardrop petals sprouted before my eyes.

"See this flower?" He asked. "How it yearns to share its knowledge with you."

I leaned down to study it closer. The flower was unlike any I had ever seen and gave off emotions of eager anticipation. God's finger slid down its petal and it changed colors. The fat petals turned blood red with two black spots dropping from the middle.

"What do you see?" He asked.

Rather than just seeing the colors, I sensed a feeling from the flower: perseverance.

"Mom," I said. At the same time, I grinned to think how smart I became in death.

God smiled and touched the dirt again to grow another flower. Though from the same stem, this flower shaded a royal blue with green-tinted outlines and red vines within. Its center shimmered gold and spoke of duty.

"Father," I said.

A third flower sprang up, though not as tall and stayed a bud. Its petals were many shades of light blue, then turned almost clear at the ends. The emotions it gave off were confused and not quite solid. All that was sure was the flower wanted to be the best it could be.

God turned to me. "What about you? What do you see of yourself?"

I looked up to meet His eyes, alive as a flame's heart. "Potential."

God's smile broadened. "Exactly. Your mission is not yet finished. You are needed in the Valley of Death."

I looked around. I liked it here. It was very pretty and felt nice. "I do not want to leave."

His smile softened. "You may stay if you wish. However, a great life awaits you if you choose to return. You have another gift, Aeron. A gift to visit those who have passed on."

"My ability?"

"Yes. This gift can help many people on both sides, but you must return to use it. Will you do that?"

I rubbed my wrist without my bracelet to fiddle and looked out again at the golden buildings and smiling people. "Alright, but only if I can come back here."

He simply smiled and touched my heart. Instead of a flower, a warmth grew in my heart and spread to my fingers and toes. My insides swelled as if taking a breath after almost drowning.

"I am giving you these gifts until they have served their purpose," He said. "Now, you must return and fulfill that purpose. Fulfill your potential. Countless flowers on both sides of life need you, but these" —He gestured to the flowers representing my parents— "need you most of all."

My body did not need to breathe, but it was nice to do so after the heat flickered through me.

"And I can come back later?" I asked.

God's smile beamed like the sun. "As long as you fight for the good, someday you will return to stay."

Without Him saying more, I understood that "someday" meant at the end of my life. I could live to be a hundred, but while standing on that hill, one hundred years felt like the blink of an eye. I could wait that long. I started down the hill to the church. God's smile encouraged me to keep walking forward.

I stumbled through the doorway and Paul was at my side.

"Prince Aeron! You returned? Did God speak with you? What happened?"

I blinked and levitated off the ground. God's warmth urged me onward. "How long was I gone?"

"Only a second or two, but time is different with God. What happened? Children do not usually return after meeting with Him. Did He give you a purpose?"

"Yes. I need to go back to the Valley of Death."

"What? Are you—" Paul stopped as his eyes raced back and forth from quick thinking. "I do not understand, but if He wills it, then you must go."

Without even a blink of an eye, I was back at the valley. Regardless of the shadows and death surrounding me, I felt the warmth and reassurance of the sun.

My ability in life let me visit the dead. In death, my spiritual gift let me become visible to the living. Then, there were the other gifts that God temporarily gave me. My consciousness separated and multiplied so I stood several places at once. I was here, yet I was there, and there, and over there, fully aware and capable.

I understood everything as if the world was planned out and read to me like a book. It was all so simple. My mind expanded a hundred fold to comprehend ideas and concepts far beyond my five-year-old mind. One thought seemed simple enough that surely I should have understood it anyway.

"You Hauntings pretend to rule this land," I said. The remaining Hauntings stared at me with annoyance while Abadda stared with worry. She knew what I came here to do. "But you are only allowed to live here by God and His helpers. You, Fantastic usurper, pretend you can rule with your powers, but you are even more foreign. My parents are the natural rulers of you. I am their heir. The blood of Fantasy and Horror gave me life. In death, it gives me rights. You might be Hauntings, but I. am. a Horror! I. am. a Fantastic!"

And I *felt* fantastic!

I categorized everyone's emotions with wisdom beyond my own. I analyzed their wants and the paths they wanted to take.

My kidnappers were the most peculiar to examine.

Missus kidnapped me. Except, I felt her sadness and guilt. A touch of greater understanding said that she was already in enough pain. She would be a better person after this.

Mister had no remorse, but lots of sorrow. He was also confused. One of my separations touched his forehead with understanding.

A light grew in his eyes. His fury lessened. He turned to Missus and I felt his desire to be happy with her. His grip on the whip loosed and Uncle Dunstan moaned in relief.

My uncle's moan distracted Mister. He turned back to my uncle and his anger returned. He rejected my gift of understanding. He rejected the truth for his own wants. His heart spoke of wickedness.

He was going to kill Uncle Dunstan!

I reached forward to knock him out, but something stopped me. It was a glimpse of the future. I saw what was about to happen, and that greater understanding told me what should be done.

My separations went to each of the liches around Missus. I punched my little arm out, fully confident that my power was beyond my regular strength. They screamed and crumpled to the ground.

I left the rest up to Missus. My separations returned to my main spirit above the altar, where my frail body lay dead.

Abadda sneered at me from across the stone circle.

"Thou hast many giftsss," she hissed.

"No," I said. "I have *every* gift."

I thrust my fist forward to strike her. She dodged! She was fast!

I barely ducked before her claws reached for my face. It quickly became clear that one of my fancy punches would not be enough to dispel her. I floated back to create some distance between us, but she followed. I recalled my self-defense lessons from Master Bahr. I was still a beginner, first mastering the stances and building my physical strength with correct forms. Being dead threw all of that out the window. Flight and unlimited energy had a way of twisting combat. I needed Ruezdad's fairy captain to teach me how to fight in the air. Until then, I had to change tactics.

One lesson held true as Master Bahr taught me to find my advantages and use them. One advantage: my small size. Second advantage: my gifts. With so many gifts, my advantages multiplied as easily as myself.

I separated again into a dozen different Aerons. I traveled at the speed of thought. Some of them disguised themselves as my parents or other spirits I knew. Others transformed into animals. I could handle objects from the living realm, but understood that my best weapons were my hands and my capacity to use these gifts.

I looked into Abadda's past and concentrated on her feelings. Before she could even swing a kick at me, I learned everything about her. I knew her childhood—of her lust for recognition and power, of her trickery to marry my grandfather, and her plots to curse my family to put herself on the throne. I knew of her hatred for my family—of Queen Alóvera, of Grandfather Konrad, of my mom and father. I saw her past as she waited and plotted to be rescued from the depths of the ocean. I knew her plots as her cursed mirror prophesied of my birth and ability, then as she overheard the prophecy of her destruction by a royal bridge between life and death. I felt her fear of me.

I knew her so well that I knew her actions before she made them. I dodged her kick and blocked her punch. I surprised her with a punch of my own.

I spoke to her mind the words from the God of Everything. He condemned her. She did not belong here. She could not stay.

She shrunk under the authority of the all-powerful God. She could not fight Him, and at that moment I was His mouth-piece. I was His hands.

A flame ignited within me, pushing me to act. It was time.

Chapter 27

HOW TO AVOID A HAUNTED ROMANCE:

Don't meet in Horror
Don't date the haunted
Don't marry the cursed
Don't dance with death
If you think it's true love at first sight,
suspect trickery

- *Oz's Haunting Survival Book,*
with notes by Pansy Fromm

THEO

Hearing Pansy's screams, I struggled to make it to my wife. The wraiths pushed me back. Each push sliced long and stinging cuts into my skin. Ribbons of my flesh peeled from my chest, arms, and legs. I screamed as never before.

"At last," a wraith grumbled, "the child is dead and—"

"Aeron?" I asked, my heart plunging into despair.

"—Abadda gained the power to banish those pesky Supernaturals. Let us finish this."

Before I could worry more about my son, my dark aura became pitch. Their next strike would kill me!

Time slowed as I sensed their nearness. One had its blade at my neck. Another had its blade at my temple, ready to slice

251

across my eyes. Pricks of blade tips pressed against my wrists. A small rip in my clothes announced another blade at my chest.

What could I do against them? What could I do for Aeron, who was proclaimed dead by the dead? What could I do for Pansy as she struggled in pain on the valley floor?

I failed. Even after all my schooling, all my training, all my understanding of my ability and magic, I was useless to save those I loved.

This was my death? My black aura said that it was.

I was blind to any escape as the wraiths surrounded me. Their unseen blades pressed into my skin. I closed my eyes.

My ending reflected how I began: useless. I did everything I could. It was not enough.

BERWYNA

Without the liches to hold me back, I ran for Urien. He would kill Dunstan if I didn't stop him. I knew what had to be done even if I hated it.

"Stop, Urien!" I screamed and ran into him with full force. His whip jerked and Dunstan yelled.

Urien snarled, "You'll have to kill me to stop me!"

"Please," I cried, "don't make me do that."

Urien spared me a glance and laughed. "As if you could! You thought you could change destiny and love a terrorist? You're a fool, Berwyna! You're fortunate I still care about you!"

"Unfortunately for you," I sniffled, "I care about you too."

He paused to give me a hopeful sneer. That twisted look held no resemblance to the Urien I once knew.

"I care so much," I continued, "to kill you when you've become corrupted."

"What?"

I drew up my arm and plunged my large needle into his chest. With both hands on his whip, Urien had no way to block. I pierced his heart, and he jerked back. Dunstan's cries stuttered.

Urien made no sound. His mouth broke open, but nothing could vocalize his pain. His grasp on the whip slackened then let go. His hands trembled as he reached up to the needle stuck into him.

I stepped back, crying more than ever.

DUNSTAN

Released from the scourge, I fell to my hands and knees. Berwyna called my name, though my attention was drawn to a ghostly child hovering beside me. He looked at me with the same blue-green eyes as his father.

"Aeron?" I asked.

"You might have betrayed the God of Fire, but you didn't betray the God of Everything. He grants you back your priesthood for one last expulsion."

Aeron touched my shoulder and a warmth spread through my body. Bullbeggar, I *really* needed to get to know my nephew better.

One last expulsion? Berwyna was safe, but my brother needed my help. Theo's right arm hung limply as invisible Hauntings pushed him to his knees.

I offered Berwyna a small smile of thanks, then used my ability to evaporate all light. The fire burning through my veins gave me just enough energy to raise my hands from the bedrock.

"You cannot hide!" The group of wraiths laughed. "We are Hauntings! We own the night!"

The fire and power of faith coursed through my body. "The darkness is mine," I snarled. Then, I commanded the heat within me. White hot fire broke through my darkness as it surged from my fingers and latched onto the monsters around my brother.

The wraiths screamed and screeched an unholy pitch that made the last werewolf shudder and whine. The wraiths dissipated into smoke and wails.

I released the light, too exhausted to hold it in, then fell to the ground.

THEO

I gasped, inhaling relief and hope as the wraiths crumbled within their white flames, screaming with every last second of their miserable lives. Dunstan had saved me. As much as I wanted to help and thank my fallen brother, my eyes went to Pansy and Aeron. Aeron was trapped on the Altar of Moloch with an ominous shadow engulfing him.

Rage and terror filled my veins. If they killed either of them, that would likewise destroy me.

I wanted to run to Aeron, though Pansy was closer and she had one last werewolf hunched over her, pinning her down with a dead werewolf. There was little I could do against such a beast, especially without my magic. That did not stop me from charging it.

Pansy's wide eyes found mine, screaming at me for my sanity. Yes, there was a tightrope between stupidity and bravery, and I sprinted on it.

The beast howled in pain from the wraiths' screeches, momentarily distracted from my mad advance. It was enough.

I smashed into the Haunting as a bull into a wall. Curses! I barely forced it off!

My wife moved with a strangely sluggish blur. Even with her speed, she moved slowly enough for me to track her movements. She pushed herself from underneath the dead werewolf, then managed to slip between the last werewolf's limbs. Her blurring stopped, and she growled to match the ferocity of every Haunting of that valley. "You forgot a rule of survival."

With enormous effort, she shoved her silver stake into its heart. The werewolf jerked, and Pansy snarled, "Never get between a mother and her child."

The werewolf finally stilled, and Pansy collapsed. I slid to my knees at her side. Three horrendous claw marks raked down the left side of her face.

"What happened?" I asked. My wife was unconscious. Did she lose too much blood? There was so much. "Just hold on. Let me grab Aeron and burn the teleportation spells. You need a healer."

My attention was distracted by the faint image of a dozen spirits floating above the altar. They were all copies of a young boy who was dead with no aura.

"Aeron?"

His little face looked determined and wise beyond his years. As much as I feared for his ghostly presence before Abadda, his confidence spoke of faith and knowledge I understood not.

My son punched at my wicked stepmother. It was similar to the punch he showed me on the oak board days ago. It was the punch of a child, yet he had power and speed beyond his practice.

I gaped.

That was my son? I helped create that?

With my right arm broken, I struggled to pull Pansy to Aeron. The dark shadow and snakes were gone, leaving his lifeless body open. Setting Pansy beside the altar, I slid Aeron from the stone and into my lap. I held my wife with my good arm. She trembled.

"Shh," I stroked her hair. Tears welled in my eyes as I fumbled for our teleportation spells. I saw Aeron's spirit. His body was still. Our child was dead.

"Do not cry for me, Father."

I looked up, startled.

One of Aeron's spirits stood beside me. He pointed at his spirits that hovered high above us.

"Look at me," he said, excited. *"I am a Fantastic Horror!"*

My son's spirit fought with my stepmother. Even as fear clenched my heart, an odd comfort settled over me. I watched in awe as two of his copies grabbed her hands to pull them to her sides. Another two held her feet down. One Aeron stabbed his hand directly through her head between her eyes. Another one jabbed through her heart.

Abadda screamed. She shook as black smoke emanated from her skin. A white light, brighter than the noonday sun, exploded from Aeron's hands and burst across the valley. I had a déjà vu of Oz's spirit destroying a poltergeist in a basement and Pansy overcoming Oswald's hypnosis in Ruezdad.

The light faded. My surroundings became no more than an ancient stone structure in a dead valley. The decapitated zombies, unraveled mummies, and piles of skeleton bones disappeared to dust. The red stains of our bloody massacres dried under the afternoon's heat. Aeron's spirits were also gone.

Any remaining Hauntings fled to the dark crevices and pits where they belonged. Someone coughed behind me. Berwyna ran to Dunstan, who lay prostrate on the ground.

"Dunstan!" Berwyna and I shouted. She helped him to stand. His arms hung limp and bleeding. His shirt tore across his stomach and back where the scourge cut into him. My brother draped heavily over the woman as they shuffled to me. I held my shaking wife and dead son.

"Pansy needs a healer," I said. "Merlin's beard, you do as well."

"And Aeron," Dunstan whispered, his voice hoarse.

"Aeron?" I asked, daring to hope.

My brother tapped my son on the chest and put his ear to Aeron's mouth. "He's mostly dead, but not entirely. Part of his spirit lingers. Miracle Mark should be able to restore him."

I grasped onto that frail thread of hope and held tightly to my broken family.

Dunstan gestured to Berwyna. "Do you still have that teleportation spell that I gave to you?"

Nodding, she pulled out a piece of parchment.

I grabbed the spell and gaped at my brother. "You gave her your spell? Are you insane?"

He shrugged. "I was a Romantic. Still am, when it comes to Berwyna."

"You lost your mind to your heart, same thing," I agreed. Rummaging through Pansy's emergency pack, I found her matchbook and struck one to all four spells. "We only have four teleportation spells. You would have been left behind."

"I'll stay," Dunstan said.

"No!" Berwyna coughed even as she shoved Dunstan closer to me and stepped back. "You're hurt! You need a healer!"

"You are too," he said, gesturing to her arm. "You sound ill."

"Dunstan," I said, wrapping my arms around my wife and child. The spell pages were halfway gone and burning faster. "Your aura is darker. You look as if you will fall apart."

"Of the five of us," the young woman said, "I'm the least injured. Go. I'll find my own way back to Fantasy."

"I'm not leaving you," Dunstan said.

"It is for the best," I grunted and grabbed his arm. We had perhaps two seconds before the spell activated.

"I'll find a way to bring you back," Dunstan said. "Stay at the Pinnacle Hotel. I'll come—"

The last corner became ash, teleporting my broken family to Fantasy, and far, far away from Horror.

Epilogue

One Week Later

The full moon sank below the horizon and a new day dawned with hopeful rays reaching into our bedchamber in Ruezdad. My eyes fluttered open from the touch of Theo's gentle fingers across my forehead. He softly brushed my hair away, revealing the werewolf scars down my face that refused to heal. I curled my face away to hide them.

"Pansy—"

"Everything else healed," I complained. "I look like a Haunting."

Theo frowned. "You do not. You are as beautiful as ever."

"I'd say you're lying, but you're a terrible liar." I blushed. "And maybe I exaggerated. Not everything healed." I nodded to his pillow, where he hid the Wand of Gandiduz. It was nothing short of a miracle that a wand maker was able to fix the legendary stick. Still, Theo cringed to use magic. We could only guess if it was lingering effects of his excessive magic use in Horror, or if some of the tainted magic of Horror leaked into the wand when it splintered.

There was also the matter of the lost abilities. Theo held onto a small hope that his friend and others would regain their stolen abilities when Abadda was killed. Apparently, they were lost forever.

"Life may never be the same," Theo said, "though I confess, some pieces are better than before." He caressed my face again and smiled his glorious smile. "Now, I have front row seats for your sleep-talking and snoring."

"Did I say anything ominous?" I panicked. "And I don't snore! I'm a lady! If anything, I breathe heavily."

Theo laughed. "I was just teasing. You do not snore. Though you did mumble something about me as the embodiment of goodness, beard and all."

I blushed harder, and he pulled me close.

"Is that how you feel about me?"

"We're connected, right? Not even lucid dreams can change my love for you."

He kissed me tenderly, then more than tenderly. We had a full day ahead of us, but we had time before it started.

A couple hours later, we went together to the dining hall for breakfast. Soon after we arrived, the doors creaked again. Aeron struggled to open the door himself, and Master Bahr kept watch nearby. Our son slipped a little, and Master Bahr flashed out one of his giant bear paws to help.

"I...can...do it," Aeron said through gritted teeth. He pushed the door open and gasped for breath once he was through. His struggles pained me, but we were eternally grateful for Miracle Mark's chocolate-coated pill to restore our son. Restoring his strength was another process though.

Aeron sat beside me with a huff.

I smiled to my husband. "Do you want to tell him, or should I?"

"May I tell him?" Theo's eyes lit with excitement.

"Tell me what?" Aeron asked.

"Eimad wants to title you," Theo said, and Aeron's eyes went wide. "They see you as a Hero for vanquishing Abadda. They decided on Aeron, the Haunted."

"The Haunted?" he mused.

"It fits you," I said, "with your half-Horror blood and ability to visit the dead in your sleep." I reached over and rotated in my seat to meet his eyes. "Aeron, I'm sorry we suppressed your ability. If we knew they weren't simple nightmares, but visits to the spirit world, we never would have made you that bracelet."

Aeron shook his head. "They scared me before. Now they do not. Uncle Oz teached me—*taught* me about my ability. He was a much better teacher than Tutor White."

I grinned. "Yes, he taught me everything I know. I'm glad you met him."

"On that topic," Theo said, "have you met any spirits here in Fantasy?"

"Yes, Father!" Our son beamed. "Lots of them! Queen Alóvera says you know her."

"Yes," Theo said with a smile. "She was my aunt and King Aneirin's mother."

"She is a nice queen," Aeron said. "She has a gift for healing. Oh, I remember! They call her the Goddess of Re—" He struggled with the word "—of Regerashun."

"The—what?" Theo blinked.

I inwardly groaned. Our son's understanding of theology just became more complicated.

"The Goddess of Regerashun?" he repeated.

"You mean regeneration?" I tried.

"Yeah! I remember they say dead people with great magics and abilities became gods and goddesses, like Horrors become Supernaturals or Hauntings. Oh! And the God of Dust was very unhappy and wants a shrine built like Great-Grandfather King Fromm's."

Theo and I shared confused looks.

"There is no shrine for the Valiant King," Theo said. "Do you mean the memorial?"

"The God of Dust calls it the shrine to the God of Conquest."

"God of—" Theo blinked and turned to me. "Fantasy's gods were once people?"

"Not to mention your relatives," I pointed out. "I think our five-year-old son confirmed that Fantasy's gods are only equal to angels and Horror's Supernaturals. The abbeys will have a fit. Can I tell Aeron the second bit of news?"

"Oh, sure," Theo said, his mind distracted with the fact that he'd worshipped his ancestors all his life.

"What news?" Aeron asked.

"First of all," I said, "how are you feeling?"

Aeron squished his face into a pout. "I feel fine. I am not weak."

"Maybe tired?" I offered. "I ask because we wanted to take a family vacation."

"What does vacation mean?"

"It's a trip to somewhere new, to see new sights and learn about different cultures. No events to attend or duties to fulfill. Simply us having fun."

"You know," Theo added, "by that definition, our trip to Horror was a holiday."

"You forgot the last part about having fun," I said with a smirk. "And this will be *planned*. We'll go to Children's for a whole week, then you'll spend a week with your cousins in Sci-Fi."

Aeron cheered for joy while Theo and I shared a secret smile. That second week was actually a separate trip for Theo and me, a much needed vacation to Romance for the two of us.

We continued our meal with idle chitchat, teasing, teaching, and simply enjoying each other's company. Theo finished before Aeron and I did. He could have left to accomplish something during the ten minutes before our first appointments. Instead, he sat with us as I finished and Aeron played with his food more than he digested.

Our appointments were put on hold, however, as a footman entered the dining room.

"Marquis, Marchioness, you have a message from the abbey. The Night Shade has returned."

Theo immediately stood from the table. I put down my silverware and reached for Aeron. "Let's go greet your uncle."

It took us all of a half hour to get out the door with Aeron, then arrive at Eimad Abbey. We found Dunstan with Berwyna in the infirmary, laying on cots as a priestess prayed for their healing. Berwyna's burnt arm looked much worse than I feared without its bandages, and they both had several more bleeding cuts and purple bruises across their bodies.

"Curses," Theo swore. "What trouble did you start this time?"

Dunstan grinned back. "Hey, Theo! You wouldn't believe the mess that goes down in Horror on the full moon."

Berwyna smirked. "It was almost as bad as Halloween night. Though the locals said this year was the calmest they'd seen in decades, as if the Hauntings were strangely absent…"

"Supernaturals," I cursed, then rushed to their bedsides. I surveyed the situation for the worst damage.

"Priestess," Theo said, interrupting her healing spell, "the marchioness is in charge of their healing now. Do what she says."

"Oh?" The priestess blinked, then turned to me for further instructions.

"Your prayers will be more effective if we clean their wounds and suture them first."

Dunstan gestured to his ankle that looked like it'd been caught in a bear trap. "Hey, do I need to do your creepy 'alive and human' test, or is this blood good enough?"

I smirked while Theo moaned. "You were barely well enough from your injuries at the Valley of Death. Did you have to go back to Horror in person?"

"Of course I had to go." His brother scoffed, his tone synonymous with "duh." "Oh, it turns out that Berwyna's sickness was due to Abadda's potions. Go figure, our wicked stepmother never spared any tears for anyone. She gave Berwyna a daily potion that made her feel better, only to return the next day worse than before. We figured that out pretty quickly since she didn't have the duchess's potion on Halloween."

"Marquis and Marchioness Fromm," Berwyna peeped. "I am so sorry for my deeds. I am guilty of kidnapping your son, and will accept punishment for my crimes."

"Berwyna—"

"No, Dunstan," she cut him off. "They deserve justice, and I am indebted to you for bringing me home to Eimad."

Her eyes met mine, then Theo's. When they reached Aeron—who hid behind Theo's leg—her lips quivered and she looked away.

Theo and I shared an uncomfortable glance. A small piece of me enjoyed the sight of her groveling. This was the woman who helped restore Duchess Abadda. This woman helped kidnap our son. She also ran from Abadda and told us where to find Aeron.

"Do not cry," Aeron said, stepping forward and reaching one of his small hands to her less damaged arm. "You are a nice person."

Berwyna's lip trembled harder. Theo and I shared another glance. This one was a smile only parents understood. Maybe one day we'd teach him as much as he taught us.

I shrugged. "Her week in Horror was probably enough of a prison sentence, don't you think? The Supernaturals execute their own form of justice. If she was truly wicked, Horror would have found a way to snuff her out. Especially during Halloween night and a full moon."

"Believe me," Dunstan chuckled, "it tried."

I smiled back. "I'll need a full report of what happened. You know, to make sure no Hauntings will follow you."

Theo rubbed his chin. "Just in case, perhaps you should spend the next year in a place that could handle a carryover Haunting."

I pursed my lips in thought. "They should have a six month reprieve, and they'll need to heal first. But sure. Sword and Sorcery has some people and tools to fight a possible Haunting."

My approval sent Theo grinning at his brother. "What do you think about visiting Di? Perhaps you could stay on the border of Urban."

Dunstan brightened. "Really? As long as I can keep my personal promise to be a better uncle to Aeron. I heard he has a nickname now. Congratulations, Aeron Fromm, the Haunted."

THE END

Want More?

Oz's rules to survive
Horror with new notes
from Pansy.

Available on
BarnesAndNoble.com

Coming Soon:

Aeron's grown-up Adventures and Romances in Mystery!
Follow me on Facebook or Instagram for more
announcements!

Acknowledgements

As with every book based in Novel, I had a lot of fun writing this. If you enjoyed reading it, I'd really appreciate a review! I'm truly grateful for those who make the effort to say kind words.

I initially wrote "Don't Date the Haunted" and "Don't Marry the Cursed" without plans for sequels, but the first two books would not be the same without this one.

I have one main person to thank for this book, and that's my husband. He supported and encouraged me in every step. Every major change in the story was discussed and bounced off of him—no matter how busy he was.

Thanks to Noelle from Eschler Editing, for helping me to dive deeper into each character and to understand the thoughts of a parent with a missing child. It's a situation I don't wish on anyone. Another thanks goes to Jeigh Meredith from Salt and Sage Editing for the proofread and encouragement.

Robyn Cheatham deserves a huge thanks from her alpha reading and fan-girling over Dunstan. Sorry, I couldn't base Berwyna off of you, but their first kiss was influenced by your comments. Thanks, also, for helping me to decide which ending to use. Who knows if we'll write that crossover with Kamo?

A stand out thanks to Jim Doran for suggesting the God-helps-us-to-help-each-other ending. Other awesome Beta readers who helped me to solidify this book include Lisa Gartner, Abby Smith, and Colleen Dowda. Thank you so much for jumping in without a back cover blurb to forewarn what was coming!

I'd also like to thank the classic and inspirational horror stories that openly promote morals and God. One of the main reasons I set out to write a horror (back in the early stages of book one), was to direct others toward God. As a Latter-day Saint Christian, I believe that God loves each of us, despite our past or present failures. I also believe that no matter our obstacles, God can lift us above, guide us through, and give us hope. The protagonists of this story will never be the same after these events, but they'll be stronger than ever with hopes for the future.

ABOUT THE AUTHOR

C. Rae D'Arc has been involved in every stage of a book's life. As a writer, editor, retailer, reader, and reviewer she has worked four part-time jobs at once. Thankfully, one of them actually paid her. She received her Bachelors in English from Brigham Young University, and now lives in the Tri-Cities of Washington with her husband and Aussie dog.

PS. To save you from hiccups, D'Arc only has one syllable.

You can check out more from C. Rae D'Arc on her
website (craedarc.com),
Facebook (facebook.com/c.rae.darc), or
Instagram (instagram.com/craedarc)

www.ingramcontent.com/pod-product-compliance
Lightning Source LLC
Chambersburg PA
CBHW071415300726
48976CB00006B/2110